From the fall? Jeff didn't seem to think so. Rachel rubbed her arms, cold in spite of the afternoon heat. She stifled a laugh of hysteria. Someone was still taking pictures out back. The flash flickered like lightning through the shadowy main floor as she closed the carved wood door. "He should have torn the walkway down," she said out loud. "I told him . . ."

"I agree with you." Jeff came around the corner of the hotel. "Are you all right?" He searched her face, looking worried. "Do you need a ride home?"

"I'm okay." She shivered. Henry was dead. Someone had maybe hit him and pushed him over the Gorge cliff. The town had the bright unreality of a calendar photograph . . .

MORE MYSTERIES FROM THE
BERKLEY PUBLISHING GROUP...

CAT CALIBAN MYSTERIES: She was married for thirty-eight years. Raised three kids. Compared to that, tracking down killers is easy . . .

by D. B. Borton

ONE FOR THE MONEY	TWO POINTS FOR MURDER
THREE IS A CROWD	FOUR ELEMENTS OF MURDER
FIVE ALARM FIRE	SIX FEET UNDER

ELENA JARVIS MYSTERIES: There are some pretty bizarre crimes deep in the heart of Texas—and a pretty gutsy police detective who rounds up the unusual suspects . . .

by Nancy Herndon

ACID BATH	WIDOWS' WATCH
LETHAL STATUES	HUNTING GAME
TIME BOMBS	C.O.P. OUT
CASANOVA CRIMES	

FREDDIE O'NEAL, P.I., MYSTERIES: You can bet that this appealing Reno private investigator will get her man . . . "A winner."—Linda Grant

by Catherine Dain

LAY IT ON THE LINE	SING A SONG OF DEATH
WALK A CROOKED MILE	LAMENT FOR A DEAD COWBOY
BET AGAINST THE HOUSE	THE LUCK OF THE DRAW
DEAD MAN'S HAND	

BENNI HARPER MYSTERIES: Meet Benni Harper—a quilter and folk-art expert with an eye for murderous designs . . .

by Earlene Fowler

FOOL'S PUZZLE	IRISH CHAIN
KANSAS TROUBLES	GOOSE IN THE POND
DOVE IN THE WINDOW	

HANNAH BARLOW MYSTERIES: For ex-cop and law student Hannah Barlow, justice isn't just a word in a textbook. Sometimes, it's a matter of life and death . . .

by Carroll Lachnit

MURDER IN BRIEF	A BLESSED DEATH
AKIN TO DEATH	

PEACHES DANN MYSTERIES: Peaches has never had a very good memory. But she's learned to cope with it over the years . . . Fortunately, though, when it comes to murder, this absentminded amateur sleuth doesn't forgive and forget!

by Elizabeth Daniels Squire

WHO KILLED WHAT'S-HER-NAME?	REMEMBER THE ALIBI
MEMORY CAN BE MURDER	WHOSE DEATH IS IT ANYWAY?
IS THERE A DEAD MAN IN THE HOUSE?	

DEVIL'S
TRUMPET

Mary Freeman

BERKLEY PRIME CRIME, NEW YORK

DEVIL'S TRUMPET

A Berkley Prime Crime Book / published by arrangement with the author

PRINTING HISTORY
Berkley Prime Crime edition / April 1999

The Penguin Putnam Inc. World Wide Web site address is http://www.penguinputnam.com

ISBN: 0-425-16821-2

Berkley Prime Crime Books are published by The Berkley Publishing Group, a member of Penguin Putnam Inc., 375 Hudson Street, New York, New York 10014.
The name BERKLEY PRIME CRIME and the BERKLEY PRIME CRIME design are trademarks belonging to Berkley Publishing Corporation.

PRINTED IN THE UNITED STATES OF AMERICA

10 9 8 7 6 5 4 3 2 1

For Hank and Joyce

ACKNOWLEDGMENTS

I'd like to thank Lucas Wortel and Kevin Roberts, of Big Sky Landscaping, for cheerfully answering all my questions about the landscape business; Bob Daum and Ken Nakanishi for their great automotive advice; and John Stoutamyer for his knowledge of jazz. Thanks also go to Debbie Cross and Sage Walker for reading my first draft and finding all the holes and slow spots. And finally, thanks, Elizabeth and Mark Bourne and Frances Groover for looking over my shoulder and cheering me on.

CHAPTER

1

July

Her boss was on another rampage.

Rachel O'Connor jumped at his furious shout and came within a hair of taking off her index finger with the Japanese pruning saw she was using. Staring thoughtfully at the thin line of crimson blood welling from the cut, she counted slowly to ten before turning to face the stocky, red-faced man standing behind her. "What's wrong, Henry?" She fished a relatively clean bandanna from her pocket and pressed it to the cut.

"You're cutting down the lilac!" Henry Bassinger's usually genial face was mottled like an angry moon, and his thinning hair stood up in ginger tufts. "You can't do this! How dare you? Grandfather planted these lilacs. Rudolph Valentino and Clara Bow had their picture taken right *here*." He pointed dramatically at the ground. "Together. I have a copy of the photo. The hotel was their private hideaway. They would never agree to this. Never!"

"They're both dead," Rachel said gently. "Long ago." This episode was worse than usual. "And I'm not cutting the lilac down.'' She made her voice soothing. Ruth at the Blossom City Market said he probably had a brain tumor. Well, he was her best client. If he ever paid his bill. ''Henry, don't you remember? We talked about this yesterday. The trunk is rotted, see?'' She tapped the hollow cavity low in the ancient trunk. ''The first winter ice storm will split it right off and may kill the whole shrub. If I cut it now,'' she went on persuasively, ''it'll look fine by this time next year. Really.''

''What about in the meantime?'' Henry was still wound up. ''I've scheduled the hotel's grand reopening for the Christmas Holidays. The trunks will be bare then. It will be *ugly. You're* the landscaper.'' He shook a finger at her. ''This is your responsibility, young lady.''

Rachel managed not to glance back at the derelict Columbia River Inn with its fallen shutters, boarded-up windows, and moss-covered, rotting roof. Christmas. Maybe Ruth was right. ''What if I put up a framed lattice panel to fill the space?'' she suggested cheerfully. ''It would balance the row nicely, and I'll use a nice clear redwood. It'll be a perfect backdrop for people who want to take pictures. The lilacs on either side will frame it beautifully, in leaf and bare-branched. Nobody will ever know you didn't put it there on purpose.''

''Well . . . maybe. I . . . we did have this conversation already, didn't we?'' The anger drained from Henry's face. ''I . . . I must be getting forgetful.'' He essayed a smile, but his eyes worried. ''You . . . you do whatever you want, dear.'' He mopped his face with the starched white handkerchief he always carried. ''I . . . I trust your judgement.''

''Are you all right?'' Rachel put her saw back in its holster. ''Do you want to go lie down?'' His face had turned an unhealthy shade of gray, and his jowls gleamed with sweat in the July heat. ''Are you sick?''

''No, no, my dear, I'm fine.'' He waved away her concern, but his lips trembled as he folded his damp handkerchief and replaced it in his pocket. ''I'm fine. Father's mind was clear as a bell when he died, you know, and he was nearly ninety. No Alzheimer's disease in my family, thank you!'' He cleared his throat and tugged at the sports jacket that he wore no matter how hot it got. ''The flowers you bought for the front beds—they're wrong.'' He tugged at his jacket again. ''They need to be white. We always had white flowers in front. That's important. I know I told you.''

''White?'' Rachel blinked. ''I don't remember that you mentioned it.'' She had spent an entire morning selecting and hauling those flats.

''Of course I . . .'' He broke off, looking briefly confused. ''I am sure that I mentioned it,'' he said more firmly. ''Quite sure.'' Turning on his heel, he hurried back along the stone path toward the old hotel perched on the rim of the Columbia River Gorge.

''White.'' Rachel blew out a breath that lifted her dark bangs. ''Now he tells me.'' Hands on her hips, she watched him disappear through the hotel's hand-carved wooden doors.

''*El señor,* he is *loco,* no?'' Julio Peron, her young Guatemalan employee, had come up beside her. ''He have not paid—has not paid,'' he corrected himself, proud of his English. He frowned. ''That is not good, *señorita*—that he does not pay.''

''We might have to quit the job, yes.'' She sighed. Julio didn't approve of Henry's temper tantrums either. He seemed to have appointed himself as her big brother— a situation that sometimes amused her and more often exasperated her. Especially since he was way younger than her twenty-five years. His documents gave his age at eighteen. Maybe so. ''Put those flats we bought in the shade, and I'll take them back later.'' Maybe the nursery had enough white-blooming annuals in stock that she could just swap for these.

''Not good.'' Julio frowned disapproval at the hotel. ''You pay me, he not pay you.'' He made a chopping gesture with his hand. ''No money. No work.''

''We'll finish the week out.'' She sighed again. ''He owes us too much—we can't afford to quit without at

least trying to get the money.'' That wasn't the real reason she kept on working here. Rachel let her eyes wander
across the overgrown shrubs and weed-choked gardens
of the old hotel. No one had touched them for well over
a decade. Small trees had sprouted in some of the beds.
Once upon a time, the sprawling Columbia River Inn had
housed some of the most famous celebrities of its day. It
had offered fabulous food, attentive service, and the
lovely privacy of its famous gardens. It had even had its
own dock where the Columbia River steamboats had
stopped to let off guests. A small, horse-powered incline
had lifted visitors and their luggage to the hotel terrace.
Both dock and incline were gone now, but the hotel walls
were lined with grainy old photos of the rich and famous
smiling from antique cars, posed with freshly caught
salmon, or lounging in the manicured gardens.

The gardens kept her here, money or no money. They
had been a masterpiece once and her private childhood
fairyland as a kid growing up in Blossom. You could still
see the genius that had gone into the design, back when
Henry's grandfather had built the hotel. Hidden fountains
and private nooks had offered romantic glimpses of the
river through the tops of the firs that lined the Gorge wall
along here. Stone benches and still pools created ro-
mance. A flagstone terrace outside the lounge offered
guests a view of a tiny waterfall that gushed out over a
lip of stone to fall onto riverbank rocks hundreds of feet
below. A wooden walkway of thick planks carried guests
over the waterfall and out to a stone gazebo complete
with fireplace that jutted out over the river below. That
had been quite a feat of engineering, she thought. And it
offered a stunning view, although the sawed-log walk
that led to it now lacked a railing and was dangerously
rotted.

''If he doesn't pay us by the end of the week, we'll
quit,'' she said firmly. Julio was right. She couldn't afford to pay him if she wasn't getting paid.

The first notes of a jazz trumpet solo blasted from the
gazebo, shattering the quiet. Rachel put her hands over

her ears. Henry's favorite album. She heard that trumpet in her sleep. "That whole thing is going to fall into the river. Go move the flats," she told Julio. "I'll finish here." She cast a last glance at the gazebo, just visible through the trees that edged the Gorge. "One of these days," she muttered, reaching for her saw, "it's going to fall." She went back to work on the tough lilac wood.

When she finished and had stacked the cut branches on the burning pile, she went looking for Julio. He was working on the overgrown front gardens. At least you could tell they were gardens now, she thought with some satisfaction. Excavated from their blanket of weeds, some of the old shrubs were even putting out new leaves. "I'm going over to the nursery to drop off the plants," she told him. "I'll be back after I interview the new client."

"He will hire you." Julio beamed at her. "This is a good day." He pulled a crisp bill from his pocket and waved it at her, grinning. "*El señor,* he give this to me."

A hundred-dollar bill. "Wow!" Rachel whistled. "Maybe he'll pay me, too."

"He say yes." Julio assumed his older brother face. "I ask him. I tell him you are paying me. That you have not much money," he said fiercely. "I tell him he must pay you."

For a moment Rachel was speechless. Julio was—to say the least—shy around whites. Sometimes he surprised her. "Thanks," she said with a smile. "I sure hope he listened to you." Shaking her head, she got her first aid kit from her truck. Never meet a new client with a bloody hand. Bad image.

"Bad." Julio jerked his head at her hand. "*Mi hermano*—he get a cut. Like so." He mimed playing a guitar, then shook his head, frowning. "No more."

He had never mentioned a brother before. But then he never talked about his family at all. Except his sister, whom he lived with. "Your brother's hand probably got infected. And this isn't really a bad cut." Rachel smeared the gash with betadine ointment and covered it with a guaze pad. "How did your brother cut his hand?"

"*Un machete,*" Julio said very softly and turned quickly away. His expression closed, and he began to chop weeds with short, violent stabs of his hoe.

For a moment, Rachel studied him, wondering about the past he never referred to. Then she sighed and pulled out her checkbook to check her balance. It wasn't good. She made a face. If the nursery wouldn't do a swap, she'd have to wait on the plants. She'd only been in business a year and a half, and there wasn't much demand for landscaping services in the Hood River area as yet.

There would be. Wealthy retirees and vacation-home people had discovered the Hood River area, drawn by the scenic Columbia Gorge, the windsurfing, and the hiking. They would want nice yards, shade trees, and shelter from the wind. They'd need drip irrigation systems, because there was only so much water in the local aquifer. Summers were hotter and drier than folk from the rainy Willamette Valley were used to. It would be a good business in time.

Her uncle Jack didn't think so. *I don't see why the orchard isn't enough for you,* he'd grumbled. *It's a solid and respectable way to make a living. We've done it for four generations now. But if you want to have a fling at planting flowers for pay, have at it.*

It wasn't a fling. And she wasn't just planting flowers for pay. Well, yes, she was, right now. Rachel blew another bangs-lifting breath and eyed the flats one more time. Squaring her shoulders, she marched up the wide, flagged walk that led to the hotel's porch. The hand-carved doors stood ajar, giving her a view of the wide, oak planks of the floor and the carved staircase that led up to the second-floor balcony. Cool air brushed her face, freighted with the scent of flowers and the tang of mildew. A huge vase filled with wildflowers, zinnia, and dahlias stood on a marble-topped table at the foot of the stairs. The huge fieldstone hearth at the far end of the room held another huge vase that masked the soot stains of old fires.

The cleaning lady—Dora or Darla or something like that—did the arrangements. They were always lovely. There was an old greenhouse out behind the hotel, beside the remains of an extensive herb garden. All vegetables for the hotel kitchen had been grown here, along with the flowers. She had picked flowers in the old greenhouse as a child.

"There you are." Henry appeared at the top of the stairs. "I was just coming to give you this." He smiled, his round face genial, without a trace of his earlier temper. "Here." He skipped down the stairs and thrust a slip of paper at Rachel. "On account."

She looked down at the check, and her eyes widened. Made out to Rain Country Landscaping, it was for five thousand dollars.

"I probably owe more than that. I couldn't find your invoices." He mopped his face with his handkerchief again and began to refold it into a neat square. "Will this do for now?"

"Uh—yes. It will. Thank you." Rachel folded the check carefully. "I'll give you a receipt."

"Later is fine. I trust you." His eyes glittered with excitement. "I've changed my mind. I want you to buy another lilac." He nodded briskly. "Get something as close to the same size as you can and simply replace that old one. I don't care what it costs. There is no reason I should struggle with plants that were old in my father's day. This is a new day." He beamed at her. "It's my day and my hotel. In fact, if you can't find an adequate replacement, cut down the whole lilac hedge, and we'll put something else in."

"Uh . . . I'm not sure . . ."

"In fact, we'll do just that! I want you to bring a list of alternative species for me in the morning. I'll decide then." He waved a dismissal and started back up the stairs. "Remember, we open for the Christmas season."

"Yes, sir."

Halfway to the top of the staircase, he stumbled and clutched at the railing to save himself. "These stairs will have to be repaired,'' he grumbled as he regained his balance. ''They're warped.''

''Yes, sir,'' Rachel said again, eyeing the stairs. The steps were ruler straight, every one of them.

''Está loco?'' Julio leaned against the door frame, his expression wary.

''I don't think so. Well, maybe.''

''He paid, yes?'' He stared moodily after the vanished Henry. ''Good time to quit, eh?''

She looked past him at the gardens, just beginning to emerge from their weedy shroud. Shook her head. ''Not yet.''

Julio gave a heavy, martyred sigh, shook his head, and turned away.

''You made your point,'' she muttered, glowering after him. She had a sneaking suspicion that he was being smarter about this than she was.

Still shaking his head, he went back to weeding.

CHAPTER

2

It was early yet. Rachel decided to deposit Henry's check on the way to her interview with her prospective new client, Dr. Meier, so she detoured into downtown Blossom. It was a small town—four blocks of Main Street lined with storefronts, flanked by a block or two of residential homes on either side. The whole town perched on the bank of the Columbia River, surrounded by cherry and apple orchards that climbed the steep slope rising from the river.

Main Street hadn't changed much since she was a little kid, Rachel reflected as she parked her truck. You could still buy penny candy from big glass jars in Hermanson's Pharmacy—although the wrapped pieces bore images of Mutant Ninja Turtles and Disney characters and cost five cents or more. There were no fast-food chains in town. Just the Homestyle Cafe, the Main Street Tavern, and Fong's Restaurant at the edge of town.

But a cluster of sleek new condominiums had sprouted along what had once been a freight dock on the river-bank. Barges had loaded boxes of fruit for the Portland market here. Now a handful of upscale shops had taken over the old warehouses, proffering espresso, gourmet lunches, clothing, and local specialties to the tourists who trickled over from Hood River. A scatter of bright sails danced across the water as a few morning windsurfers enjoyed the brisk breeze, adding to the holiday atmosphere. The booming tourist industry in nearby Hood River was beginning to make itself felt. Not everybody welcomed it.

A whiff of fresh bread drove all introspection from Rachel's head as she walked along the sidewalk. Joylinn must be taking the afternoon batch of bread out of the oven. Rachel breathed deeply, her stomach growling instantly. Bread—any kind of yeast goodie—was her downfall. No willpower. Joylinn Markham, her friend since third grade, had opened a small upscale bakery and espresso bar called The Bread Box on the shoreward end of the dock. She had left Blossom after high school to work in a San Francisco bakery. Open for less than a year, The Bread Box was rapidly earning a reputation locally, and with the tourists.

Rachel eyed her reflection in the window of the First Interstate Bank and made a face. Her father had been tall and lanky like his brother, and her mother was a fine-boned, petite woman who never gained an ounce no matter what she ate. Where her stocky frame came from, she didn't know. "Peasant type," she muttered. "Good for hoeing and plowing. Not bred for looks . . ." Opening the glass-paned door in the old stone building, she marched into the bank.

Built in the early part of the century, when the Columbia River still teemed with salmon, the marble counters and wooden wainscotting might have come from the set of a Hollywood Western. The glossy wood and soaring windows made her instantly conscious of her dirt-stained jeans, work boots, and T-shirt. Fortunately the lobby was empty except for her friend Sandy at the counter. Sandy's wide, freckled face brightened when she caught sight of Rachel, and she waved vigorously.

"We close on the house this afternoon!" Her clear soprano voice sounded like the trill of an exotic bird in the echoing cavern of the old bank. "I'm so excited. Bill's already groaning about all the work we need to do. Honestly! That man."

"He's just teasing you." Rachel pulled a deposit slip from the pad on the counter and filled it out. "He's as excited as you are, and you know it."

"Oh, I do." Sandy winked as she took the check and deposit slip from Rachel. "Our own home at last. I can't wait!" She glanced down at the check, and her smile faltered. "Wow, that's kind of big, isn't it?" She chewed her lip, not meeting Rachel's eyes. "I think I'd better check with Mr. Lanier first." She wrinkled her nose. "Sorry."

"Hey, it's okay. I'm not sure I believe it's real either." Rachel gave Sandy a reassuring smile as her friend departed with the suspect check. Everyone knew that Henry lived on a trust fund established by his father—and it wasn't much of an income.

To her surprise, Sandy was back in a matter of minutes, beaming. "It's good! Do you want to deposit the whole amount?" She scribbled on the slip and tapped keys on her terminal. "Or do you want cash back?"

Rachel remembered Julio's hundred. Money after all . . . "I guess I'd better get two hundred back." She needed groceries and the new annuals.

"I guess Henry made a *big* deposit," Sandy confided as she counted out twenties. "If he sold that property through another realtor, my dad's going to have kittens. He's been after Henry to list it with him for ten years now."

"I can't believe he'd sell it." Rachel took the bills and folded them into her wallet. "Maybe this nephew of his really did come up with money to renovate the old place. I hope so."

"Ha." Sandy rolled her eyes and grinned. "I met his nephew once. He's with some big architectural firm down in California somewhere. He seemed much too . . . well . . . city to get involved in something like this. I'll bet you dinner at Fong's that he sold it to one of those developers who are sniffing around.'' Her grin turned mis-chievous. "Speaking of dinner, want to come over to the new house tomorrow evening? It's empty, so we can move right in if we want. I'm grilling steak for fajitas, and we'll do the grand tour. It's kind of a 'before' party. That way you can all be impressed when we do the 'after' party.'' She winked. "I'll even make sure Bill goes easy on the salsa.''

"He'd better, or I'll end up in the ER.'' Rachel gave her friend a narrow look. "Okay, what's up? You look like my uncle when the price of apples goes up.''

"Oh, nothing.'' Sandy waved her hand airily. "I've got a little surprise for you, that's all.''

"What kind of surprise?'' Rachel leaned her elbows on the marble countertop. "Oh, my gosh—are you preg-nant?''

"No, silly.'' Sandy rolled her eyes. "We aren't even trying yet. Seven o'clock tomorrow?'' She gave Rachel an arch smile. "Don't bring anything. We're celebrating. Just don't sneer at our wasteland of a backyard.''

"I guess I have to come now.'' Rachel grinned and pocketed her wallet. "See you.'' She turned to leave— somewhat to Sandy's disappointment. Sandy loved to be coaxed for a secret, but Rachel didn't have time today.

So Henry's check was good. She touched her wallet as she exited the bank, wondering if he had sold the hotel after all. It would be a shame if the old building was demolished to make way for a vacation development of the sort going in locally. The beams were fastened with wooden pegs and hand-forged nails. The stone had been quarried locally. She felt a pang for the gardens, just beginning to reemerge from the weeds.

She was so absorbed in her thoughts as she pushed through the bank's glass doors that she ran right into a pas-serby on the sidewalk. The man grunted, and she stumbled backward, cheeks flaming with embarrassment. "I . . . I'm so sorry,'' she stammered. "I guess I'm sleepwalking this morning. I hope I didn't hurt you.''

"Not likely.'' A grin colored the man's tone. "Although you pack more of a wallop than I remember.''

Rachel's eyes widened as she focused on her victim's face. ''Jeff!'' She laughed, delighted. ''Jeff Price, is it really you?'' But there was no mistaking his tawny, hawklike profile and startlingly blue eyes. His father had run a small truck farm, offering a variety of gourmet and ethnic vegetables to the U-Pick crowd and restaurant buyers. His customers had come clear out from Portland to buy his produce.

When he had been killed by a hit-and-run driver, his wife had taken their only son and moved back to Los Angeles to live with her sister. ''You left a hole,'' Rachel said breathlessly. ''A threesome wasn't like the old four-some.''

''I saw Sandy the other day. I never doubted that she and Bill would get married.'' His eyes held hers briefly. ''They were the perfect couple.''

Rachel felt her cheeks warming again and looked away. ''So what are you doing back here?'' she asked lightly. ''Just visiting?''

''Maybe not.'' Again his eyes sought hers. ''I took a temporary job with the Blossom Police. One-year contract. In fact, I was just on my way to work.''

''You always said you were going to become a homicide detective.'' Rachel smiled. ''Sounds like you're well on your way.''

''I thought I was.'' He looked away briefly. ''At least I'm a cop. I'll settle for that for the moment.'' He put the smile back on his face with an obvious effort. ''I was on the Los Angeles police force for a couple of years. I didn't like it there.'' His tone suggested that this subject was closed. For a moment Rachel studied his face without speaking. There was a hard edge to him that hadn't been there, back when he and Sandy and Bill and herself had been The Foursome.

Back then he had been the one who never lost his temper, the one who cooled Bill off when his hot blood threatened to get the better of his common sense. ''I missed you," Rachel said. "I kept hoping you'd write. Or visit."

"I did write." He looked surprised. "You never answered my letters."

"I never got a single letter from you. Did you get the address right?"

"Not likely I'd forget it."

"How odd," she said. For a moment silence stretched between them, then Rachel looked at her watch. "I'd better get going," she said, feeling suddenly awkward. "I've got an interview with a new client this afternoon."

"Sandy told me you had your own landscaping business." He walked beside her as she headed for her truck. "Nice." He eyed the new white Toyota with the neat green lettering on the door: *Rain Country Landscaping.* "Very professional."

"Very expensive." She made a face. "But I needed a truck for the job, and appearances count in this trade." She opened the door and paused, that unexpected awkwardness seizing her again. "Let's get together, okay?"

"I'd like that." He grinned. "How about tonight? Are you free?"

"That would be great." She took out her wallet, extracted a business card, and scribbled her home address on it. "It's up above Main," she said. "A big white house. I have a separate apartment upstairs, in the back."

"Seven?" He pocketed the card. "I noticed there are a ton of new restaurants in Hood River."

"Seven is great." She was blushing again. "It's nice to see you."

"It's nice to find you looking so good." Jeff turned quickly and strode off down the sidewalk in the direction of Blossom's tiny brick City Hall. It housed not only Blossom's four-officer police force, but also the two-cell city jail.

Rachel got into the truck, started the engine, but didn't pull away from the curb right away. Jeff Price. She had long ago given up on ever seeing him again. Rachel shook her head, smiled, and pulled out into Blossom's negligible traffic.

With a screech of tires, a new white Toyota Camry rounded the corner, heading straight for her door. Rachel gasped and stomped on the gas. Her pickup roared across the narrow street, just missing a pickup as she fought the wheel. Brakes screeching, the Toyota swerved wildly, its driver's side wheels bumping up onto the empty sidewalk. Then it roared on up the street and swung around the corner.

Slowly Rachel unclenched her fingers from the steering wheel and wiped cold moisture from her face. Her hands were trembling. She squeezed them between her knees and took a deep breath, waiting for her pounding heart to slow. "Talk about a close one," she said weakly and glared after the vanished car. She wished she had had the presence of mind—and the time—to memorize the license plate. It was a rental car. She was pretty sure of that much.

Her knees still felt a bit shaky when she stopped at the Riverside Nursery to return the rejected annuals and see if she could get some whites. Iko and Daren Rhinehoffer carried a small stock of standard annuals and perennials, as well as an eclectic assortment of less common species, and some natives. Iko also offered custom grafting—a service that Rachel had more than once promoted to clients. Her Bonsai collection—some of the pieces had been in the family for several generations—took Rachel's breath away. Their nursery had been featured in the Portland paper's Sunday supplement for their antique varieties of fruit trees and roses. As a consequence, they had about as many customers from Portland as they did from Hood River. But, like Rachel, they just scraped by.

Iko waved away her apologies when Rachel returned the flats. "Customers," she said cheerfully. "They're always right, eh?"

"There are times . . ." Rachel rolled her eyes and paid the difference for the new flats.

"I could still open an account for you." Daren pocketed the money with the squint-eyed smile of someone who had lived his whole life in the sun. "Hey, people are beating down the door to get credit from us," he grumbled as she shook her head. "And I can't *give* it away to you."

"One truck loan is enough debt for now." Rachel laughed as she closed the truck's tailgate. She waved at Iko, who had gone back to potting up seedlings, helped out, more or less, by their three-year-old son. If nothing else, the kid had a lot of nice dirt to play in, Rachel thought with a smile. She checked her watch, discovered that she had plenty of time to swing by Joylinn's bakery and drop off the plants at the hotel. Julio liked Joylinn's cinnamon rolls, too. It would be nice to bring him one.

She was finishing a huge, gooey roll as she turned into the hotel's circular driveway. Licking the last of the vanilla frosting from her fingers, she nearly ran into the white Toyota Camry parked smack in the middle of the hotel's overgrown drive. With a gasp, she hit the brakes, spilling the bag with Julio's roll onto the floor. Her left headlight nearly touched the Toyota's taillight as she brought the truck to a halt. It was a rental car. *The* rental car. She glowered at it as she got out of the truck, then waved the bakery bag at Julio. He was staring at the house and didn't respond. Rachel broke into a trot as she heard the shouting coming from the rear of the hotel. "What's going on?" she called as she reached him. "Who's there?"

"*Yo lo no conozco, señorita.*" Julio shook his head vigorously, his careful English deserting him. "*Hombre. Joven.* Young. He is . . . in anger."

"I think we nearly met," Rachel said. She took a step toward the house, then halted as glass shattered. "I'm calling the police."

Too late. Julio was already on his way around the side of the hotel, his expression determined and frightened at the same time. Muttering a curse on his adolescent machismo and big-brother complex, Rachel ran after him.

"No." She caught up with him and grabbed his arm as he reached the rear terrace. "We'll let the police handle it." As she tried to pull him away from the terrace, the French doors that led to the hotel's lounge burst open, and Henry Bassinger rushed out onto the flagstone terrace. His eyes were wild, and he waved a pair of pruning shears like a small sword. *Her* pruning shears, Rachel noted.

"You will leave here this instant!" He waved the shears at the slender young man who had followed him out onto the flagstones. "I have nothing more to say to you," he wheezed, struggling for breath. "Not now! Not ever!"

"Uncle, don't get so upset. Your asthma . . ."

"You're trying to kill me! Whose fault is it that I'm upset?" Bassinger thrust the pruners at the stranger, who skipped nimbly backward. "I told you I had to approve any changes to the plans."

"Which is why I'm here, for God's sake." He brandished a roll of paper in his hands. "So that you can approve them."

"Approve this *rape*? This *desecration*?"

"Uncle, they're minor and necessary changes." A diamond flashed in the man's earlobe as he spread his hands. "I can't turn back the clock. This isn't 1920. We have to obey today's building codes."

"Clock ohmock. Nobody asked you to turn back any clocks." Henry brandished the pruners again, driving the young man back into the lounge. "*Minor* changes? You call a health club *minor*? And this . . . this *spa* thing? I'd have to tear out the mermaid fountain to put it where you want it. No." He thrust at his retreating nephew as if he meant to run him through. "No, no, *no*! I *refuse*!"

"Look, Uncle, if people want a bed for the night, they go to a Motel Six. We're offering a *vacation experience*. We're offering real relaxation." The man's voice emerged muffled from the lounge. "A vacation today means you give people something to do besides stare at the river and drink martinis."

"People came here for years to stare at the river. They seemed to think it was relaxing."

"Nowadays people relax by playing games. Will you stop living in the past, damn it? People want to windsurf. They want to work out, or hike, or play tennis. We need a pool, too. And a hot tub. We need a connection with a local riding stable. We discussed all this—or don't you remember?"

"I never agreed to any of this!" Henry flung the shears onto a wrought iron table with a glass top. "Over my dead body!" he yelled as the thick glass cracked across.

"If you want this place to succeed, you have to give people what they want." Henry's nephew sounded shaken. "Look, I'll give you some articles to read. Market surveys." He emerged briefly from the lounge, then retreated as Henry made a grab for the shears. "Uncle, what's *wrong* with you?" His eyes lighted on Rachel and Julio, and he halted instantly, a brilliant flush staining his cheeks. "Uh, Uncle? We have company." He nodded in their direction.

"Who?" Henry turned on them, his fists clenched, still gasping for breath. "Oh. I . . . I'm sorry." With an effort, he managed a thin smile. "I'm sorry you had to overhear this . . . petty altercation."

"Petty?" His nephew was breathing hard. "Try major mental meltdown."

Henry glared briefly at him, his composure returning. "This is my nephew Alex Cresswell. He is an architect of sorts . . ."

"*Of sorts?* Thanks."

"And sadly lacking in manners," Henry went on as if Cresswell hadn't spoken. "He has been interested in participating in my restoration of the hotel. But his ideas are . . . childish."

"Childish?" Alex yelped. "Look who's talking. And I *am* the restoration at the moment. It's my money funding it until we get some other investors in place. Do you know how hard it is to find capital for this kind of risky venture?"

"You are not the only financing available," Henry said frostily.

"Really? You could have fooled me." Alex brushed off his expensive linen slacks, his face still pale with anger. "Well, if you've got another source of financing, feel free, Uncle. It's your property, not mine. If I didn't love this place so much, I'd walk out right now. I have a waiting list of people who want to pay me money for my childish ideas." He turned on his heel and vanished into the dim recesses of the lounge.

"You come back here." Henry took a step after him, then stopped, his expression agitated. "Young hothead. He can't handle criticism is all. I just don't understand what upsets him so. We can't even have a civil discussion about plans without an upheaval like this." He turned back to Rachel. "*You* don't lose your temper when I ask you to make a small change. Health club? Tennis court?" He pulled out his handkerchief. "He wants to turn a fine hotel into a summer camp!"

Rachel noticed that the usually starched square had been wadded into a damp ball. Henry looked at it with distaste, then stuffed it angrily into his pocket so that a limp corner jutted out. "If he insists on controlling everything—well, I don't need him. He's right. He doesn't own this property, I do." His face crumpled. "But I don't understand." He looked after his vanished nephew, bewildered and hurt. "We used to get along so well. We talked about this project oh . . . ever since he was a small boy. And now . . ." He looked down at his hands. They were shaking. "I don't understand." He shoved them into his pockets.

"I think you should sit down," Rachel said, alarmed by his gray face. "Can I get you some water?"

"I'm not going to have a heart attack! Oh, dear." Henry raised his eyebrows at the cracked table. "That was Mother's favorite piece. How did that happen?" He sounded as if he was going to cry. "I just don't understand . . ." Before Rachel could stop him, he stumbled across the terrace and nearly ran along the plank walkway that led to the gazebo.

Rachel wanted to cover her eyes, half expecting him to fall to his death right in front of her. But the walkway was quite wide, and Henry was steadier on his feet than it had seemed. She breathed a sigh of relief as he disappeared into the shelter. A moment later, the familiar jazz erupted from the open windows, loud enough to make Rachel wince.

"I guess he'll be okay." She glanced at Julio, whose fierce scowl didn't quite hide his unease. "Keep an eye on him while I'm gone, okay? You can call me on my cell phone." Her mother would know what to do about Henry. But her mother was back east, taking care of her aunt. "I'll be back as soon as I can."

"*Sí.*" Julio nodded, his eyes hooded, as they went out front to unload the new flats. At least the familiar trumpet solo was bearable out here.

"Ms. O'Connor." Alex Cresswell straightened from where he had been leaning against the side of her truck. "I'm sorry to interrupt you—but what the hell is wrong with Uncle Henry?" He cast a worried glance in the direction of the hotel, oblivious to Julio's glare. "Has he been like this long? My God, he acts like he's on drugs."

"I've only worked for him for a few weeks," Rachel said cautiously. "He does seem a little . . . unpredictable."

"He was fine three months ago—when I was up here last." Cresswell was obviously worried. "He was clear as a bell. I don't think he even remembers that I was here. There's no history of Alzheimer's disease in our family."

Henry had mentioned Alzheimer's disease, too.

"And what do you mean by unpredictable?" Cresswell took a step toward her. "Is he forgetful? Irrational? My God, it was like meeting a stranger today. Has he seen a doctor lately?"

"I don't know." Rachel shook her head at Julio, who quivered at her side like a dog about to attack. He caught her look and set his jaw, then fixed his eyes on Cresswell.

"I don't mean to sound like I'm blaming you." Cresswell looked down at his clenched fists and relaxed them with an obvious effort. "I'm sorry. This just . . . upset me. My uncle . . . this place . . ." He gestured at the old hotel. "He was my family when I was a kid. I spent summers here." He gave the hotel a troubled glance. "I don't know what to do."

That made two of them. "He seemed pretty upset about his argument with you, after you left." Rachel chose her words carefully. "Maybe you should come back later and try again."

"So he's been like this ever since you started working for him?" Cresswell gave her a searching glance.

"Well, not quite this upset—but touchy. Yes." She frowned, remembering the lilac incident this morning. "He's pretty forgetful at times," she admitted.

"I hope I don't have this to look forward to at age fifty." Cresswell sighed, then gave her a tentative smile. "Sorry you got the fallout today. I think I will come back later. I'm going to try to talk him into seeing a doctor—for a checkup." He grimaced. "He'll love that advice." He climbed into his car and pulled out of the driveway in a flurry of gravel.

Rachel watched him thoughtfully. So the restoration was a reality. That explained Henry's deposit anyway. Julio had unloaded the flats while she and Cresswell talked—without once taking his eyes from the architect. Her watchdog. She sighed and fished the directions to Dr. Meier's house from her glove box. Frowning at her hurried scrawl, she climbed into her truck. "Call me," she told Julio as she started the engine, "if anything happens."

Dr. Meier lived south of town, up high on a newly paved road that wound up into the hills above the Gorge. This was old cherry orchard land. It had belonged to the Preuss family. They had moved to Portland after three bad harvests in a row, when Carolyn Preuss had been diagnosed with breast cancer. Some people in town had grumbled when Tom Preuss had sold the land to a developer. Her uncle—who had made an offer on it—was one of the more outspoken critics of the sale. She decided not to mention her new client's address at the orchard. The view of the Columbia from up here was spectacular, but the slope looked barren without its cloak of cherry trees.

Dr. Meier's house turned out to be the one farthest up Cherry Way, as the developer had named the road. It faced north, with a sweeping view of the Columbia and a glimpse of distant Hood River. Not a single tree softened the bare, weedy slope. The builder had spread a thin layer of topsoil over the fill around the house, but there the landscaping effort had ended. Erosion channels gouged the rocky soil, and scattered dandelions blazed beneath the summer sun.

No shade. Rachel eyed the slope. No shelter from the wind that howled up and down the Gorge in the winter. She wondered just what this Dr. Meier had in mind.

A small bald man with the flat belly and muscled legs of a serious runner emerged onto a side deck as Rachel parked in the circular driveway. He skipped down the wide wooden steps, beaming and offering his hand before she'd even managed to get the truck door closed. "You must be Ms. O'Connor." His gray eyes twinkled above his broad smile. "Glad to meet you. I heard great things about you from Penny Roth."

"I did a wildflower and water garden for her." Rachel returned Dr. Meier's firm handshake. That had been her biggest job to date—and her best chance so far to really get creative with the design. Penny Roth, a retired state senator who had purchased an old farmhouse near Hood River, had given her a few requests and free rein. She had been delighted with the small, intimate garden Rachel had created for her. "I enjoyed working for her," she said.

"It was lovely. I liked your use of native plants, especially." Dr. Meier shook his head and sighed. "We

can be so stupid. We have dozens of lovely plants that
are already adapted to the local climate, so what do we
do? Import fragile aliens from the tropics. And then
spend a fortune trying to keep them alive. Wasteful. I
hate waste.'' He gave her a twinkling smile. ''I want you
to think long-term, dear, and keep ecology in mind. I had
a second well drilled for watering. My contractor suggested it. But I don't want to waste water, even if I have an
extra well.'' He shook a finger at her. ''No overhead sprinklers. I want everything in drip irrigation.''

''I always suggest drip systems.'' Rachel nodded. She
was beginning to feel more at ease with her prospective
client, but writing up a job estimate still scared her to
death. It was so easy to overlook details that could cost
you your profit. And sometimes the numbers frightened
the client off. People didn't realize how much it cost to
landscape a yard.

''Let me tell you what I have in mind.'' Dr. Meier
beckoned peremptorily.

For the next hour they wandered around the property
discussing water features, tree species, and native shrubs
for privacy. Dr. Meier had done his homework, Rachel
discovered with pleasure. His suggestions for plants were
thoughtful, and mostly reasonable, although he was disappointed when she told him that deodar cedars wouldn't
work. Their shallow roots wouldn't stand up to the Gorge
winds, she explained. They settled on pin oak and ginkgo
for shade, along with Bloodgood maples for added color.

He went along with her suggestion of pines for the
mid-sized plantings, and was delighted when she suggested a hedge of espaliered apple trees instead of
wind-fragile photinia.

''I've always admired those fancy tree fences,'' he said
gleefully. ''I didn't think anyone did them anymore.''

He was similarly pleased with her suggestion of ornamental grasses, blueberry, native huckleberry, Oregon
grape, and salal for the plantings around the house. The
water feature was their one sticking point. He wanted a
duck pond. She patiently explained that on this slope,

made up of thin soil over rock, he'd need a liner to keep the water from seeping away, which would be expensive and ugly. "Duck ponds are built in naturally wet areas," she told him. "How about something small? With a fountain or water trickling over a rock formation? We can get some gorgeous Columbia basalt locally." She and Julio could hand-dig it, which would cut down significantly on the cost.

He agreed reluctantly and told her he'd consider the herbaceous lawn she recommended, although he wasn't terribly enthusiastic. The mix consisted of grass, sweet clover, wildflowers, and herbs that required less care and water than a turf or seed lawn. It wouldn't require much mowing either, she told him. That got his attention, at least.

Generally she found him easy to work with and realistic about time, which was a relief. Most of her clients wanted a final effect within days. Or months at the most. Someone who was willing to think in terms of years was a refreshing change.

"I'll need a weekly maintenance service, too," Dr. Meier decided as they returned to the house. "Unless you do that, too? I suppose I could do all the work myself, but I'd much rather have fun and pay someone else to weed and prune." He grinned like a muscular leprechaun. "That's why I worked so hard to earn all that money, after all."

"No problem." Rachel nodded. "I can recommend a man who does excellent work." That was how Julio earned a considerable chunk of his income—servicing some of the projects they'd worked on. He wanted to start his own business eventually. "He's very reliable," she said.

"Fine, fine. How soon can you give me an estimate?" Dr. Meier waved his hand airily as he opened a set of French doors. "Lemonade, dear? Or may I offer you a beer?"

"Lemonade, thanks. My day isn't over yet. I can have

an estimate for you tomorrow afternoon. Is that all right?"

"Wonderful." Dr. Meier's voice came from the big open kitchen visible through the huge expanse of glass. Copper pans hung from an overhead rack above a tiled work island. A moment later he reemerged carrying a tray with pitcher, glasses, and a plate of small, plain cookies. "I'd like you to start working on the project right away, if you can. I feel like I'm living in the middle of a cow pasture."

"It was an orchard once. The developer cut most of the trees down." Rachel accepted a dewy glass of lemonade and took a cookie. Music was playing in the house. A jazz ensemble. Rachel frowned. "That trumpet sounds familiar." She was pretty sure it was the same CD that Henry seemed to play night and day. "Who is it?"

"That's Clyde Montaine. He's backed by studio musicians on this CD, but he's good—a Cajun from Louisiana. You can hear a bit of zydeco in his rhythms." Dr. Meier nodded briskly. "I think he's going to turn out to be one of the best horn men alive." His eyes twinkled. "You must be quite a jazz aficionado to recognize him. He's not very well known yet—and certainly should be."

"I don't really know much about jazz. My dad listened to it a lot. But one of my clients—Henry Bassinger—plays Montaine's music all the time."

"He's only got a single CD out at the moment. Mostly he plays the small clubs. Bassinger, hm?" Dr. Meier's eyebrows rose. "Now there's a name I haven't heard in years. I wondered whatever happened to him. So he lives around here? What a coincidence."

"You know him?" Rachel took a bite of cookie and blinked. She had expected something sweet, but instead found her mouth filled with the tang of cheddar cheese and a fiery hint of cayenne.

"Cheese crackers." Dr. Meier chuckled at her reaction. "People always expect vanilla. Hope it's not too much pepper for you. I like 'em hot."

"You made these? They're great." Rachel reached for another.

"After Ruth, my wife, died, I got tired of eating out all the time. Not bad for a man who only learned how to boil an egg at age forty-five, huh?"

"Very good." Rachel eyed the copper pans hanging in the kitchen with new respect. With a start she realized that the kitchen was filled with afternoon shadows. Julio would be waiting for his ride home. She wondered how Henry was doing. "I've got to go, Dr. Meier." She drained her glass and stood up quickly. "I'll call you as soon as I have some numbers for you. And I'll draw up a set of plans for you to look at."

As she brushed crumbs from her lap, her cell phone rang. Excusing herself, she answered it, recognizing Julio's agitated voice with difficulty.

"Señorita O'Connor, vamos pronto! Por favor. El señor es muerto!"

Muerto. Dead. The word sent a shock wave of numbness through her. "Are you sure?" Rachel thought of stroke. Or a heart attack. "What happened?"

"No sé. Yo no sé, señorita. He . . . fall. *Señorita,* please . . . I did not do it. I did not." The call ended abruptly. For an instant Rachel listened numbly to the buzz of the vanished call.

"Is something wrong?" Dr. Meier looked worried.

Rachel shook her head. "I'll call you," she said quickly. "Tomorrow." Then she hurried down the steps to her truck, forcing herself not to break into a run. As she started the engine, she dialed 911 on her cell phone. As the operator answered, and she pulled out of the driveway, she noticed Dr. Meier on his bright new deck, watching her departure with a frown on his face. As she reported Julio's call, she wondered if she had just lost a big new client. It would be just her luck.

CHAPTER

3

"So tell me more about this nephew." Jeff Price sat across from her on the stone terrace of the old hotel, looking strange and official in the pale blue uniform shirt and dark pants of the Blossom City Police Department.

"There's not much more to tell." Rachel's eyes kept wanting to fix on the black leather holster on Jeff's belt. "They were arguing about plans for the renovation when I got here. Then I left to go meet with a client. Julio stayed here. I told him to finish the front beds—and to call me if anything went wrong. Henry was acting strange."

"Strange?"

"Upset. More than I've ever seen him." She looked into the lounge where Julio sat bolt upright on the edge of a chair. He stared back at her, his eyes shiny with anxiety.

"It's all right, Julio," she said and turned back to Jeff. "I was on Dr. Meier's deck when Julio called me. You can't think he had anything to do with this!" She glared at him. "That's *stupid,* Jeff. He's a kid. Why would he want to hurt Henry?"

"He was here." Jeff looked unhappy. "That makes

him a suspect. If there *is* a suspect.'' He frowned. ''It could have been an accident. We should know soon enough. Did Bassinger go out to that stone building often?''

''The gazebo? All the time,'' Rachel said grimly. ''It still has electricity, and he'd go out there to play music. I warned him . . .'' She fell silent as two uniformed paramedics maneuvered a stretcher across the terrace and over to the waiting ambulance. A blanket covered the bulky shape on the stretcher.

''Did he fall from the walk?'' Rachel asked softly.

Jeff nodded. ''Did Peron ever need to go inside the house?''

''No! But he went in to call me.'' She pressed her lips together. ''There's a phone in the lounge.''

''He says he didn't touch anything else.'' Jeff turned and looked through the lounge doors. The place looked as if a fight had taken place—a small table had been overturned. Shards of glass and sticky puddles of some liquid gleamed on the tiled floor.

''Come off it,'' Rachel snapped. ''What? You think Julio attacked Henry? Threw him over the terrace wall?''

''Probably not.'' Jeff evaded her glare. ''But I can't just dismiss him as a suspect. Until I'm sure.''

''He didn't do it, Jeff!''

''*Señorita?*'' Julio stepped into the doorway, his eyes wide and ringed with white. ''*Yo sé*—I know.'' He struggled for English, speaking very slowly. ''The music—it stop. *El señor,* he come to the door. Front, you know? Close it. Tight.'' He made a key-turning motion with his hand. ''Afraid. I dig. Time passes . . . I hear voices. I hear *el señor* yell. Very afraid!''

''Why didn't you tell me this before?'' Jeff asked sharply.

Julio shrugged, his expression frightened. ''Afraid,'' he repeated.

''Of what?'' Jeff frowned. ''What was he afraid of?''

Julio turned around without answering as Blossom's other police car pulled up beside Rachel's truck. A uniformed officer got out and opened the passenger door for Alex Cresswell.

"Him." Julio pointed. "*El señor está* afraid. Of him."

They all looked at the architect as, face pale, mouth set, he climbed the terrace steps. He moved woodenly, as if he was sleepwalking. His eyes skimmed across Rachel without the slightest flicker of recognition. "Where is he?" he croaked in a hoarse voice. "Where's Uncle Henry?"

"We removed the body." Jeff stood. "Have a seat, Mr. Cresswell. I'd like to ask you a few questions."

Cresswell moved his head like a cow bothered by flies. "Whatever you want." He collapsed onto a chair as if his legs would no longer hold him up. "I want to see him."

"You'll get a chance," Jeff said gently. "I'm afraid I'm going to have to ask you to identify the body."

Alex swallowed, his Adam's apple jerking, and looked away.

"When did you arrive in Blossom?" Jeff flipped to a new page in his small notebook.

"Late this morning. I caught a six A.M. flight from LAX, rented a car at the Portland airport, and drove straight here. Uncle called me last night. He was upset about some plans for our restoration of the hotel, and I had a couple of days between projects, so I came on up to straighten things out."

"Straighten things out," Jeff repeated.

"Yes." Cresswell's eyes focused suddenly, and he gave Jeff a sharp look. "What's going on here? The officer told me Uncle Henry had an accident."

"Possibly."

"What the hell do you mean, *possibly*?"

"So what did you talk about?" Jeff asked.

"Mostly he yelled at me. We never really got to the talking stage." Cresswell glanced at Rachel. "Ask her. She was there."

"Why did he yell at you, Mr. Cresswell?"

"He didn't like the changes I'd made. He was acting . . .

crazy. I don't . . . I don't know what was wrong with him."
His voice caught. "I think there *was* something wrong with
him. A brain tumor maybe. My God . . ." Cresswell got
control of himself with an effort. "He was never like that—
hostile. Forgetful. He was a kind and thoughtful man. He
didn't throw temper tantrums."

"Where did you go when you left your uncle?" Jeff
scribbled steadily in his notebook.

"I booked a motel room in Hood River. Then I bought
some lunch stuff at the grocery store there and went for
a long drive. To think. I was worried about Uncle Henry.
I had to figure out how to get him to see a doctor. He
hates . . . hated doctors." His face worked briefly.
"When I got back to the motel, the cop was waiting."
He jerked his head at the parked car.

"And you didn't come back here to talk to your uncle
again?" Jeff asked blandly. "Say, about three o'clock?"

"No." Cresswell crossed his arms, his expression
stubborn. "I did not, and, no, there's nobody who can
confirm that if you're asking for an alibi. I don't have
one. I was out driving the back roads. Someone murdered
him," he said numbly. All color had drained from his
face. "My God, why?"

"Do you need a glass of water, Mr. Cresswell?" Jeff
put a hand gently on the architect's arm. "Are you
okay?"

"I . . . I'm not okay, but I'm not going to pass out on
you or get hysterical if that's what you're asking." He
shook himself. "Murdered," he said softly.

Jeff cleared his throat. "During your discussion with
your uncle, did he attack you?"

"No." Cresswell glanced briefly at Rachel. "Well, he
sort of waved a pair of pruning shears at me, but he
wasn't really trying to hurt me."

"I see." Jeff's face gave nothing away. "Did you
have to grab him? Maybe hard enough to leave bruises?
Maybe hit him?"

"No!" Cresswell looked horrified. "I'd never lay a
hand on Uncle Henry. He yelled, and I yelled back. I

yelled . . ." He buried his face in his hands.

Jeff closed his notebook and got slowly to his feet. "Mr. Cresswell, I'll have to ask you to come downtown with me. We'd like to ask you a few more questions and, with your permission, take fingerprints and a sample for DNA analysis."

"DNA analysis?" Alex bolted to his feet, twin patches of color staining his cheeks. "And just why do you want that?"

"It might . . . clarify a few matters for us. You can call your lawyer first if you'd like."

"Are you arresting me?"

"No."

"I'll come along." Cresswell's face looked skeletal. "Why should I refuse? If you think someone murdered my uncle, I want to know who. And I want to know what was wrong with him. Something was. I sure didn't do anything to hurt him. I . . . he wouldn't commit suicide." His voice faltered, and he got abruptly to his feet. "Do all the tests you want." He nodded at the second officer, turned on his heel, and marched down the walk to the waiting police car.

"What about suicide?" Jeff tapped his notebook with his chewed pencil.

"I don't know. Henry was acting kind of strange." Rachel frowned. "He didn't seem like the suicide type to me—but what do I know? Maybe you should ask his cleaning lady. She was there twice a week."

"I will." Jeff closed his notebook decisively. "The autopsy should tell us if his behavior was caused by a brain tumor or drugs. You can go home." His eyes filled with sudden sympathy. "It's tough—walking into something like this."

"What about Julio?" Rachel lifted her chin stubbornly.

Jeff sighed, his expression unhappy. "I can't dismiss him as a suspect. Not yet."

"But I know—" She broke off abruptly. His eyes had taken on an opaque gloss, and she wondered just what

lessons you learned as a cop in Los Angeles. "I know
he didn't do it," she said softly. "Can I give him a ride
home now?"

Jeff hesitated, then nodded. "Let me know if he
doesn't show up for work." He didn't smile.

Rachel nodded, then beckoned to Julio. He was shivering like a nervous dog as they walked to her truck,
glancing back over his shoulder as if he expected Jeff to
charge after them. "He did it, *señorita*." Julio spoke in
a hissing whisper. "I saw him. His car. When I took *los*
weeds by *el invernaculo* . . . the house of glass."

"Greenhouse."

"It is . . . *escondrijo*." He made motions with his
hands, as if covering up an object.

"Hidden?" Rachel suggested.

"*Sí*. Hidden." He nodded vigorously. "Why, *señorita*? *Está* family. *Por que* hide?"

"The car was back by the old greenhouse?" Rachel
said, frowning. "You're sure it was his car—*el coche del
sobrino?*"

Julio nodded mutely, his dark eyes glossy with judgement.

Henry had been bruised. That was what Jeff had implied. From the fall? Jeff didn't seem to think so. Rachel
rubbed her arms, cold in spite of the afternoon heat. Wind
gusted suddenly, shoving the heavy front door open with
a groan that made her jump. It was starting to get dark.

She started to go back and lock it, then halted. The
police were here. She stifled a laugh that tasted of hysteria. Someone was still taking pictures out back. The
flash flickered like lightning through the shadowy main
floor as she closed the carved wood door. "He should
have torn the walkway down," she said out loud. "I told
him . . ."

"I agree with you." Jeff came around the corner of
the hotel. "Are you all right?" He searched her face,
looking worried. "Do you need a ride home?"

"I'm okay." She shivered. "I guess it just hit me . . .
that he's dead. That someone . . . killed him." She shiv-

ered again. "I need to take Julio home." She walked
with him back to her truck, where Julio was rolling a
cigarette while he waited. He stiffened as Jeff approached. "It's all right," Rachel told him mechanically.
"We're going."

"About our dinner date . . ." Jeff hesitated.

"You're busy." She nodded. "It's okay."

"You usually solve the case in the first few hours or
not at all. Thanks for not being pissed." He gave her a
tentative smile. "See you later." He lifted a hand to her
and walked away.

Rachel drove Julio to the small mobile home on the
edge of town where he lived with his oldest sister and
her husband. Refugees from Guatemala, Gloria worked
at the O'Connor family orchard in the busy seasons,
while her husband was a cook at a Hood River restaurant.
They had owned a restaurant in the city of Flores before
they had had to flee, Julio had told her. It had taken his
sister four years to get permission for Julio to remain in
the U.S., after he had fled Guatemala to join them.

Rachel told him she'd call when she knew about the
Meier job and drove back into town. Joylinn was closing
up The Bread Box, cranking down her colorful awning.
Rachel drove past without stopping, thankful that Joylinn
hadn't spotted her. She felt strangely distant—as if she
was a stranger, as if she'd never been here before.

Henry was dead. Someone had maybe hit him and
pushed him over the Gorge cliff. The town had the bright
unreality of a calendar photograph. She turned onto the
dead-end street where she lived. It stood at the upper
edge of town, where streets and houses ended abruptly
in orchard. Mrs. Frey owned the renovated farmhouse
where she rented a small upstairs apartment. Cherry trees
spread their thick canopies beyond the backyard fence.
In the spring, the orchard was a blanket of white blossoms. Now, the cherries picked and shipped, the dark
leaves rustled in the freshening breeze. The house—usually welcoming—looked stark and lonely tonight.

The curtain twitched as Rachel climbed the stairs that

led up to her small second-floor apartment. Blessedly Mrs. Frey, an elderly widow who lived alone in the main house, didn't come out to chat tonight. She'd know right off that something was wrong. Rachel reached the landing outside the neat one-bedroom apartment that Mrs. Frey's son had created years ago. She unlocked the bolt lock, then ducked as a gray shape streaked up the steps and launched itself at her head.

"Oof!" She staggered as the wiry cat landed neatly on her shoulders. "I should rent you to the circus," she complained, but she hugged him against her.

With a low yowl of complaint, the cat batted her ear. Purring like a motorboat, he let her carry him inside. Peter had come with the apartment, although Mrs. Frey denied all knowledge of his antecedents. They fought a perpetual and usually good-natured war over possession of the rose garden out back. The phone began to ring as Rachel closed the door. "I'll get your food in a minute, Peter." She tugged on one of his chewed ears, dumped him onto the sofa, and grabbed for the phone. Peter leaped onto the sofa back and fixed her with a steely glare, obviously dissatisfied with Rachel's priorities.

"Hello?" She carried the phone to the small formica breakfast bar that separated kitchenette from living space in the large, airy room.

"Rachel? I expected your machine." Her mother's voice came over the wire. "You're home early."

"Hi, Mom!" She swallowed a lump in her throat, wanting nothing so much as to pour out the whole dark history of this afternoon. But her mother would only worry. Rachel tucked the phone under her chin and pulled a can of cat food down from the cupboard. "I've got to write up an estimate for a new client this evening." She made her voice cheerful. "How's Aunt Esther?"

"*Mazel tov* on the new client. And Esther is about as well as can be expected." Her mother sighed. "It's hard to go from living in your own apartment to living in an institution—even one as nice as this place. She's always been such an independent person."

"That's a very nice way to say it." They both laughed, and Rachel felt her heart lighten at the warmth in her mother's voice.

"She's as settled in as she's going to get," Rachel's mother went on. "And after our third argument today, she told me I'd better go home before I ruined her good blood pressure." She snorted, then laughed. "She's as opinionated and stubborn as she ever was. I told her I'd worry about her when she stopped arguing with me."

"So you're coming home?" Rachel smiled, realizing suddenly just how much she had missed her during these past months. "It's about time. Sunday dinners at the house are awful without you. If I hear one more description of the newest thing in spray nozzles, or eat one more tomato-soup-covered meatloaf, I'll die."

"Well, your aunt Catherine does treat her *Campbell's Soup Cookbook* like a Bible, I must admit," her mother said briskly. "But she feeds a lot of people well during harvest. Conversation *you* can fix. How's the crop coming along, by the way?"

"I could fix it if I could get a word in edgewise." Rachel rolled her eyes. "The crop looks great, and the prices should be good, with the new Asian markets opening up. Uncle's whistling a Sousa march." This time her mother laughed. You could always tell the price of apples by the tune Uncle Jack chose to whistle. Sousa was good. Irish laments were bad. "It'll be so good to see you, Mom," Rachel said as she opened the cat food can.

"Five months is a long time." Her mother sighed. "But this was a tough change for Esther. It was worth doing."

"And you're the only member of the family who can stand up to her." Rachel forked cat food onto a plate and winced as she felt the most delicate of claw-pricks on her ankle. "Okay, okay," she mouthed, and bent to set the plate on the floor.

"Well, I live three thousand miles away. That makes a difference. I'll be on a one o'clock flight into Portland tomorrow," her mother went on. "No need to pick me up. I'll catch the Amtrak Empire Builder out to Hood River.'' She had always loved the train and took it between Portland and Hood River whenever possible.

"I'll meet you at the train station," Rachel promised.

"Heavens, girl, I can call the Taxi Sisters."

"What if they have a tow job? Forget it." She tossed the can into the recycle bin. The Taxi Sisters, as they were known, ran Blossom's only taxi and towing service. "I'll come get you. I want to hear about life in New York. And I'm sure you'll tell me about all of the relatives."

"Of course. In great detail. Why shouldn't you suffer, too?" They both laughed again.

They said their good-byes, and Rachel hung up, feeling a twinge of guilt over not mentioning Henry's death. But her mother would only worry, and she deserved a peaceful flight home at least. Peter was licking the last crumbs of food from his dish, and it was definitely dark now. Shower, Rachel thought, then something to eat, and get to work on the estimate.

Showered and dressed in clean jeans and T-shirt, she set out paper, her notes, and calculator on her small dining table. Eat dinner, she told herself, but she wasn't really hungry. Later, she decided, and began to concentrate on the task at hand. Estimates were tricky. She had to figure her costs carefully—number of plants, number of sprinkler heads and emitters, how much pipe. She'd need to diagram her irrigation and electrical trenches, figure out how many man-hours would be required for their digging. Add to that the cost of grading and the hardware for the low-voltage lighting system. She tapped her teeth with her pencil, adding up the cost of grading the lot, topsoil, and rock from the quarry over in Camas.

Unexpected expenses lurked like snags beneath still water—the vein of basalt that might lie just below the thin soil, preventing her from trenching for water pipe. Or an inadequate well. They could set the project back and run the cost up quickly. But if she figured everything in, then the cost might send Dr. Meier looking for someone else.

A firm knock at the door made her jump, jolting Rachel out of a fog of watering zones and plant lists.

"It's me, Jeff." His voice sounded through the thin wood panels of the door. "Are you there?"

"Well, hi. I didn't think you were coming by." Rachel pulled the door open, unexpectedly flustered.

"I had to take a dinner break." His smile was tentative as he entered. "You've probably eaten by now."

"I wasn't hungry." She looked away, uncertain, and not sure why. "I guess . . . it hit me harder than I realized. Henry's . . . murder."

Peter, who had retreated to the back of the sofa, hissed loudly, and they both started. "Hi." Jeff sat down on the edge of the sofa and offered his fingers to Peter. "Pardon me for not introducing myself."

Peter glowered, then sniffed his fingers cautiously. After a moment of consideration, he shoved his head once against Jeff's hand, then began to wash himself vigorously.

"Wow, you passed." Rachel smiled. "I'm impressed."

"I like cats. I fed a couple of back-alley visitors down in LA." He stood. "Want to go to Fong's? I'm buying." He sounded unexpectedly anxious.

"I would like that very much." Her stomach rumbled agreement. "Remember when Bill made that sculpture with every pair of chopsticks on the table?"

"And the soy sauce bottle."

"I thought the waitress was going to take him by the ear." Rachel smiled. "Then old Mr. Fong came out and applauded, and everybody else did, too, and Bill ended up a hero."

"That's Bill for you." Jeff ushered her down the steps. "He always ends up with the brass ring, even when he falls off the merry-go-round."

A black Nissan pickup was parked beside her truck. Rachel felt mildly relieved that he wasn't driving one of

Blossom's two police cars. She climbed into the truck and rolled the window down, resisting the temptation to wave to the invisible Mrs. Frey. The cool night air combed her curly hair back from her face, and she breathed the scent of the river and dust as they drove down to Blossom's main street. Only night-lights glowed in the storefronts, but at the west end of town, the Main Street Tavern and Cafe glowed with neon. A few dusty cars and pickups stood at the curb, along with a couple of Jeep Cherokees, Suzukis, and a Volvo with sailboards racked on the roof.

At the other end of the street, Fong's, a clapboarded example of classic roadhouse, advertised CHINESE AND AMERICAN FOOD and COCKTAILS in red and green neon letters. The parking lot was nearly full, but the hostess greeted them immediately. "Jeff Price, I don't believe it." She touched her honey-blond hair quickly, giving him a dimpled smile. "I heard a rumor that you were back in town. You got tired of the big city, too, sweetheart?"

"Hi, Mandy." He smiled a bit awkwardly. "It's nice to see so many old friends. I figured everyone would be gone by now."

"Not me." Mandy tossed her head and fluttered her eyelashes. "I tried LA, too. Made a start in pictures, but the lifestyle was too much." She waved vaguely. "So I'm back, and back on my own again. We should compare stories one of these evenings." Her eyelashes fluttered again. "Will this do for you?" She led them to a booth near the wall, where they would be in clear sight of her cash register, Rachel thought uncharitably.

"It's fine." Jeff slid onto the bench across from Rachel. "Rachel, you know Mandy Benther, don't you?"

"Hi, Mandy." Rachel nodded. "How are you doing?" Mandy's father was the town dentist, and Mandy had been one of the golden crowd—cheerleader, homecoming queen, class president. Rachel had never been one of her crowd, although they had both raised 4-H guide dog puppies from the same litter one year.

"Oh, I'm doing fine, honey." Mandy gave Rachel a vague smile, then turned back to Jeff as she handed out the menus. "I hope I'll see you around." Her smile brightened. "We just have to get together and have a good old talk about that City of Angels. And the good old days."

"Sure thing." Jeff began to study the menu obsessively. "One of these days."

"She sure hasn't changed much," Rachel said dryly.

"She noticed me. That's new." Jeff looked up from the laminated sheet with a grin. "I was pretty invisible when I was in high school—except the one time she wanted me to dissect her frog for her in Mr. Bell's biology class. I want Kung Pao chicken." He laid down his menu. "What else?"

"Pot stickers," Rachel said firmly. The tender dumplings were her absolute favorite at Fong's.

Their waitress—one of Fong's many relatives—took their order and departed, leaving a pot of pale fragrant tea on their table. "I got the feeling I scared you a little this afternoon." Jeff frowned as he poured golden tea for them both.

"Yes." Rachel hesitated. "You kind of did," she said softly. "It hit me that you could suspect anyone. Even me."

"I have to." Jeff picked up his chopsticks and slowly began to strip away the white paper wrapper. "You do that or you're a lousy cop. *You* have an alibi." He gave her a brief grin.

"Julio doesn't."

"No." Jeff sighed and laid the chopsticks down. "He doesn't. A part of me has to be that way—a stranger to everybody. Suspicious of everybody. If I'm going to do my job right. I saw . . . what happens when you don't do that—keep that distance. I guess . . . I just wanted to tell you that. So you'd know." He raised his eyes to her face, a crooked smile on his lips. "So now you know. Do you want me to take you home?"

"No." Rachel looked up at the waitress, who appeared

at that moment with a steaming platter of pot stickers.
"I want to eat pot stickers." She inhaled blissfully as the
young woman set the platter down and arranged small
dishes of dipping sauce. "I know it matters to you—
doing a good job." She leaned forward as the waitress
departed. "It always has." She touched his hand lightly.
"I don't think you scare me anymore, anyway."

He smiled tentatively, then picked up a dumpling with
a deft snatch of his chopsticks and deposited it on her
plate. "Tell me about your business," he said. "Why
didn't you leave Blossom?"

"I discovered I didn't really want to." Between bites
of food, Rachel told him about her father's death, school,
and her final realization that she hadn't felt at home since
she had left the town. "I guess I'm a small-town type,"
she said.

The Kung Pao chicken came, and they devoured it.
Tingling with Szechuan peppers, chicken, vegetables, and
peanuts, it vanished quickly. She told him about her decision to design outdoor living spaces for people instead
of running the family orchard. "We crowd closer and
closer," she said. "We're forgetting what the outdoors
is like. It's just a space between car door and office door.
I want to give people a little bit of nature—their own
backyard ecosystem. I want them to have a private bit of
green space—a retreat. Their own mountain peak."

"You're passionate." Jeff was smiling at her, his eyes
warm and blue as a summer sky. "You always were—
when you cared about something. You know . . . you
were my best friend."

"You were mine," she said, a little shy, because she'd
never put it into words before. But it was true. She'd
always known it.

They finished dinner, and he told her a little about LA,
about the shabby little neighborhood he'd moved into,
not far from the edge of the barrio. He didn't tell her
much at all about his time with the LAPD. There was a
dark space there. And a closed door, Rachel thought.

As they were waiting for their check, a stocky man in

slacks and a chino shirt walked by the table on his way
from the men's room. Rachel recognized Herbert Southern, Sandy's father, who ran Western Realty. He waved
and came over to their table. "So has my daughter cried
on your shoulder about the new yard yet?" he asked her
cheerfully. "It's a desert—sunburned grass and clay. I
told her to go with bark dust and a deck, but she wants
plants."

"I haven't seen it yet," Rachel said, and introduced
Jeff.

"I remember you. Better than you think." The realtor
twinkled at Jeff. "You four thought you were getting
away with a lot, didn't you?"

"Didn't we?" Rachel asked innocently.

"Maybe, maybe." The stocky Herbert beamed at her.
"And maybe not as much as you thought. So I hear
you're working for old Henry these days."

"I was." Rachel gave Jeff a quick, sideways glance,
wondering if she should say anything. He shrugged.

"Was?" Herbert asked sharply. "Did the old fool fire
you?"

"He . . . had an accident this afternoon. He fell. He's
dead."

"What?" Herbert looked for a moment as if Rachel
had punched him. "Henry Bassinger is dead? You're
sure?"

At Rachel's nod, he clucked his tongue, eyes fixed on
the gilt-patterned wallpaper, his gaze distant. "Well, I'll
be," he said faintly. "You never know what's going to
happen in this crazy world."

"I guess not," Rachel said, but he didn't appear to
have heard her.

Without another word, Herbert Southern turned on his
heel and hurried off across the restaurant in the direction
of the restrooms.

"He was upset, wasn't he?" Thoughtfully Jeff stared
after him. "Were they close friends?"

"Not that I know of." Rachel shook her head. Jeff
was back in officer mode, she thought. "Maybe he

thought Henry was going to sell after all.''

"Maybe," Jeff said as Mandy bustled over with their fortune cookies and a determined look on her face.

They managed to extricate themselves from her clutches and escaped into the cool darkness. As they drove back to her apartment, Rachel felt a small stab of regret. They really had been best friends, sharing a closeness that had grown out of afternoons spent lying in orchard grass, finding patterns in clouds, and searching for patterns in life. She had missed him—and that sharing. At her apartment Jeff climbed the stairs with her, but he seemed impatient, and she caught him glancing at his watch.

"You need to get back to work," she said, kissing him lightly on the side of the mouth. "Thanks for dinner."

"Thanks for taking the time. And listening to me." His smile warmed his eyes. "I'm glad I don't scare you anymore. Good night." He lifted his hand and clattered down the stairs to his truck. For a few moments Rachel stood on the tiny landing, watching his receding taillights vanish around the corner, filled with a jumble of odd feelings.

"What a day, Peter," she said as she let herself inside. "What a crazy day."

Peter yawned from where he lay stretched out along the back of the sofa. Then he flattened his ears as someone knocked loudly on the door. "So what did you forget?" she asked as she opened the door. It wasn't Jeff.

"H'llo," Alex Cresswell mumbled. "C'n I come in?" He swayed forward and would have fallen if Rachel hadn't grabbed his arm. He was heavy and off balance, and together they waltzed across the living room in a staggering zigzag. Peter hissed and bolted out the front door. With a grunt Alex flopped into the easy chair across from the sofa and buried his face in his hands.

"Are you all right?" Rachel caught her breath, poised between worry and outright anger. "What's wrong with you? And how did you find out where I live?"

"Saw yer truck. I'm jes' drunk," he mumbled through

his fingers. "Uncle's dead, an' . . . an' . . . I don't know. I bought a fifth of Scotch. I drank it. Maybe all of it. Don't remember." He made a sound between a hiccough and a sob. "They think I killed him. All of 'em. That's crazy, y'know? He was . . . I could talk to him. Not like with Mother. She didn't want to hear me. I guess she lived in her own world, too, you know?" He hiccoughed again. "Never thought of that. That she did. But Uncle Henry and I . . . we're both kind of alike. Just tryin' to make it. An' be safe. Even if you have to do it alone. Mother made fun of him, but Uncle Henry was . . . special. Really special. And I never told him." Tears seeped from his eyes. "I never told him," he whispered.

"I think he knew, Alex." She put a hand on his shoulder as he buried his face in his hands again. "I'm going to fix you some coffee." She went around to the kitchen side of the breakfast bar, wondering who she could call. One of her cousins, maybe, but this close to harvest, they were already putting in long days. Bill, she thought. Sandy's husband. "When you've had some coffee," she called over her shoulder, "we'll drive you to your motel. Where are you staying?" He didn't answer, and she turned the gas flame up high under the teakettle, hoping he wasn't throwing up on her rug.

He was still quiet when she carried the steaming mug of coffee into the living room a few minutes later. Too quiet. He lay curled on his side on the sofa, sound asleep, one arm trailing on the floor.

"Wake up!" She set the coffee down to shake him. "Alex? Alex!" He smiled without opening his eyes and mumbled something. He smelled like a distillery.

"Time to get up," she said, shaking him again. This time his only answer was a snore.

With a sigh, she straightened, her hands on her hips. Relaxed in slumber, he looked young. As if maturity was a mask he put on for the day. What had he said? Something about being safe. *Even if you have to do it alone.* As if the world hadn't been a very safe place for him or his uncle. With a sigh Rachel went to the closet and pulled an extra blanket down from the top shelf. Opening the front door, she called Peter softly. "You can come back in now, cat. He's harmless."

Peter was having none of it.

Rachel looked down at the pool of yellow light from the outside security lights. Maybe Mrs. Frey was asleep. Maybe it was past her bedtime, and she hadn't noticed Alex climb her stairs.

Yeah, maybe. She sighed and closed the door. Locked it.

CHAPTER

4

The phone jolted Rachel from a dream where Henry Bassinger followed her around, pulling up every shrub on the hotel grounds, shaking them in her face and yelling at her. He was saying something very urgent and important, but she couldn't understand him because he had left his stereo on, and the trumpet solo blasting from the gazebo drowned out his words. Then she was out in the old wooden octagon, searching for the trumpet player. Only the gazebo was breaking apart—falling down into the river.

She woke with a cry to the shrill ring of the phone beside her bed. "Hello?" She fumbled it to her ear, still shaky from her nightmare.

"I hope I didn't wake you." Dr. Meier's agitated voice came over the line. "I wanted to catch you before you got started on a job."

"This line rings my cell phone if I don't answer." Rachel stifled a yawn. She had worked on the estimate until after two A.M. "You can always reach me." She didn't tell him that she didn't have a job scheduled for the morning. Except for the hotel job, which was certainly on hold, she had no clients at the moment. "I'm almost finished with your estimate."

"Look, everything has changed." Dr. Meier sounded harried. "Your references are wonderful. I trust you. We'll just work out costs as we go. This is an emergency."

"An emergency?" Rachel rubbed sleep out of her eyes. "What's wrong?"

"My daughter is what's wrong." Dr. Meier let out a gusty sigh. "Or maybe it's my fault for bringing her up to be a headstrong, spoiled, stubborn . . . Let me start over."

Rachel reached for her terry robe, thinking that would be a good idea.

"She just called to tell me that my granddaughter is getting married."

"Congratulations."

"Hardly." Dr. Meier's tone was acerbic. "Brianna is barely eighteen and a spoiled child who thinks her daddy is going to take care of her forever. But for good or ill, it's going to happen. And Elaine—my daughter—is bound and determined to make an Affair of the mess." His tone capitalized the word. "Maybe she wants to scare the boy off. He's only nineteen, for God's sake, and not even in college. What are they going to do with their lives?"

"I see," Rachel said cautiously, not at all sure that she did.

"I'm sorry. I'm not being coherent, am I? Elaine wants to put on a fancy wedding, and she's determined to have it at *my* house. Because Hood River is in, she says." Dr. Meier sounded resigned. "There's no way I can talk her out of it. And she tells me it's set for September tenth. I'll need to have the landscaping done by then or listen to my daughter kvetch forever."

Rachel whistled softly, all traces of slumber banished from her brain as she grabbed for the calendar on her desk.

"Can you do it?" Dr. Meier asked anxiously. "I want

it to look nice. We can finish the real long-term work afterward."

"That gives me nearly seven weeks," Rachel said slowly. Standing up, she paced the length of the phone's cord. Outside her window, the morning crowd of chickadees and sparrows fluttered around Mrs. Frey's bird feeder. "If I get started right away, I can have the main work done by then. But I'll have to hire more labor than I planned in my original estimate." She frowned, thinking hard. "It'll cost more."

"Money we can do." Dr. Meier sounded immensely relieved. "You'll have to change our design, I suppose," he said ruefully. "Too bad."

"Oh, we'll stick with it. I'll space the plantings much closer than we'd planned. As they grow, I can transplant out the extras."

"Wonderful, wonderful. Sounds like a plan," Dr. Meier said enthusiastically. "Can you give me your estimate this afternoon? Then you can get started right away."

"No problem." The estimate was mostly complete, and the changes wouldn't take long to make. "How about if I come by at eleven?"

"Thank you," Dr. Meier said in heartfelt tones. "If you can pull this off, I'll sing your praises across the entire Northwest. My daughter is incredibly conscious of status and appearance. And that," he said grimly, "is what comes of marrying a lawyer with ambitions. He should have stayed in the family furniture business."

Rachel shook her head as she hung up, smiling. No love lost between the good doctor and his son-in-law? Well, this was the biggest job she'd landed so far for her fledgling business, and it would be a golden reference in the growing community of affluent retirees who were moving into the Gorge. Belting her robe, she padded into the front room to make coffee.

Peter sat on the sill outside the front window, glowering at the snoring figure on the sofa. Alex! Rachel clapped a hand to her forehead and groaned. Wait until this got around town. Which it surely would, unless Mrs. Frey chose today to go blind and deaf. With a sigh she opened the door for Peter. At least Alex hadn't parked his rented car in the driveway. "Come on, cat. Come get your breakfast," she told him. "Mandy will love this bit of gossip."

Tail erect, Peter stalked past her, walked deliberately across the room, and leaped neatly onto the middle of the blanketed sleeper. Peter was not a small cat. With an explosive grunt Alex jerked into a sitting position, staring around wildly. "What the hell?" His eyes fixed on Rachel and widened. "Oh, Lord. How did I get . . . Oh, yeah." He leaned his forehead in his hands and groaned. "I barged in, didn't I? I think I was pretty drunk."

"To put it mildly."

"Why didn't you kick me out?" he mumbled.

"Believe me, I tried." She had to smile in spite of herself. He seemed so *embarrassed*. "I was too tired to go borrow a wheelbarrow. As long as you're up—want some coffee?"

"Coffee—oh, God, please." He lifted his head and rubbed at the stubble on his chin. Winced. "I do remember. Sort of." The words came out muffled.

"There's aspirin and such in the bathroom medicine cabinet," she called back to him. "When you're ready for it." Taking the coffee beans out of the freezer, she ground enough for a whole pot and filled the machine's reservoir with water. If she was going to get her estimate finished by eleven, she was going to have to get to work pronto. With one eye on the wall clock she got the half-and-half out of the refrigerator and checked the egg carton.

Peter had decided to ignore the intruder long enough for breakfast at least and now entwined himself around Rachel's ankles. She opened a can of cat food and scooped it onto a plate, which she set beside his bowl of dry food—an item he disdained until faced with starvation. Cracking eggs into a bowl, she grabbed the phone and called Daren Rhinehoffer at Riverside Nursery.

Explaining the situation, she grabbed a pad from the drawer and went down the list of plants she had drawn up yesterday. If she could limit her trips to Portland for nursery stock, it would save her a couple of full days. At least. Fortunately they had a number of species in stock. Feeling more hopeful, she set her enamel omelette pan onto the stove and dropped a lump of butter into it.

Sprinkling a generous amount of marjoram over the eggs, she added a dollop of half-and-half and a couple of drops of Tabasco sauce and whisked vigorously. Water was running in the bathroom as she poured the foamy mixture carefully into the hot pan. As the eggs cooked, she leaned on the counter with a pad and her calculator, figuring costs. When the eggs were done, she sprinkled a bit of grated cheddar over them, folded the omelette in half, and got down two plates.

"Think you could eat some breakfast?" Rachel asked as Alex emerged from the bathroom.

"I wouldn't blame you for hitting me with the frying pan instead of cooking me breakfast." He sniffed wistfully. "Wow, that smells good. Listen, I'm really sorry. I was . . . I just don't do that kind of thing." His face was crimson. "You must really think I'm a jerk."

"Drunk, yes, jerk . . ." She gave him a mischievous smile. "I don't have enough information yet. Here." She handed him a mug of coffee. "There's cream. And I've got sugar if you want it."

"Real cream. And good coffee." He poured in a generous portion of cream and took an appreciative sip. "I think I might live after all." He drank some more coffee as Rachel set out silverware and divided the omelette onto two plates.

"I'll try." He eyed the food doubtfully, then took a tentative bite. "That's good. Where did you learn to do this?" He forked up more egg. "This is just what I needed. And a whole lot better than anything I'd get in a restaurant in this town. Or Hood River."

"My mother believes that everyone needs to know how to cook well—male or female. My cousins Jerry and

Eric learned, too. I'm not sure they ever admitted it to their girlfriends, though.''

"Jerry O'Connor? I played baseball with him when I was up here for the summers. Over in the park.'' He drank more coffee. "He was a good hitter.''

"He still plays on the Blossom team. They beat Hood River last year.''

"I met you, you know.'' He gave her a brief smile. "You and another girl rode your horses out to the hotel. I showed you the greenhouse, and we picked roses. I remember your horse stepped on my foot.''

"That's right. I'd forgotten.'' Rachel laughed. She studied his lean, tanned face. "You've changed a lot,'' she said.

"No more acne.'' He managed a straight face. "I used to look for you after that—when Jerry and I were playing baseball. But I guess you didn't hang around with him much.''

"Are you kidding?'' Rachel rolled her eyes. "Last thing Jerry wanted was his kid-sister cousin tagging along to games.''

"Too bad. We talked about the solar system, I remember. You knew more than any girl I'd met.'' He carried their plates to the sink and began to wash them. "Can I at least buy you dinner sometime? As payment?'' He gave her a tentative smile. "And to give myself a chance to prove I'm not really a jerk?''

"That would be nice,'' she said.

"Tonight?''

"I'm sorry.'' She shook her head. "I'm supposed to go to a friend's house.''

"I'd better call you.'' A shadow crossed Alex's face. "I may be in jail,'' he said darkly. "That hick cop yesterday sure seemed to think I pushed Uncle Henry off that walkway.'' His knuckles whitened briefly on the plate he was holding. "I guess I'm a prime suspect. Since I inherit the place,'' he said bitterly. "Like it matters now.''

"Do you really think someone murdered him?" Rachel asked slowly.

For a moment Alex's face was still, and he stared unseeingly at the wall. "I . . . I guess what I'm really afraid of is suicide. He was acting so . . . strange." He shook his head sharply. "But I don't know. Real estate prices are going wild out here. That property has tripled in value in the last few years. It's a prime spot for a small resort or even a bed-and-breakfast. That's the reason I was able to find some financing possibilities." He turned back to face her. "Uncle Henry wasn't doing it for the money. I don't think he ever quite lived in the real world. I think that's why he was special. He fit right into a kid's magical universe. He was kind of a Peter Pan. We played together. We could talk to each other. It's not the same without him." He hesitated. "I guess you'd better stop work over there. I don't know what's going to happen to the property, and to be honest, I don't know if I'll go on with the restoration. I'll pay you whatever Uncle Henry owed you."

"He paid me most of it." Rachel tilted her head. "I thought it was from the money he'd received for the renovation."

"Oh, no." Alex shook his head. "I hadn't been able to give him any real money yet. I was looking for financing, but everything was still in the negotiation stage. If he paid you, it was out of his own pocket."

Interesting. Rachel wondered where that big deposit had come from.

"I'd better go see if the cops are done scouring my car for incriminating evidence. They had a search warrant before you could say boo." Alex laid the folded blanket carefully on the sofa, wary of the glowering Peter, who had reclaimed his perch on the back. With a wry smile and another round of thanks, he left, hurrying down the stairs as if in retreat. There was no sign of Mrs. Frey behind the curtain. Rachel breathed a sigh of relief.

"If that man didn't genuinely care about Henry, then he's a world-class actor, cat." Rachel put the blanket

away and poured herself a final cup of coffee. "Time to
stop thinking about Henry, or Alex, or anything except
that estimate." Carrying her coffee over to the drafting
table that along with a file cabinet and computer made
up her office, she got out her design plans from the night
before.

She lost track of time as she reworked her plans, adding the new plants, altering the watering system accord-
ingly. They could plug the extra emitters after they
moved the plants, but it would add to the initial cost. She
called a couple of nurseries in the Willamette Valley that
offered mature shade and ornamental trees—up to forty
feet tall. Then she sketched, erased, and sketched some
more. Finally satisfied, she looked up to discover that it
was half past ten. With a yelp, she leaped to her feet,
startling Peter, who was catching up on his sleep on *his*
sofa. She had meant to swing by the hotel to water the
flats of plants that Julio hadn't been able to finish planting and to look for her shears—if they hadn't been
bagged as evidence.

Peter exited ahead of her and vanished around the corner of the house, headed in the direction of Mrs. Frey's
rose garden to spend the day lounging hopefully beneath
the bird feeder. Rachel stowed the estimate and the rolled
plans safely in the locked box behind the cab, hopped in
the truck, and headed west through town. She should
have just enough time to water the plants, take a quick
look for her shears, and still get to Dr. Meier's on time.

Traffic was light, and she made good time. To her
relief, the shears lay on the cracked glass table on the
terrace. She picked them up, then froze. The French
doors stood ajar, and the sunlight that filtered through the
boughs of the cedars that overhung the terrace glinted on
shards of glass scattered across the flagstones. One pane
in the left-hand door gaped, glassless. Rachel peered into
the gloomy interior, the hairs prickling on the back of
her neck. Nothing moved as she backed cautiously away
and hurried back to her truck. She called the Blossom
Police Department on her cell phone, reading the number

from the emergency sticker she'd finally gotten around to pasting on the inside flap of the leather case.

Jeff was there. "Get in your truck and get out of there," he said sharply when she'd told him what she'd seen. "I'm on my way over."

"I'm leaving." She started the engine as she spoke. The plants would have to wait.

She drove to Dr. Meier's house, gooseflesh still prickling her neck and arms. By now, of course, everyone in town probably knew that Henry was dead. Ordinary burglary? she wondered. Kids looking for cash or valuables, or maybe daring each other to visit the scene of a murder?

She didn't think so.

She was still feeling jumpy as she parked her truck in Dr. Meier's roomy driveway. He came bounding around from the east deck with enough energy to make her feel tired. Vitamins, she thought, and swallowed a nervous giggle. This was the moment of truth. . . .

"I'm so glad you're here," he said as he hurried her up the wide steps that led to the deck. "Come on—we can talk out here. The mountains are lovely this morning." Indeed they were. The deck, facing north, gave them a breathtaking view of St. Helens' truncated top and Jefferson's huge profile. A wooden table had been laid with a platter of cold cuts, a plate of bagels, and a pitcher of iced tea. "I don't want hunger to distract us," he said with a grin.

"Thank you," Rachel said, although all vestiges of an appetite had vanished. She unrolled her plans across the end of the table and weighted the corners against the brisk Gorge breeze with a jar of mustard and a glass. "I marked in everything. The permanent plantings are done in green." She snagged a bagel from the platter and used it as a pointer. "The short-term fill-ins are in red. We can spread them out down here, along the northern border, when they get crowded. The view should keep folks from noticing how barren it is at the moment. We'll barkdust the beds and arrange the boulders. It'll have a minimalist effect—sort of like a Japanese sand garden.''

Dr. Meier nodded, his lips pursed, eyes narrowed. Rachel drew a deep breath and went on.

"For now, the extra shrubs and plants will give the upper beds a nice full profile. The irrigation lines are drawn in black.'' She pointed. "These orange lines are for the electrical lines. I've marked the floods in blue.'' She took another deep breath. "Here are the final numbers.'' She laid the page in front of him and took a huge, nervous bite of bagel.

It tasted like sawdust.

For what seemed to be a small eternity, Dr. Meier frowned down at her numbers, his eyes traveling occasionally to the neatly drawn plans. Finally he straightened.

"Do you want half now and half on completion?'' He pulled a leather checkbook from his pocket.

"Uh . . . yes.'' Rachel struggled to swallow her dry mouthful of bagel. "That would be fine.'' Feeling a little dazed, she fumbled the two copies of their formal agreement from her folder. She signed them, then handed them to him. He slipped a pair of reading glasses from his pocket, read the agreement carefully, then signed both copies with a flourish.

"Everything looks fine.'' Dr. Meier laid a check on top of the signed agreements, then reached for some sliced turkey breast. "This place will be just what I've dreamed of for all these years.''

"I'll sure do my best.'' Rachel folded the check and tucked it into her wallet. The sum made her a little breathless. Rain Country Landscaping had just stepped into the big leagues, as far as she was concerned.

"I was thinking about our little baby pond last night.'' Dr. Meier's eyes sparkled as he nibbled on another handful of turkey. "I think I want to put koi into it.''

"I wouldn't.'' Rachel shook her head. "Blue herons,'' she explained to his blank look. "They love koi. Very picturesque to find a great blue heron wading in your koi pool. But koi are expensive heron food.'' She gave him a lopsided smile. "There are some gorgeous goldfish out there in the pet stores. Some of them get pretty big."

"Hmmm." Dr. Meier raised his eyebrows and laughed. "I'm not sure but I'd rather have the herons than the koi."

They went over the garden plans detail by detail, oblivious to the increasing heat of the day. Rachel explained how she would handle the job—grading first, then soil amendment, irrigation and electrical lines, and finally the plants.

"I'm happy." Dr. Meier finally sat back, a satisfied smile on his face. "And you can really have it looking good for the wedding?"

"Barring unexpected catastrophes." Rachel stretched, discovering that she was exhausted. Well—the two A.M. bedtime hadn't helped much. "I called Harvey Glisan last night," she told him. "He can get the grading done this afternoon if you want. He's got a DC-8 Cat—a bulldozer," she amplified. "And a track hoe for placing the rocks. He does very good work at a good price."

"Sure of yourself, weren't you?" Dr. Meier's eyes twinkled.

Rachel blushed. "Well . . . I bid low. And since you're in a hurry . . . I did say that it wasn't for sure, that I'd call him if the job was off."

"Relax." The doctor chuckled. "I like someone who doesn't wait to be told to breathe."

She hoped he didn't change his mind on that one. Rachel reached for another bagel and yelped as she checked her watch.

"What's wrong?" Dr. Meier, on his way to the kitchen with the empty iced-tea pitcher, paused.

"I'm supposed to pick up my mother at the Amtrak station in Hood River in half an hour." If she left this minute, she'd barely make it on time. "I'll have to call Harvey and put off the grading until tomorrow," she said regretfully.

"Let's not ruin a good start." Dr. Meier waved a hand. "I can go collect your mother. It'll keep me out of your hair, and I'm really harmless." He gave her an impish grin. "I haven't attacked an old lady in . . . oh, weeks now. It'll give me something to do besides sit here and think black thoughts about my granddaughter's misbegotten essay into matrimony."

"That's nice of you to offer," Rachel said cautiously. She really did want to get started. Harvey could have a job lined up for tomorrow.

"It's an excuse to take my MG out for a spin." He looked suddenly anxious. "Is your mother up to a ride in a sports car?"

"She'll survive." Rachel decided not to mention that her mother drove a Triumph TR 6—that ran only because the local mechanic who worked on all the orchard's vehicles was a Brit whose passion was the Triumph in all its incarnations. It was a standing family joke for someone to ask daily if the Blue Monster was running today or not. Frequently it was not. "For an old lady, she's pretty tough," Rachel said with a straight face.

"Good, that's settled then." Dr. Meier's smile sparkled. "Call in your bulldozer. I'll get going right away." Whistling, he was off before Rachel could say another word.

She half rose, intending to call him back and describe her mother to him, but he had already disappeared into the house. A moment later the garage door rumbled open out front, and a powerful car engine revved. Rachel shook her head and went back to her irrigation design with a smile. They would find each other, she had no doubt. Not many people got off the train at Hood River. This kind of thing wouldn't flap her mother at all, but she had a feeling that Dr. Meier was in for a bit of a surprise.

It turned out to be a good thing that she had chosen to stay and work. Rachel was just dialing Harvey's number on her cell phone when his dump truck rumbled up Dr. Meier's driveway, towing the big DC-8 behind it on a flatbed trailer. *Glisan and Son Earth Movers* had been painted on the door of the black truck in flowing gilt script.

"You didn't call." Harvey leaned out the cab window as his lanky son Carl hopped down to uncouple the trailer. "So I figured the job was a go. Gonna be busy the rest of the week." He spat, shut off the engine, and climbed down. As Harvey stood in the driveway, his head didn't quite reach Rachel's collarbone. Small and wiry, he had shoulders like a boxer, with a broken nose to match. Harvey never backed down from a fight, but no one had ever seen him lose his temper either.

"It sure is a go." Rachel walked to the edge of the deck with the small man. "Nice lettering on your truck, by the way. New?"

"Got it from the guy who did yours." Harvey shaded his eyes, jaw working on a wad of chewing tobacco, as he surveyed the slope. "So what do you want here?"

Rachel described the proposed lawn area. He would have to work the slope down into a terrace that curved across in front of the house. "Just contour the lower slope a little, so we don't have all the water running straight down the hill." It had bothered her the first time she had used Harvey that he didn't survey first and plant stakes before he began. He worked by eye, and she'd heard a rumor that once an irate foreman on a big job had bet him a hundred dollars that he was at least a foot off from the site plan.

The foreman had lost.

True or not, it made a good story. By now Carl had the Cat warming up. The low mutter of the powerful diesel engine sounded like the rumbling purr of a giant feline. Rachel perched herself on the deck as Harvey swung onto the patched black vinyl of the Cat's seat and touched the levers. The blade rose, and the Cat lumbered forward, its metal tank-tread churning up the thin layer of topsoil that the builder had dumped, mixing it with the tan rocky soil below. Good thing she'd figured in the cost of a few truckloads of topsoil, Rachel thought, or she'd already be hurting.

Oblivious to the hot afternoon sun, Rachel watched Harvey work. He made the Cat dance, gouging out a deep trench in the hillside one moment, shaving off a few centimeters on a contour the next. As he carved the hillside with the skill of a sculptor, Rachel began to believe the story of his hundred-dollar win.

Harvey had finished the terrace and was contouring the slope when she heard the roar of the returning MG. Rachel realized with a jolt of surprise that it was late afternoon. Glancing at her watch, she was shocked to discover that it was nearly five o'clock. A fly buzzed hopefully about the plastic-covered platter of lunch meat and a yellow jacket investigated the rim of her iced-tea glass. It was a half-hour drive to Hood River. Even if the train was late, Dr. Meier should have been back here by three.

Rachel reached the driveway just as the MG screeched to a stop behind the parked truck and trailer. Carl, waiting patiently, was all eyes and teenaged lust as he eyed the sleek sports car. Her mother's three suitcases were strapped precariously on the luggage rack. It was a miracle none of them had fallen off, Rachel thought.

"I told you it was well trained," Dr. Meier announced as he shut off the growling engine.

"Good brakes is what you have, not training." Deborah O'Connor was laughing, her head thrown back, her fine-boned face flushed with wind and mirth. Her curly, shoulder-length hair was nearly as dark as Rachel's— touched only at the temples with a light frost that denied her fifty-one years. Unconsciously Rachel brushed at her own mop of hair, a little startled by how pretty her mother still was. At that moment her mother looked up, a wide warm smile lighting her dark eyes as she hopped out of the tiny car.

"Rachel, what have you been up to?" She swept her daughter into a bear hug. "Joshua told me that poor Henry Bassinger was murdered. I can't go away for a minute, girl, without you getting into trouble."

Joshua? "Mom, where have you been?" Rachel pulled out of her mother's embrace, feeling unexpectedly

cranky. "Was the train late? I was worried." Well, she
would have been worried, if she hadn't lost track of time.

"I'm so sorry." Her mother looked genuinely penitent.
"We stopped for lunch on the way back, because the
dining car was closed and the snack bar only had pop
and overpriced flavored water. And we ordered a nacho
plate to split, and it took forever to show up, and we got
to talking, and . . . and . . . I should have called." Deborah hung her head in theatrical contrition. "I was bad."

"Oh, come on, Mom." Rachel rolled her eyes and
laughed. "You'll make Dr. Meier think we're both
nuts."

"Aren't we?" her mother asked innocently.

Dr. Meier chuckled. "It was mostly my fault," he said.
"We got started talking cars, and then jazz . . . then I told
her about Henry Bassinger's murder."

"Poor Henry." Her mother shook her head. "How
terrible."

"We lost track of time." Dr. Meier shrugged, his eyes
sparkling as he regarded Rachel's mother. "I want to
hear that old Charlie Parker 78 of yours. I'm still not
sure I believe you about it." He turned to Rachel. "I
certainly had no trouble recognizing your mother. She
could be your older sister."

"Oy, what a line." Rachel's mother laughed. "Hey,
at my age I'll take it."

"I'm impressed." Dr. Meier nodded at the grumbling
bulldozer. "I never thought he'd have this much done so
soon."

"He should finish by dark." Rachel collected her scattered thoughts with an effort. "I can have the topsoil and
amendments delivered tomorrow and get a crew out here
to spread them."

"Wonderful!" Dr. Meier rubbed his hands together
gleefully. "My poor daughter may not have anything to
complain about. What a shame."

"Don't be hard on her." Rachel's mother wrinkled her
nose. "She has to live with that man, after all."

What had these two been doing? Exchanging lives?

Rachel glanced at her watch, feeling a bit as if a medium-sized earthquake had shifted the landscape slightly. "I'm supposed to be at Sandy's celebration barbecue at seven," she said. "I'd better cancel . . ."

"Why don't I spend the night with you?" Her mother smiled at her. "That way you don't have to run me out to the orchard tonight, and we'll have a little time to catch up before I go home."

"That'll be great, Mom," Rachel said and squeezed her mother's hand. "We could have an early breakfast, before I come over here. I can run you home at noon."

"You take your time in the morning," Dr. Meier instructed Rachel. "A few hours lost won't ruin the wedding. Here, Deborah. If you like King Henry, you'll like this, I bet." He handed her a compact disc. A young black musician hunched over a horn in the dramatic black-and-white cover shot.

"Thank you, Joshua." Giving him a sparkling smile, she climbed into the cab of Rachel's truck. "See you at seven?"

"Seven?" Rachel started the engine and pulled away from the house. Dr. Meier was still standing at the foot of the steps. He waved, and her mother waved back. "What's at seven?"

"Joshua and I are going into Hood River to have dinner at the new brew pub. The Flecktones are playing. I haven't heard them in years."

"I always thought Dad was the big jazz fanatic," Rachel said, feeling a trifle dizzy.

"Well, he was, honey. But I'm the one who introduced him to it." She wrinkled her nose. "He thought Spider John Kerner was the ultimate musician when I first met him. Blues or bluegrass—that was music. Period." She laughed and shook her head. "He loved jazz from the day I played him Brubeck's album *Time Further Out*. That was when I decided he might be worth pursuing after all."

Rachel looked at her sideways, feeling oddly uncomfortable in the face of this conversation. "So now you've got a date."

"We're simply going out to drink beer and listen to jazz. I was going to invite you, but you have this barbecue." She leaned over to tweak a stray lock of Rachel's hair into place. "My dear, you sound so disapproving."

"I do not sound disapproving." Rachel took the turn into town too fast and winced as the pickup's rear end fishtailed slightly on the pavement. She kept her eyes fixed studiously on the road, pretending not to see her mother's slightly amused expression.

When they reached the apartment, Mrs. Frey was out back pruning her roses, watched carefully by the languid Peter. She was wearing her sunflower hat today—one of a collection of huge straw garden hats whose size and silk-flower decorations seemed to belong to another century.

"Hello, dear. Hello, Deborah." She waved her pruning shears, hat brim swaying with her movements. "Goodness, I just heard the news about poor Mr. Bassinger. Murdered, how awful!" She hurried over to the truck, her china-blue eyes wide with a mixture of horror and curiosity in her pale face. "And how awful for you, my dear. Your employer and everything . . ." She turned her china-doll gaze on Deborah. "You must be worried terribly about her."

"Oh, I don't think she's in any danger." Rachel's mother smiled at the elderly woman as she got out of the truck. "I didn't know they'd even decided it was murder."

"Oh, yes, it was murder. That nephew of his did it. Mrs. Bonner over at the Bingo Hall told me. He wants to turn the old hotel into another resort for all those awful windsurfers." She shuddered delicately. "He's from Los Angeles, you know." She lowered her voice and leaned closer to Rachel. "He wears an *earring*."

"A lot of men do," Rachel said.

"Robert would never let my grandsons do that," Mrs.

Frey said firmly. "I just don't know what the world's coming to these days. I really don't."

"I think we'll just have to wait and see," Rachel's mother said lightly. "Those pink roses are lovely. What kind are they?"

"Queen Elizabeth." Mrs. Frey nodded at them approvingly. "Very tall habit, strong and open. An excellent all-round rose."

"I'll have to add one to my rose garden." She lifted one of the suitcases that Dr. Meier had placed in the bed of Rachel's truck. "Rachel, honey, would you grab the other two, please?" She smiled sweetly at her daughter. "I'm an old woman, after all."

"Ha." Rachel swung the two bags out of the bed and escorted her mother up the stairs, preceded by Peter, who rubbed himself enthusiastically against her mother's ankles while Rachel unlocked the door.

It was nearly six o'clock. "Shall we flip a coin for the shower?" her mother asked as she opened a suitcase on the coffee table and peered thoughtfully at the folded clothes it held. "A simple dress," she decided. "I'm not in the mood for slacks."

"Go ahead. I have to run back to Dr. Meier's house. Harvey should be finishing up. I hope." Rachel opened a can of cat food, dumped it onto a plate. "So how is everybody?" she asked, and winced at her formal tone.

"Oh, Aunt Esther is nagging me as usual. She wants the two of us to move back to 'a real city,' as she puts it. I think she still believes that cowboys and Indians have shoot-outs at the brew pub on Saturday nights."

"Don't they?" Rachel set the plate down on the floor, earning a disdainful glance from Peter, who had apparently decided that he had not yet forgiven her for Alex's trespass. "You take the bed tonight. I'll fight with Peter."

"No, dear, I rather like your sofa. It makes me feel more like I'm camping out and less like a guest. Much more fun. How about this? With a single gold chain and sandals, I think." Her mother held up a sleeveless linen shift of teal blue. With her olive Sephardic complexion, dark eyes, and raven hair, it would be stunning. Especially since she had what Rachel considered to be a perfect figure.

"Very nice," she said.

For a moment, her mother looked at her, then she laid the dress carefully down across the back of the suitcase, gave Peter a warning glare, and walked over to put her hands lightly on Rachel's shoulders. "I have to look up to meet your eyes. I remember the first day I noticed it. I thought it was so wonderful that you had your father's height. You remind me so much of Will." Her voice caught. "I miss him so much. I thought I'd never laugh again after he died. It has been a long time, dear. I told myself I was fine on my own. I have Jack and Catherine, after all." She paused. "It . . . was such a surprise to find myself laughing with Joshua, to really want to go listen to music and drink beer with him. Don't worry." She smiled. "I'm not falling in love with him. But it *is* a date, I suppose."

"I'm sorry." Rachel bent slightly and kissed her mother, noticing for the first time the tiny lines around her eyes and mouth. The record of past grief? "I'm being silly. I didn't mean to. Go have a good time."

"I intend to." Her mother tweaked another of Rachel's curls back into place. "So I'd better get into the shower."

"The dress will floor him," Rachel called as she let herself out the front door.

"I hope so." Her mother's voice came faintly from the bathroom. "That would be nice."

CHAPTER

5

Harvey was just finishing up when Rachel arrived back at Dr. Meier's house. The smoothly contoured hillside and lawn area impressed her all over again. She paid him and watched him disappear down the drive with the big Cat in tow. Dr. Meier wasn't home. But it was almost seven. He would be picking up her mother.

That bothered her. Rachel scolded herself for being provincial as she drove back to her apartment. She showered and headed—late—to Sandy and Bill's party.

It still bothered her.

By the time she arrived, several cars had parked along the low hedge that fronted Sandy and Bill's new house. A tall, straggling boxwood hedge bordered a dusty strip of trampled yard in front. Sun-scalded rhododendrons and azaleas flanked a tiny front porch, below twin wood-framed windows. Their leaves drooped from skeletal branches in the slanting beams of the setting sun. Rachel shook her head over the fool who had planted these sun-sensitive shrubs against the west side of the house. A battered swing set and a weathered doghouse with a rusty chain still attached filled the narrow side yard. Paint peeled from the window frames, and some of the wooden siding had curled.

A genuine fixer-upper, Rachel thought as she parked her truck. Bill would love the challenge. Sandy met her at the wooden picket gate set in the sparse hedge. The last vestiges of paint had vanished long ago, and the untrimmed branches of the box pushed against it as if to prevent anyone from entering. "It has tons of potential," Sandy chirped, her eyes glowing. "Bill is going to raise the roof and add another bedroom and a family room. We'll put a deck out back, and a real front porch with a swing, and . . ."

"Sandy, it's neat." Rachel hugged her, smiling at her enthusiasm. Heaven help anyone who disparaged this house, she thought with an internal grin. "And Bill's a talented carpenter. I bet you turn this place into a showcase."

"That'll sure take some work outside here." Sandy glanced around the beaten earth of the shadeless yard with a grim expression. "Bill says we should just pave it over and use it as a parking lot."

"Well, you would have plenty of space for parking that way. . . ."

Sandy made a face. "You're the last to arrive. Come get something to drink, and we'll do the grand tour." She pulled Rachel down the walk. A stubborn rugosa rose grew at the corner of the house. Its arching canes had obviously blocked the concrete slab walkway at one point, but Sandy's ministrations were visible in neatly pruned canes and a fresh mulch of composted manure around the roots. The elderly rose had responded by putting out a host of new green shoots and even a few pink blossoms.

Rachel ducked around the rose on Sandy's heels. A concrete slab served as a patio, leaving another expanse of scuffed dirt and sunburned grass between it and the back of the long, narrow lot. The backyard would get the full morning sun, Rachel reflected. In fact, with the house's east-west orientation, there was no part of the yard that couldn't do with some seasonal shade. At the moment, a folding trestle table held an array of potato and green salads, vegetables, dip, bowls of chips, and all the condiments for the hamburgers Bill was grilling over charcoal. A cooler full of ice, beer, and pop stood at the end of the table, along with a glass pitcher of lemonade and two bottles of inexpensive merlot.

Rachel recognized Herbert, Sandy's father. He was talking to a dark haired older woman, and near them stood Jeff. She smiled in pleased surprise, and realized that Sandy was watching her closely, a smug expression on her own face. "Ha." Rachel punched her lightly on the arm. "Jeff was your secret, right?" She nodded as Sandy's giggle confirmed it. "I ran into him yesterday, thank you very much." She grinned at her friend. "If I'd had my head on straight, I would have invited him to come along."

"Isn't it great that he's back in town?" Sandy's eyes sparkled with mischief. "Bet you were glad to see him."

Rachel made a face at her. Sandy had been setting up dates for her for the last three years—ever since she and Bill got married.

"Hi." Jeff arrived at her side, grinning. "Have you tried the salsa?" He pointed to a clay bowl full of a pepper-studded tomato mixture next to a platter of corn chips. "Bill made it. It's dynamite."

"I hope he left out the Habanero peppers this time." Rachel sighed. Nobody could equal Bill's tolerance for hot food, and he had a hard time remembering the frailties of mere mortals in that respect.

"I'm not so sure he took it easy." Jeff grimaced. "I think I've finally stopped sweating anyway. Beer?"

"Thank you." She took the local ale he handed her, waited while he uncapped another. "How's your case going?" she asked as Sandy scooped up the chips and salsa and began to offer them around. "Anything new?"

"We brought Alex Cresswell in for more questioning today."

With the beer bottle halfway to her lips, Rachel paused.

"Henry's cleaning lady corroborates Peron's sighting of Cresswell's rental car. She was on her way to another job yesterday afternoon." Jeff gave her a brief look. "Cresswell has no alibi for the time, and he had a lawyer in the room within minutes. I guess he flew up here from Los Angeles last night. Not very cooperative, either one of them. If we get a shred of conclusive evidence back from the lab, he's coming in to stay," he said grimly.

Rachel took a swallow of beer, her mind whirling. "I can't believe he did it," she said slowly. "He just doesn't seem the type."

"There is no type when it comes to murder," Jeff said wearily. "It's a hard lesson to learn, Rachel. Sometimes it's a costly one."

The shadows in his eyes silenced her briefly. Rachel touched his arm, then took a chip from the bowl Sandy was offering around and absently scooped up a pile of salsa. "Yikes!" She gasped, tears starting in her eyes, and gulped hastily at her beer. "Sandy, you promised!"

"Honey, this *is* mild." Sandy managed to get the words out without giggling. "Honest."

"That man is dangerous." Rachel drank some more beer, and Jeff chuckled, and the brief shadow passed. "If I ate some of his 'hot' salsa, I'd probably go into cardiac arrest." She fanned herself.

"Time for the tour," Sandy announced, clapping her hands. "I'm only going to do this once, so you all better come see it now. There will be a quiz."

Jeff fell in beside Rachel as the group shuffled after Sandy toward the kitchen door. "Henry's lawyer doesn't have a will on file," he murmured to Rachel as Sandy described the large deck she and Bill were going to build to replace the patio. "He claims that Henry kept it in the house somewhere, even though he'd been nagging him for years to put it in his safe-deposit box."

"Well, it took the whole family to pressure Uncle Jack

to make a will. I guess it was an admission he might actually die.''

"People are funny." Jeff shook his head. "If we don't find a will, then Cresswell inherits. His mother—Henry's sister—died two years ago, and there are no other living relatives that we know of.'' He gave Rachel a sharp sideways glance. "He can do what he wants with the property now.''

"He *wanted* to renovate the hotel.''

"Maybe." Jeff shrugged. "I talked to Herbert about it. He values that property—without the buildings—at close to a million dollars.''

Rachel whistled softly.

"Maybe Cresswell changed his mind.''

Rachel shook her head, but at that moment they were filing into the kitchen where Sandy was pointing out the shabby 1950's fixtures with something like pride. ". . . and we'll put a freestanding counter in here, with one of those countertop ranges in it. Bill's going to put in French doors here, which will make this corner into a perfect breakfast nook with the morning sun streaming in and access to the deck . . .''

"Be careful if you have any dealings with this guy," Jeff murmured. "I don't want you at risk. And there's a lot of money at stake here.''

Rachel opened her mouth to tell him that Alex's grief wasn't an act, but closed it without speaking. A part of her balked at telling him that Alex Cresswell had spent last night in her apartment. She wasn't sure why she felt so reluctant; she shook her head, annoyed with herself. For the rest of the tour, she kept reviewing their conversation in her apartment, looking for a hint of greed or calculation in his tone and manner. Couldn't find anything. She blinked as they exited into the backyard, realizing that she hadn't paid much attention to the tour at all.

If there really was a quiz, she was going to fail.

"Oh—excuse me." The dark-haired woman who had been talking to Herbert nearly collided with Rachel as she turned abruptly away from the table. The glass in her hand sloshed, and a few cold drops spattered Rachel's arm. "I'm terribly sorry." The woman snatched a paper napkin from the pile and blotted the moisture from Rachel's arm. "I hope it didn't get on your clothes?"

"Oh, no." Rachel gave her a reassuring smile. "Not a drop."

"It's just lemonade." Fine lines around the woman's eyes crinkled when she smiled. She had been beautiful when she was younger, Rachel realized with a twinge of envy. She must be in her fifties, but she was stunning still. Gray frosted her chestnut hair so lightly that Rachel could almost believe that it had its origins in a beauty salon rather than the passage of years. Her gaze was almost disconcertingly direct, and her eyes were an unusual dark gray, without the faintest trace of blue. Rachel was sure she had met her before, but she couldn't remember where or when.

"I put a few herbs into it along with the lemons," the woman went on. "Try some. It's different. I'm Doreen Baldwin, by the way. Sandy and Bill's neighbor. The owner of the jungle." She laughed and nodded toward the tall cedar fence that separated this yard from the property to the south. Lush greenery and a row of espaliered trees almost hid the small cottage.

"I'm so pleased that they bought here," the woman went on. "The couple who lived here before were so unpleasant—always fighting, always screaming at their children. Their dog barked all night. Poor thing—it was always chained up out here." She shook her head and smiled ruefully. "I get headaches easily, and I had a lot, let me tell you. May I pour you some lemonade?" She lifted the glass pitcher questioningly.

Rachel accepted a glass and arched her eyebrows in surprise. She had expected mint, but the sprigs of greenery in the pitcher added a complex herby taste that accentuated the lemon.

"Borage and lemon verbena." The woman smiled at Rachel's expression. "And a few dried high-bush cranberries to give it that pink blush. They're full of vitamin C.''

"It's delicious." Rachel emptied half her glass, realizing how thirsty she was, in spite of her beer. "Not too sweet either." She glanced over the fence at the riot of lush plants in the next yard. "Did you grow them?"

"Oh, yes." Doreen smiled. "I have a small greenhouse out back, too. I use a lot of herbs. And I like to grow the odd vegetables—the ones the supermarkets don't carry, like salsify and radish pods."

"It's lovely." Rachel walked over to the tall fence. Bean vines climbed trellises, offering clusters of red and purple and white flowers to the sun. Squash ran below, shading lettuce plants tucked into shady nooks, trained away from tall, staked tomatoes. Herb plants thrived everywhere. Rachel identified thyme, lovage, lavender, rosemary, and at least three varieties of mint.

"I make up a few herbal remedies for friends."

"Her stuff is great." Sandy wandered by, making the rounds with the chip bowl again. "She gave me a syrup for my sore throat when I had that cold. It worked."

"Hyssop and horehound with honey." The woman smiled modestly. "Old remedy. A lot of our modern medicines derive from herbal origins, you know. With every acre of rain forest we cut, we lose possibly dozens of valuable medicines. There are a lot of species there that we'll never even identify before they're gone," she added.

Rachel nodded cautious agreement, afraid she had just invoked a fanatic tirade, but Doreen merely shook her head.

"I decided long ago that we'll never learn as a species. One can only make an individual effort. So what do you do?" She changed the subject brightly.

"How lovely," she responded when Rachel told her. "I recognize you now—you were working on Henry's place. I cleaned for him. You were there once while I was working, but mostly I think we missed each other. I came in the late afternoons. Poor Henry." She lowered her voice. "That nephew of his bullied him so. I think Henry was afraid of the man. I told him not to invite him back, but he said his nephew would just show up—whether he wanted him to or not. I think it was affecting his mind." She leaned closer, her tone confidential. "He was getting so nervous . . ."

"I brought you food." Jeff appeared at Rachel's side with two ladened plates balanced in his hands. "I hope you're hungry."

"Uh . . . famished, actually." Rachel took a plate, her mind whirling as she introduced him to Doreen.

"We met." Her smile was cool.

"You were very helpful."

"I hope you catch the terrible person who killed him." Her voice trembled, and Doreen turned away to whisk the plastic from a crockery bowl. "Do try the bulgur salad. It's flavored with lovage and lemon balm. Lots of protein and roughage. I'm a vegetarian," she said with a vague smile. "So I always bring an extra hearty salad to these barbecues."

"Thank you." Jeff spooned a very meager portion of the herb-flecked grain salad onto his plate. He looked relieved as she made a beeline for Sandy, bearing her bulgur salad. "She was very cooperative," he told Rachel.

"She didn't have much good to say about Alex," Rachel said thoughtfully.

"No, she didn't. She was pretty outspoken about her disapproval. There're a couple of chairs over there." He steered her toward a pair of yard chairs. "Deliver me from devout vegetarians," he muttered under his breath as he sat down. "Bet she does crystals, too. Do you think she channels?"

"Only plants," Rachel said with a straight face. She forked up some of the bulgur salad. "Hey, this is good." She chewed contemplatively. "It has some kind of cheese in it, too."

"Probably soy cheese." Jeff poked at it dubiously, then abandoned it for the large burger he had loaded with onion, tomato, and—from the look of it—all available condiments.

Rachel regarded her own burger doubtfully.

"Don't worry. I stuck to mustard and pickles for you. Mmm." He closed his eyes and chewed blissfully. "Bill does a great burger." He caught a steady drip deftly on his plate. "I'll let you have my share of the New Age salad."

"Try it, you'll like it." Rachel took a bite of her own burger. Bill was indeed talented with a barbecue grill, she decided. The meat was suffused with rich flavor and cooked just enough. "So where are you living?" she asked. "In town?"

"Up on the rim of the Gorge," Jeff said with his mouth full. He paused to swallow. "The old Ferren place. Remember it?"

"The haunted house?" Rachel wrinkled her nose, remembering a cottage huddled in the midst of black winter tree trunks, its windows boarded up, shutters sagging. "You're kidding."

"It's not that bad," he said defensively. "I've been working on it. The new owner fixed it up as a rental." He broke off as Sandy wandered over to lean against the fence.

"My gosh, Jeff, you must be starving." She giggled. "I'll bring you another burger. How about you?" she asked Rachel.

"I wish I had room." Rachel patted her stomach ruefully.

"I do." Jeff bounced to his feet. "I'll get it, Sandy." Plate in hand, he headed for the grill like a shark homing in on a kill.

"I bet he doesn't cook for himself." Sandy looked after him. "He's skinny." With a sigh, she plopped into his vacant chair and extended her feet. "So." She blew out a breath that lifted her blond bangs. "What do you think?"

"The house is perfect for you." Rachel nibbled at the

last of her bulgur salad. "And this is a good party—but your parties are always good."

"I guess." Sandy gave a preoccupied glance in the direction of the grill.

"Okay, what's wrong?" Rachel put her plate aside.

"Nothing."

"Oh, sure." Rachel touched her friend's knee. "Honey, you are as clear as glass. Tell me so I don't have to pry and guess and maybe get it wrong. Plumbing troubles? Bill's in bed with your herbal neighbor?" That wrung a giggle out of Sandy, but it lacked its usual chime.

"It's just Dad." Sandy propped her chin in her hand. "Something is worrying him, but he won't tell me what it is. He had a physical last week." She frowned down at her knees. "He says everything is fine, but . . ." She shook her head. "I've never seen him like this. I think he's . . . scared." She lifted her chin as if she expected Rachel to challenge her. When she didn't, Sandy's shoulders drooped. "He's not getting any younger."

"I don't think your dad would lie to you about his health." Rachel shook her head. "He might not tell you exactly what was wrong, but he wouldn't say he was fine if he wasn't. He's too honest." If anything, Herbert was blunt to the point of tactlessness. Sandy nodded reluctantly, twirling a blond curl around one finger.

"That's what I've been telling myself, but . . . I don't know." She shrugged again. "I've never seen him like this. Oh, well." She started to get up. "I'd better go get the ice cream and cookies."

"I'll help you." Rachel gathered up a pile of plates from the end of the nearby table and followed Sandy into the kitchen. Jeff and Bill were laughing over by the grill, waving beers around for emphasis. "You know, I never gave you much of a wedding present."

"Hey, that platter you gave us is beautiful. I was going to put the cookies out on it." Sandy took twin half gallons of ice cream from the freezer. "They're over by the stove."

"Well, nice or not, I did want to give you something more, but I wasn't sure what you needed." Rachel opened one of the bakery bags piled on the counter. "Ooh, no fair. You bought Joylinn's gingersnaps. You know I'm addicted to those things."

"Yep."

"Evil girl." Rachel took a bite of one crispy round, rolling her eyes at the nuggets of candied ginger studded through the cookie. "Well, even though you did such an awful thing, I'll still give you your housewarming present."

"Rachel, you don't have to—"

"I'll help you design your landscaping and I'll put it in for you. You pay for the materials. The rest is on me."

Sandy stood as if turned to stone, the spoon she'd been using to serve ice cream dripping in her hand. "Oh, Rachel." Her voice faltered. "I wanted to ask you . . . just to do a design. But we decided we couldn't really afford it, and we knew you'd do it for free if you thought we were asking you to, so we didn't say anything, and the yard is so ugly, and I don't know how to make it really nice, and neither does Bill and . . . and . . ." She flung her arms around Rachel. "Thank you so much, girl. You are really, really, really wonderful."

"You're welcome." Rachel gasped. "But if you break my ribs, I can't work on your backyard."

"Oops. Sorry." Sandy released her, and, laughing, the two of them finished scooping ice cream into two big serving bowls.

Outside, it was beginning to get dark. People had settled in the available yard chairs around the grill full of embers, and a ragged chorus of laughter wafted across the yard as Rachel carried a tray full of bowls and spoons out to the partially cleared table. Movement caught her eye, and she glimpsed a dark figure at the fence that separated Doreen Baldwin's garden from Sandy and Bill's yard. The harsh aroma of a cigar tickled Rachel's nose, and she sneezed. "Herbert?" she called.

The leaning figure straightened with a jerk, and the

glowing coal of his cigar trembled. "Just trying to keep
my filthy habit—as my daughter refers to an excellent
Cuban—out of people's eating space," the realtor said a
trifle too heartily. He hurried over, stooping to put out his
large cigar on the heel of his shoe on the way. "So . . .
have you recovered from your grisly experience?"

"You mean finding Henry? Julio, my assistant, actually found him. I just called the police." Rachel peered
at his face, because the middle-aged realtor sounded
tense. "Sandy's bringing out the ice cream," she said.
"She has fresh strawberries and some of her brandied
peaches to put on it."

"She'd better not have gotten into my Courvoisier for
those peaches, or she's in big trouble," Herbert grumbled. He laughed. "I remember the one time you four
imps tried out my whiskey. And topped the bottle up with
water." He shook his head, his profile massive as a bull's
in the near dark. "You were all sick as dogs the next
morning."

"You knew?"

"When all four of you get the flu on the same day that
I discover my whiskey has been well watered . . ." Herbert chuckled dryly. "I conferred with your mother, and
we decided that all in all, you'd probably learn a better
lesson if we stayed out of it."

"I . . . I don't know what to say. *Mom* knew, too?"

"Your mother is a smart woman, my dear." Herbert
stowed his extinguished cigar in his shirt pocket. "She
had already guessed that your 'flu' might have unusual
origins."

Rachel shook her head wordlessly. "She never said
anything," she managed at last.

"Dad? Rachel?" Sandy emerged from the darkness.
"The ice cream is melting. And Sam and Georgie are
leaving. Want to say good-bye?" This last was directed
at her father, and Herbert departed with his daughter,
calling cheerful farewells and predicting great things for
the new residence. He had the air of someone escaping

an uncomfortable conversation. Which seemed odd, considering his light tone just now. Thoughtfully Rachel followed them, turning aside as Jeff beckoned from the table.

"I saved you some peaches. They were going fast." He handed her a bowl of melting ice cream mingling with the alcoholic fruit. "Herbert is certainly conversational tonight."

"You're joking, right?" Rachel spooned up ice cream.

"I wonder what's eating him? I tried to ask him about the new building restrictions in the Gorge—and he just cut me off. Walked away. That's his favorite soapbox." Jeff shook his head. "I guess he's mellowing in his old age."

"Not recently." Rachel wondered if Sandy's worries had some foundation after all. "Whew!" She swallowed a spoonful of mostly brandied peaches and fanned herself, changing the subject. "These are potent. I don't know if I'd better drive home—not with an officer of the law hanging around."

"The officer of the law can always give you a ride."

"Hey, you had one more beer than I did. At least." Rachel could feel his eyes on her and kept her voice light. "If I eat too much of this, I may end up calling a cab, though. Do you remember that Saturday night when we went over to Sandy's house and nobody was home and we got into her dad's liquor cabinet? Bill got sick, and I nearly did."

"I managed to hang on until I was on the way home." Jeff shook his head and laughed. "It sure cured me of any desire to get drunk again."

"Herbert knew."

"You're kidding?" Jeff's eyes widened. "If he'd told Mom, she would have tanned my backside to shoe leather. He knew?" He sounded incredulous. "And he didn't say anything?"

"He called my mother. I guess they decided to keep quiet."

"Huh." He shook his head, chuckling softly. "That's

a side of Herbert I never would have guessed. I'd have expected him to ground Sandy for the whole year and threaten us all with death. But hey.'' His eyes twinkled in the dim glow from the single anemic floodlight mounted on the back of the porch. ''None of us ever became heavy drinkers. Not even Bill.''

''True.'' Rachel drifted toward the house where people were making their good-byes and trickling around. From the front of the house came the sound of engines revving. ''This was fun. It's going to be a lovely house when they get through with it.''

''Sandy told me what you gave them.'' Jeff hung back a little, outside the yellow pool of light on the concrete patio. ''That's a very nice thing to do.'' He touched her hand. ''Want to go for a drive before you go home? Watch the moon on the river?''

She almost said yes. ''My mom's staying the night.'' Rachel fought down a twinge of regret. ''I don't think I should abandon her utterly.''

''Oh.'' Jeff sighed. ''Another time? And why didn't she come along?''

''She . . . sort of had a date.''

''Sort of?'' The yellow light bronzed Jeff's face and touched his dark eyes with flecks of gold as he gave her a quizzical look.

''She went into Hood River to listen to jazz with Dr. Meier. One of my clients.''

''Good for your mom.''

''Yeah, I guess.'' Rachel turned to say her good-byes to Bill and Sandy, and to promise to get together with them in a few days to talk about the yard and potential designs.

''Does it bother you?'' Jeff asked as they negotiated the shadowed walk along the side of the house. ''That your mom is dating someone?''

''I guess it does,'' Rachel admitted reluctantly. ''It shouldn't, I know. But . . . it does.''

''Is he a jerk?'' They'd reached the edge of the road and were walking along the gravel to Rachel's truck, which she'd had to park above Doreen Baldwin's house.

"Not at all. He seems really nice. Older than she—but not a lot." Rachel unlocked her door. "He's a retired surgeon from Portland. I guess his wife died a long time ago."

"Sounds great for her. I wish her well." Jeff nodded. "She deserves someone good." He noticed her expression and smiled. "Relax—you'll get used to it. I remember when my mother started dating Carl. I hated him on sight. But we're good friends now."

"I never asked you about your mother." Rachel felt a rush of embarrassment, but Jeff's mother had always seemed remote and cold—as if she disapproved of her son's friends.

"She married Carl. They moved down to San Diego. She's happy, I think. I'm not sure she was ever really happy while I was growing up."

"It must be tough to be a single parent." Rachel touched Jeff's hand, hearing the sadness in his tone. "It wasn't your fault."

"I know." He leaned down suddenly and kissed her.

It was chaste and brief, and they separated quickly. As if they were both afraid of what might have happened.

"I'll talk to you tomorrow," Jeff promised as he closed her door.

"I started to ask you about the break-in at the hotel." Rachel paused, her hand on the ignition key. "Then Sandy interrupted, and I forgot."

"Someone was looking for something. They didn't take any obvious valuables."

"Looking for Henry's will?"

Jeff shrugged, his broad shoulders blocking the street-light's glare and hiding his expression in shadow. "We lifted some prints." He frowned. "Can you stay away from that place? You're not working for Cresswell, are you?"

"No . . ."

"Good." He touched her arm lightly with one fingertip. "I'll sleep better. Something doesn't feel right about this whole situation."

Rachel squirmed on her seat, wondering if it wasn't too late to mention Alex now. "I'll be careful, Jeff. I promise." She turned the key and revved the truck's engine. Jeff stepped back reluctantly and lifted a hand to wave as she pulled away from the curb.

She returned his wave, but as she turned around at the end of the block and drove past Bill and Sandy's house again on her way into town, a shadow caught her eye. A slender figure stood half screened by climbing bean vines in Doreen Baldwin's front yard. A stray beam from the halide streetlamp gleamed on raven hair. Doreen. Rachel wondered if she had been there, listening to them. Snoop, she thought, remembering the woman's comments about her former neighbors. Maybe a tall privacy fence was in order for the front yard.

As she drove across town to her apartment, it occurred to her that she hadn't seen Doreen after their conversation at the table—that she must have gone home soon after. Rachel wondered if she would have objected to Herbert's smoking near her plants. Probably, she thought with a wry smile. He was lucky she hadn't caught him.

The clock above the glass doors of the tiny brick library showed that it was almost midnight. *Mom better be home*, Rachel thought grimly, and then laughed at herself. Role reversal for sure. But she found herself wanting to speed through town and was glad that Jeff wasn't behind her.

CHAPTER

6

It wasn't until Rachel pulled into the driveway and saw the warm glow of light spilling from the upstairs windows that she relaxed. Annoyed with herself, she tiptoed up the stairs past Mrs. Frey's dark windows. If her mother chose to stay out all night, it was none of Rachel's business. But she was still relieved—even if she felt a bit guilty about it. Peter hopped down from the railing on the landing, butting hard against her ankles and telling her in no uncertain terms what he thought of her late hour of return.

"Shush," she whispered as he yowled his displeasure. "Mom might be asleep."

"She's not," her mother called cheerfully from the kitchen. "I'm making chamomile tea. Would you like some?"

"Mom, what are you doing up?"

"My dear daughter, it's not even midnight yet. Not quite." She poured steaming water into the white porcelain teapot with the dragon design that she had given Rachel years ago. "Do you really think I'm too old to stay up late?" She gave Rachel a twinkling smile. "So how was Sandy's barbecue? Was Jeff there?"

"Yes, as a matter of fact, he was." She shrugged and pursed her lips. "The house is pretty basic, but they have some good ideas for remodeling. Mom—Jeff said he wrote me letters. After he left." She hesitated, suddenly embarrassed. "What am I saying? I know you didn't pry into my mail."

"Thank you." Her mother raised one eyebrow. "I never saw anything that might have come from Jeff. In fact—I felt badly for you. Because I knew you missed him. And then your father—" She broke off suddenly. "So, how are Bill and Sandy's neighbors?" she asked brightly. "Are you sure you don't want some of this?" She poured pale golden tea into a mug. "It'll help you sleep."

"I don't think I'm going to have any trouble sleeping." Rachel yawned. "Actually, you'd probably like their closest neighbor—Doreen Baldwin. She's into herbs, too. She put some in the lemonade." Rachel wrinkled her brow. "Borage, I think she said. Or lovage. She cleaned house for Henry."

"Oh, I know Doreen." Her mother sipped luxuriously. "She cleans for Camilla Rodriguez. Also for Matthew Ferren, ever since his wife died." She clucked her tongue. "She's a caretaker rather than just a cleaning lady. Keeps to herself."

"Caretaker?" Rachel tilted her head. "What's that?"

"Oh . . . I guess you could just say she gets involved. By the way, Joshua and I had a wonderful time." Deborah's smile warmed as she changed the subject. "I've always liked the Flecktones. But they did a short set, so afterward we went over to that new little French place that opened up last year, down near the river. We ate snails and bread with olive oil and roasted garlic, and the waiter steered us to a really good Bordeaux." Deborah sighed happily. "Then we walked along the river. It was lovely." She sounded briefly wistful. "I haven't had that kind of an evening in . . . oh, in years. Then, to top it all off, we had the most bizarre adventure on the way home." She sipped her tea meditatively. "We passed this man limping along the old highway. He was kind of young. About your age. Joshua stopped to ask him if he needed help. He said he had been out walking and had twisted his ankle. And, of course, there's no room at all for a third person in Joshua's MG, but at least Joshua had his cell phone, so he called the Taxi Sisters.''

Blossom had its own taxi and towing company, which consisted of two sisters in their sixties: Roberta and Earlene Guarnieri. They owned the local gas station-cum-garage and drove identical gray Jeep Eagles with *Blossom Taxi, Independently Owned and Operated Since Forever, Cash Only* hand-lettered on the side. Known locally as the Taxi Sisters, they charged whimsically by the trip, take-it-or-leave-it, and stubbornly refused to take credit cards—although they would include a detour past the ATM machine in the bank lobby if you came up short. Since there were no other taxis, they mostly got what they asked, although they appalled the occasional tourist who strayed into Blossom and needed a taxi. For the most part, they ferried a small, steady clientele of carless, rural elderly into Hood River to medical appointments, or to shop, or just to have lunch. Rachel had heard rumors that the Taxi Sisters made some of those trips for free or close to it, depending on who was riding. She suspected that either of the women would deny it vehemently, if asked. They didn't do charity, as they announced loudly any time a passenger protested the fee.

''So did one of them actually show up?'' she asked, trying to ignore an image of her mother walking hand in hand along the river with Dr. Meier. ''At that time of night?''

''Oh, Earlene's a night owl.'' Her mother poured herself more tea. ''She showed up, all right. In her own good time, of course.'' She winked. ''So we had plenty of time to get acquainted. It turns out that the young man's name is Alex Cresswell. Henry's nephew. I didn't even recognize him. Goodness.'' She shook her head. ''I last saw him when he was—oh—fifteen or so. He looks like

Henry. You can certainly see it." She smiled. "He told us he'd met you."

"He certainly did." Rachel stifled a yawn. "That habit of going for solitary jaunts gets him into more trouble."

"So I understand," Deborah said with asperity. "He told us that Jeff arrested him for Henry's murder this afternoon. Which is ridiculous, I might say."

"He didn't arrest him. He brought him in for questioning. After all—he inherits the hotel. I guess he's the obvious suspect."

"Really?" Her mother arched one eyebrow. "So what happened to Henry's son?"

"What son?" Rachel blinked at her, all sleepiness banished in an instant. "Henry had a son? Since when? He never got married."

"I don't know about the married part for sure," her mother said as she opened the refrigerator and peered inside. "But he had a son, all right. Or at least he said the boy was his son. We met him once, when your father and I went to hear him play in a Portland club. He had the child with him then. I think the boy was about two. Cute kid."

"You went to hear him play? Play *what*? Are we talking about the same Henry Bassinger?" Rachel asked faintly. She was beginning to feel as if she'd stumbled through some kind of invisible barrier into another universe. One where Henry Bassinger had a different past, and her mother walked along rivers at midnight, holding hands like a teenager.

"He called himself King Henry." Her mother's voice emerged from the depths of the refrigerator. "He played one heck of a trumpet. He never really got the attention from the critics he deserved. Probably because he didn't do the clubs long enough to get noticed, and only brought out a single recording. Someone told me that his father was very much against his playing. Henry had to run away to do it, even though he was in his twenties. I guess he was on the road for three or four years with a band. Then one day he was back in town, and as far as I know, he hadn't played since. Not in public anyway. I never knew him well enough to ask him why he quit." She straightened, a tub of whipped cream cheese in one hand and a somewhat aged apple in the other. "Lunch meat and leftover Chinese food? Is that all you eat?"

"Better than snails. I actually cook very nice meals at least two or three times a week, thank you. Using all four food groups." Rachel made a face, then propped her chin on her hands. "If Henry has a son, everything changes. There's no will. Would his son inherit?"

"I suppose he would, if he could prove that Henry really is his father. Maybe Henry married the girl. I could see his father forbidding her to live here. He was a hard, controlling man. He had his wife and children utterly under his thumb." Deborah got out a cutting board and began slicing the apple into neat wedges. "Snails make a nice vehicle for Le Bistro's rather delicious garlic butter, by the way. You should try them."

"I could eat garlic butter on something besides snails, thank you." Rachel plucked a slice of apple from the board and dodged as her mother tried to rap her knuckles with the knife handle. "I wonder if Jeff knows about this missing son," she mused. "*Possible* son."

"I doubt it, or he wouldn't be concentrating so hard on poor Alex. I don't know why Henry would have called that child his son unless he was." Deborah licked cream cheese delicately from her fingers. "He seemed very proud of the boy. I don't remember his name, but if he was about two at the time, he'd be . . ." She frowned, her lips moving as she counted. "About twenty-six," she said. "It was the year before you were born." She eyed the cream cheese and apples doubtfully. "We need bagels. Real bagels." She vanished into Rachel's bedroom, from whence came the rasp of a garment bag zipper. A moment later she returned, carrying two glossy rings of glazed bagels reverently, as if they were priceless art objects. "From Rosenberg's Deli—remember them? They gave you that giant pickle when I took you to visit when you were ten. Surely you remember."

Actually, she did. The huge pickle had been tart and wonderful and full of garlic. No other pickle had ever quite measured up to that remembered delicacy. As for the bagels, they were good—a little harder in texture than the ones you could buy locally. She wasn't sure why they seemed so special to her mother, but she wasn't about to argue with her, either. Her stomach rumbled, and she realized that she had talked more than eaten at Sandy's barbecue. "If Henry got married, there should be a record of it somewhere." She bit into a chunk of bagel. "I could check the Hall of Records in Hood River."

"If he got married in Hood River County. Personally I doubt it, or lots of folks would know. If he married, the family certainly didn't let on that it had happened. But maybe the marriage didn't last long." She spread cream cheese on the second bagel.

"Mom?" Rachel hesitated, then set down her bagel. "Did you and Dad go listen to jazz in Portland a lot?"

"Maybe once a month. That was before you were born." A half-eaten bagel in her hand, Deborah smiled into the middle distance, her face softened by memory. "Hood River seemed so *rural* to me when we first came here. Well, it still does, but I'm used to it now." She chuckled. "Back then, it seemed like the middle of no-where. I think it was your father's way of trying to make it all work for me. Jazz was something from my youth in New York—going to the clubs with my father. He was a fanatic." Sadness tinged her smile. "Your father and I would stay in this little hotel near the freeway and go to whatever club had good music. In the morning we'd have breakfast and window-shop in the department stores, go to the Art Museum, shop the bookstores, and pretend we lived a nice urban life. Of course, there weren't very many clubs doing jazz then—certainly not like New York." She laughed. "But your father ended up liking jazz a lot. It was something nobody else in the family understood at all, so it became our private bit of rebellion, our way of remembering that we weren't quite as narrow and rural as the life we'd chosen.'' She tilted her head, her dark eyes on Rachel's face. ''Your father was a rather wonderful person. I love the bits of him I see in you.''

''Thanks.'' Rachel swallowed and looked away. ''They sound . . . neat. Your trips.''

''Oh, they were.'' Deborah swept bagel crumbs from the counter into her palm and yawned. ''I think I'm ready for bed, daughter of mine. If you want to stay up, you won't bother me.''

''I'm ready, too.''

Her mother leaned over and kissed her on the forehead. ''I hope you find such happiness with someone,'' she murmured. ''It's a gift from God.''

CHAPTER

7

In the morning Rachel fed Peter and managed to tiptoe out of the house without waking her mother. She left a note on the kitchen counter, telling her that she'd call later in the morning and drive her out to the orchard. The sky was just getting gray. It was too early to pick up Julio. She had awakened before her alarm, filled with a restless sort of energy. On a whim, she drove down to the new boardwalk built along the riverbank.

Most of the shops were closed at this hour, their night-lights still glowing faintly in the early light. Rachel parked the truck along the empty street and walked past the windows filled with bright summer clothes, wind-surfing gear, local art, and antiques. The Bread Box glowed with light, and Rachel's mouth watered at the scent of baking bread wafting from the kitchen vents. She pressed her face to the steamy glass of the door and rapped lightly.

A moment later, Joylinn herself opened it. "Another early riser." She held the door wide, grinning. "Welcome to the Crack of Dawn Club. Want some coffee?"

"Does anyone ever turn you down?" Rachel entered

the fragrant warmth of the bakery, sniffing like a hungry dog. "Mmm. What's in the oven?"

"This is Thursday. Whole-wheat-and-honey day." Joylinn featured a different type of bread every day. "I just cut a loaf. Wasn't perfect, you know." She winked. "Can't sell imperfect bread, and no, nobody's ever turned down coffee at this hour. Not that I can remember. Want some bread to go with it?"

"You are an angel." Rachel took the steaming mug of Viennese Roast coffee Joylinn handed her and watched her slice a thick slab from a dark, crusty loaf on the wooden worktop behind the counter. She picked up the still-warm slice with a sigh of pleasure. "You are the best bread baker I know." Sunflower seeds studded the crust, and local honey suffused the fragrant bread with a flowery aroma. "My mom spent the night," she said with her mouth full. "I didn't want to wake her making coffee."

"Hey, come by any morning." Joylinn pulled a huge pan of rolls out of one of her ovens. "Although I leave right after the rush today. I always bring Anne-Marie fresh rolls on Thursday and do my shopping for the week in Hood River. Thursdays are slow for some reason, and Celia can handle the place by herself, no problem."

"Let's see . . ." Rachel studied the ceiling. "Anne-Marie has been at that retirement home for, what? Not quite a year, right? By now she must run the place." Joylinn's grandmother, ninety-two, had a mind as sharp as a razor. Her tongue was equally sharp.

"Actually, I think it took her about a week." Joylinn finished transferring the rolls to a cooling rack. "Bloodless coup," she drawled.

Rachel laughed, nearly choked on a swallow of coffee, then slapped her palm on the formica counter. "Of course!"

"Of course, what?" Joylinn pushed auburn hair back from her perspiring forehead as she began to arrange more of the dark whole wheat loaves in the glass-fronted display case. "You have that 'Eureka!' look on your face."

"Anne-Marie." Rachel chortled and took another bite of bread. "She'd know if Henry Bassinger had a son."

"Henry Bassinger? The old crazy guy who lived in the closed-up hotel?" Joylinn pulled open an oven door as a timer buzzed a shrill demand. "I heard he was murdered." She banged another hot pan of rolls down on the wooden worktop. "The paper just said the police were looking into his death. Celia told me his nephew shot him or something. To get the property. She said they arrested him. Someone told me you knew him."

"I met him." Rachel winced. "And I don't think he did it."

"So what's this about a missing kid?" Joylinn leaned her elbows on the counter, her face flushed from the ovens' heat. "I thought he was a recluse who never ever left home. I remember meeting his father when I was about ten. Brr." She shivered. "My cousin and I snuck into that abandoned greenhouse out behind the hotel. We were just fooling around—not doing anything. But the old man caught us, and he was really mad. He had this big, silver mounted shotgun on his arm. I just about wet my pants." She made a face. "We ran all the way home, and I guarantee you, we never went near the place again. So what's this about him having a kid?"

"Not him—Henry. That's what I want to find out." Rachel finished her coffee and checked her watch. "I've got to get to work. Will you ask Anne-Marie if I could visit her? I'd like to ask her what she remembers."

"Sure thing. Believe me, she doesn't turn down visitors. Just prepare yourself to answer a zillion questions. There's a price for information." She smiled, revealing a dimple at the corner of her mouth. "I only escape because I tell her I have to be back to close up."

"I'll try to drop by this afternoon if I can. Thanks for the coffee and the wonderful bread." Rachel exited into the cool morning, wondering what light Anne-Marie might shed on this mysterious offspring.

Julio was waiting for her in front of his sister's home when Rachel arrived. He stowed his lunch cooler and water jug in the bed of her truck and climbed in, his young face unusually serious in the strengthening light. Rachel outlined the day's work to him as they drove to Dr. Meier's house. The topsoil would be delivered early, and she'd rented a Bobcat to do the spreading. Julio would finish the job with a rake. "Interstate Rock, over in Camas, is going to call me about delivering the boulders," she told him. "I'll get Harvey to bring his track hoe over to place them—but we won't wait for them." She sighed. "They're backed up, and Harvey's pretty busy. If they don't show, we'll go ahead and get the trenches dug for the water and lights. If we have to re-dig a few—well, we do."

Julio gave her a long-suffering look, which she ignored as she negotiated a sharp turn. She spent at least as many hours wielding a shovel as he did. And she was better with the Bobcat than he was. They picked up the Bobcat on its small trailer at the rental place and hauled it out to Dr. Meier's house.

The doctor's sports car was parked in the driveway. Left out after his date last night? Date. The word still made her flinch, and she shook her head at herself as she and Julio unloaded the Bobcat. She enjoyed driving the little machine. Her hands sure and quick on the multiple levers, she made the Bobcat spin and dart across the graded slope, pushing the new black soil mix out across the churned clay and rock.

Its tires laid a surreal pattern down across the soil, and Rachel hummed to herself, because this was fun as far as she was concerned. The little machine was quick and responsive, and although she was no Harvey, she was good with it. Courtesy of college summers spent working for a landscaper who had his own nursery and owned a lot of equipment.

It didn't take long to get the topsoil roughly spread. Reluctantly Rachel shut off the Bobcat. Julio was busy with his rake, smoothing the soil out. She climbed down and got a second rake from the truck.

"*Quien es?*" Julio jerked his chin at the deck as he joined her.

A small wiry man paced the treated planks, his legs swinging with the short, impatient flick of a cat's tail. Head sunk between his hunched shoulders, dressed in a chambray work shirt, new jeans with a silver belt buckle the size of a small dinner plate, and shiny eel-skin boots, he looked like a misplaced rodeo wanna-be. Abruptly he vaulted to the ground and marched briskly over.

"You are responsible for this mess?" He peered up at Rachel with the face of an ageless gnome. Thinning hair of an indeterminate pale color had been combed carefully across an incipient bald spot. "I am Alonzo." He announced his name as if that answered all questions. "We must talk. This is a disaster."

"Nice to meet you." Rachel gave Julio a brief sideways glance as she offered the diminutive man her hand. Julio leaned on his rake, staring at Alonzo with a mixture of fascination and disdain. "Is there something I can do for you?" she asked politely as her hand was ignored.

"You have already done enough! You have destroyed what would have been the social triumph of the season." He gestured at the raw soil behind her and shuddered theatrically. "I cannot work in mud. I demand a written guarantee that this . . . this marsh will be effectively covered in sod or turf or whatever you call those green slabs of grass—and that the paths can be trod in civilized footwear at least ten days before the event. Notarized, please." He had lost Julio. The young man shook his head, caught Rachel's eye, and raised his own gaze to heaven.

"I'm sorry." Rachel managed a straight face. "The plans don't call for sod. Dr. Meier is putting in an herbaceous lawn. But the paths will be graveled before the wedding. I guarantee it. And if it's raining, you won't be doing this outside, will you?"

"It never rains on my affairs." Alonzo fixed her with

a gimlet stare. "This is not sufficient. Herbaceous lawn?" He chopped the air dismissively with one small hand. "I am not interested. Sod! Or I simply cannot undertake this . . . farce."

"Excuse me." Rachel glanced at the steadily advancing sun. "I really need to get to work here. We're sort of on a deadline."

"I will put the arbor here—*if* I decide to go forward with this project." He waved imperiously at a spot near the center of the gently sloping backyard. "Oriented east and west, of course, so that the bride and groom face the mountain. At least the architect had the good sense to make use of the adequate view." He sniffed. "It will be clear for the wedding? But not too hot. I abhor outdoor weddings in the heat of August."

"Isn't it set for September 10?" Rachel interrupted mildly.

"It is so *hard* on the arrangements," Alonzo went on as if she hadn't spoken. "Everything *droops* no matter how much water you use in the reservoirs. Fuchsia pink." He sighed. "Well, I suppose it's better than all white. Boring, boring, *boring*. And I simply can't make these women understand the flexibility of greens and grasses. They all want gladioli. Another middle-class convention." He sighed again and blotted his wizened face with a huge, pale blue handkerchief. "At least dear Elaine is willing to listen to reason about the impact of properly chosen foliage varieties."

Light dawned. "Are you the florist?"

"My *goodness,* no." Alonzo peered down his nose. "My dear, a *florist* sticks carnations in a block of oasis, adds a handful of baby's breath, and drives it around to the doorsteps of the undiscerning. I create *events*." He tilted his head theatrically as he slipped an elegant leather case from his pocket and handed her a card.

Amused in spite of the delay, Rachel glanced down at the expensive engraved rectangle. *Alonzo and Jayne*, she read in elegant script. *Unique Moments, Incorporated.*

"Honeymoon first nights, weddings, solstice celebra-

tions, Bar Mitzvah—we create Events. I must have your
fullest cooperation. This has great potential. Although
why she chose to set it in this"—he shuddered again—
"*rural* locale is beyond me. Still, I suppose rustic charm
is popular in some quarters." His tone suggested that he
equated rustic charm with outhouses. "And she was quite
determined about it, although there are several lovely
venues available in town." He sighed heavily. "Guar-
antees—I must have your written guarantee, including a
penalty clause—my lawyer has drawn me up a nice
form—or I simply will not be able to create. I will be
too nervous. No mud. Sod, please. Immediately. And I
must have an adequate staging area." He waved again at
the place where he planned to put his arbor.

"I'm sorry," Rachel said mildly. "The water feature
goes in there."

"Nonsense." He put his hands on his hips and did his
down-the-nose stare again. "It is so . . . suburban to have
the buffet on the deck. Sod. A nice terrace instead of that
silly pond. I will give you my form."

"I'm sorry." Rachel picked up her rake. "I can't make
changes without Dr. Meier's approval. And I'm not signing your form."

Alonzo gaped at her, his chest thrusting out aggres-
sively, obviously building a head of outrage and verbal
steam. He was beginning to remind Rachel of her aunt's
fox terrier, Pepper. Lots of ego and noise.

"Alonzo, dearest, are you making a scene?"

Rachel turned at the unexpected British accent to find
herself facing a tall, distinguished-looking woman wearing a pastel shirt and chino slacks. Stylishly short dark
hair framed her pale oval face, touched with silver at the
temples.

"I'm Jayne Zwycaffer. I see you've met my husband." She offered Rachel a firm handclasp and a pleas-
ant smile. "You must be Ms. O'Connor, the landscaper.
My dear, Dr. Meier was telling me about her yesterday.
She does wonderful work." She smiled briefly at Rachel,
then turned back to the still sulking Alonzo. "She works

with native plants. You were the one who suggested a natural motif to our client, do you remember?''

"Which she flatly rejected," Alonzo grumbled.

"But, dear, that was before you could tell her that she has the opportunity to benefit from the services of an award-winning landscape designer, whose specialty just happens to be in native species. She will undoubtedly realize the esthetic advantage of coordinating her decor with the landscape." Jayne glanced at Rachel for confirmation, a hint of a smile playing at the corners of her mouth. "And she will certainly have the project finished before the wedding, darling. She's a *professional*."

"Thank you," Rachel murmured. "And the award wasn't a big one. It was simply . . ."

"Never explain an award." Jayne lifted an eyebrow. "Clients so much prefer to fill in those blanks for themselves, and they tend to be generous when they've hired your services. Justifies their good judgement, don't you see? And if the award *is* famous, then modesty befits one."

Rachel hid a smile. Alonzo frowned and said, "Dear Elaine made it terribly clear if you remember. She wants roses." He shuddered again. "No matter that they're so . . . déclassé. And it really doesn't matter." He gave Rachel a venomous look. "I cannot work in *mud*. And I will *not* arrange a buffet on a *deck*. With *roses* yet. She could order that sort of thing from the Sears catalogue." He turned and stomped off—although the effect was somewhat spoiled as his boots sank into the soft soil.

His wife glanced briefly heavenward. "He does the artistic passion a bit too well at times, but the clients actually seem to enjoy being bullied for the most part. He's a pragmatist beneath it all. And he is terribly creative." Her smile was genuinely warm. "He really is the genius of the partnership. I just do the bookkeeping and talk to the clients. We obtained a copy of the final garden design from Dr. Meier. Very nice, by the way." She smiled. "I like it a lot. In spite of my husband's opinions, we will work with your design. And we may ask you about local sources for the greenery. This is a bit out of our usual territory.'' She winked. ''Don't take Alonzo too seriously.''

Rachel returned her smile, liking the woman. ''I really will do my best to have everything ready for you.''

''Oh, I'm sure you'll succeed.'' Jayne nodded. ''I have faith in you.'' She gave Rachel a final sweet smile and disappeared into the house. Shaking her head, Rachel picked up her rake and got back to work.

Alonzo and Jayne had departed by the time they took a break—zooming off in the MG that Rachel had assumed belonged to Dr. Meier. She wandered over to where Julio was drinking from his water jug. ''Julio, when you saw Mr. Cresswell's car in the bushes at the hotel—are you sure it was his car?''

Julio followed her question with knitted brows. ''*Sí, señorita.*'' He capped his jug and nodded vigorously.

''It couldn't have been another white car? Maybe the same model and make?''

''No, *señorita.*'' His chin jutted stubbornly. ''It was his car.''

''How did you know?''

''*Yo sé.*'' He shrugged and went back to shoveling. End of discussion.

Rachel stopped working at five—because she had to get the Bobcat back to the rental outfit by six or pay for an extra day. She wiped sweat from her face, her cotton shirt sticking uncomfortably to her skin. ''We'll quit for today.'' She lifted her thick hair off the nape of her neck, wishing for a breeze on this unusually still day. ''We'll start digging trenches tomorrow. Can you get Eduardo and Jorges? *Por excavar?*'' Julio's friends, Jorges and Eduardo, worked for her whenever she needed a crew.

''*Sí, señorita.*'' Julio began to clean the dirt from his shovel blade with the hose.

It was 5:10. Rachel fought down a pang of guilt. She had meant to give her mother a ride home and stop in to talk to Anne-Marie. She had managed to completely forget. ''I'll tell *el señor* that we're leaving. Get the Bobcat

chained down to the trailer, will you?'' she called as she
headed for the house.

Dr. Meier wasn't home. Rachel hurried back out to the
truck to call her mother on her cell phone. But she got
her machine. It had a memo function, and when Rachel
checked it, sure enough, her mother's soft voice came
over the line: ''It's such a lovely day that I think I'll go
for a walk. Why don't you take your time at your job
and then come out to the orchard for dinner? You could
stay over and come back into town in the morning. By
the way, I fed your cat. He informed me that you forgot.
Bye-bye, honey.''

''Peter, you liar.'' Laughing, Rachel put away her cell
phone. Trust Mom to immediately understand that she
was feeling a bit of pressure about this wedding and to
find a way to avoid interrupting her day. Of course, she
could have called Aunt Catherine or the Taxi Sisters for
a ride if she'd really wanted to get home. Rachel suspected that she had welcomed the chance to visit in town
for a day. Since her father had died, Mom seemed a little
at loose ends at the orchard, although she'd always gotten
along well with Uncle Jack and Aunt Catherine. Still,
they didn't really have a lot in common, Rachel mused
as she loaded her tools. Aunt Catherine had quit high
school to marry Jack, and he had had two years at the
Ag college only. She couldn't recall a lot of conversa-
tions with her uncle that didn't involve weather, the func-
tionality of machinery, crops, prices, or local politics.

Thoughtfully she got into her truck and started the engine. Dropping Julio off, she drove back through Blossom and on down to drop the Bobcat in the cluttered
yard at the equipment rental company. The turnoff to
Anne-Marie's retirement home was only a mile or two
farther down the road. Rachel hesitated, then turned her
truck away from town. After all, her mother might not
even be back from her walk yet. Dinner at the orchard
was a late affair in the summer. It occurred after the sun
set and work was concluded for the day. A huge lunch
was the main meal.

The nursing home—Orchard View Retirement Village, it was called—occupied three rather barren acres with a view of the interstate between Blossom and Hood River. The buildings formed a long U with a courtyard in the center. A somewhat weedy lawn sloped gently down from the front of one long wing to a small pond. The whole thing looked as if the contractor had simply planted grass over the fill, Rachel thought. Circled by a gravel walk and a few benches, the pond lacked any plantings except a small clump of cattails at one end. On a day such as this one, the sun beat down on the gravel, and several of the few residents feeding the single swan and small flock of assorted ducks carried umbrellas as sun shades.

"Trees," Rachel muttered. "A willow. Flag iris and cedar." Lily pads and the iris would provide some cover for fish and amphibians and would attract herons. She sighed and shook her head as she parked the truck. You could maintain the entire grounds with a single lawn mower.

"Mrs. DeRochers-Smith?" The freckled young aide in the lobby looked up from helping a very old man get himself settled with the paper. She absently wiped the chin of a wispy woman in a wheelchair who was smiling at the wall and drooling gently. "She's taking her after-dinner walk. I don't know if this is a good time to bother her." She gave Rachel an appraising glance. "She has these routines, and she doesn't like anybody to interrupt them, you know?"

"Oh, I know very well." Rachel smiled at the girl's careful understatement. "But she knows I'm coming, so she probably won't bite my head off. Or yours, for telling me where to find her."

The girl laughed. "Well, she's in a good mood today, so maybe we'll both survive." Her grin was infectious. "Still, don't say I didn't warn you if she goes after you with her cane."

"I'm a fast runner," Rachel drawled. And then, because she couldn't help herself, she asked, "How come nobody planted anything but grass around here?''

"They ran out of money." The girl sighed. "It sure gets hot outside. Seems like a few trees would save a lot on air-conditioning. The south side of the building just bakes in the summer. But hey—I just work here." She wrinkled her nose. "Speaking of which, I'd better get these sheets delivered to the infirmary." She waved. "Gotta hurry. It's almost time for Mr. Bram's afternoon game of checkers."

Rachel returned the aide's cheerful wave and headed down toward the pond. It was indeed hot out here. She was sweating before she'd gone ten feet. Shading her eyes, she searched for the small, upright figure of Joylinn's grandmother. The petite woman radiated vitality in spite of the cane she used to get around. In fact, Rachel suspected the cane was used more as a theatrical prop than a physical one. Now she found Anne-Marie on the far side of the pond, perched on the edge of one of the stone benches. Her back to the setting sun, she was keeping the determined young swan at bay with her cane as she scattered crumbs for the mallards, and chatting with the man in the wheelchair next to her. He was lanky and weathered, his hair as white as the proverbial snow. He seemed entranced with Madame, Rachel noticed with a smile.

"I tell you, they would be better off to put them all to work when they're twelve, these modern children." Her clear, carrying voice came to Rachel as she rounded the end of the pond. "They are bored with the too-easy lessons at school and their endless toys, so of course they get into mischief. Mama and Papa are never home, and there is too much television. And now, this Internet, *ca*, where anyone can say he is anything at all. You had your share. *Allez!*" She poked at the advancing swan, who retreated, hissing. "Let them pick the strawberries and weed the fields. Let them pick up the trash along the road. You would think work is a disease you could die from." She snorted. "After a summer in the fields earning the blisters on one's palms, the so-boring school is now so much better, yes?''

"You might have something there, my dear." The man in the wheelchair chuckled. "But you can't pull it off in a democracy."

"And that, *cher ami*, is the failing of democracies." Anne-Marie crossed her hands on top of her cane, not a drop of perspiration visible on her long, oval face. Dressed in an uncompromising gray linen skirt and long-sleeved white blouse with a high collar pinned with an ebony brooch, she obviously made no concessions to the weather. "The people, they prefer the choices that feel good to the choices that are good for all."

"Yes, but no other system has worked any better—not for long anyway."

"Perhaps that is our own failing." Anne-Marie turned as if noticing Rachel for the first time. "Mademoiselle O'Connor. My granddaughter announced your intention to visit." Her imperious nod conferred permission to approach. "Mademoiselle, may I present Monsieur Harris McLoughlin? Monsieur McLoughlin is the only other resident here who has the capacity for intelligent conversation. Perhaps that is because he was born in Ontario."

"Ontario, Oregon. Don't let her kid you." McLoughlin laughed. "Anne-Marie, you're just too sharp for the rest of us."

"Nonsense." Anne-Marie turned bright blue eyes on Rachel. "It is because we encourage our children to chatter as they will. You, my dear, have at least managed to acquire the blessed skill of intelligent and disciplined conversation."

"Thank you." Rachel bowed her head to the old woman. "That is quite a compliment."

"It is."

"She's right." McLoughlin's eyes twinkled. "I'm honored to meet you." He wheeled forward with brisk precision and offered Rachel his hand. "Pardon me if I don't get up."

"Nice to meet you." Rachel returned his firm hand-clasp. "I'm glad somebody here can keep up with Anne-Marie."

"I wouldn't say I keep up with her, but she doesn't leave me too far behind." He grinned.

Anne-Marie raised her eyebrows. "So what is it that you wish to know?" Anne-Marie regarded Rachel with the air of a teacher calling on a student, although a corner of her mouth twitched suspiciously. "Although if you wish to pretend that you are here merely to visit a cranky old lady, then I will play the game and allow myself to be flattered."

"Anne-Marie, I confess." Rachel laughed and made a face. "I did indeed come here to ask you questions. But it's still nice to see you again."

"My child, you are refreshingly honest. A rare enough attribute." She chuckled, then coughed into a lace-edged handkerchief she pulled from her skirt pocket. "So what is it that you wish to know about our local hotelier and his family? She brought timber money to the marriage. I will not go so far as to say that Henry's father married her for her money." Anne-Marie lifted her shoulders in a very Gallic shrug. "But such things happen—then and now—but perhaps more openly then. He knew, at least, what he wished to accomplish with that money, and he accomplished it."

"The hotel?"

"*Oui*, the hotel." She nodded emphatically. "He was smart, that man. His advertisements appeared in Portland, Seattle, and San Francisco society papers, and in the best magazines. He was not interested in the stranded traveler. *Non*, he wished to cater only to the elite. So he attracted them with the promise of privacy, of elegant and personal service, comfort, and the rugged beauty of the Columbia River Gorge. His establishment became . . . a fad. Right here in the tiny and utterly unimportant town of Blossom." She turned to her companion. "Did you not say that you visited there one day?"

"When I was about ten." He nodded. "We stopped

for lunch on our way home from spending a week with
my aunt in Portland.'' He shook his head ruefully. ''I
remember my father turning red when the waiter brought
the bill. He and my mother fought all the way home
about it. Dad accused her of wanting to belong to the . . .
as he put it . . . fancy-pants class.''

''So what did they serve that cost your father so
much?'' Anne-Marie asked curiously.

''Game, I think. Quail, maybe. I was kind of disappointed, I remember. My oldest brother shot quail all the
time. I was all set for something really special.''

''What about the son?'' Rachel interjected before the
two of them could wander off on a new tangent. ''Did
Henry spend his whole life in Blossom?''

''Henry, who was murdered?'' Anne-Marie gave Rachel a brief piercing look. ''*Les pauvres petites* never had
a life of their own. They did what *le père* told them. Until
the girl ran away to Los Angeles to escape him. With a
man who claimed to be a painter—an *artiste*. He left her
and their child the instant her money ran out, and Papa
refused to send her more.''

A brief and telling history of Alex's childhood, Rachel
thought. ''What about Henry?'' she persisted. ''Didn't
he run away from home, too?''

''Oh, no, not him.'' Anne-Marie shook her head decisively. ''He was the perfect son without a shred of what
the British refer to as the 'backbone.' Papa sent him into
the military, but after a short time he returned home
again. I am not surprised,'' she said with asperity. ''He
was not officer material. So?'' She lifted one eyebrow.
''This is not what you expected to hear?''

''My mother said something about him becoming a
musician. A jazz musician. Ouch.'' Rachel yanked back
her hand, which she had offered to the swan. ''He bit
me.''

''Nasty birds, swans.'' Harris regarded the bird
through narrowed eyes. ''Wonder how they taste?''

''They are tough.'' Anne-Marie clucked her tongue.
''Goose is much better. A musician? *Le petit Henry?* Per-

haps he played an instrument." She fluttered her fingers dismissively. "I do not remember where I heard that he was in the military. One puts the best face on one's children. But I am certain that Papa would never let him play music on a stage—if that is what you mean. Papa hired musicians. For the hotel. He would never have allowed his son to become someone he could hire. *Non*." She shook her head decisively. "He was to take over the hotel from Papa. That is why he was born. Now." Her smile twinkled. "Shall I ask why you are so interested in our murdered Henry? Could it be, perhaps, because of a certain new member of the Blossom Police Force? You are perhaps assisting in this matter?"

"Heavens, no." Rachel tried in vain to keep her cheeks from heating and made a mental note to give Joy-linn serious grief for this little bit of gossip. "I don't have a clue as to what the police are doing. But I used to work for Henry." She noticed suddenly that Harris was staring at her intently. "I was talking to my mother about his death and wondering what was going to happen to the hotel. She told me that she met Henry at a Portland jazz club one night, and he had introduced her and dad to a little boy. Henry referred to him as his son."

"Ah, *ça*." Anne-Marie laughed indulgently. "Henry was forever telling stories. One could never believe what he said, unless one was present at the time."

"Maybe." She hadn't thought of that, but it was true that Henry had told her dozens of elaborate stories about the glorious past of the hotel.

"They are not all real. He likes to . . . make the old days better, if you will."

The young swan had abandoned the threesome at last and was heckling a pair of mallard ducks. "It's almost time for the party," Harris announced to Anne-Marie. "Glendora Spencer's seventy-eighth birthday," he explained to Rachel.

"A child." Anne-Marie waved airily. "And it is only six-thirty, *mon cher*. Your watch is fast."

"But you need time to dress." Harris grinned. "You

promised you were going to knock my socks off, remember? Don't deny an old man one of his few remaining pleasures of the flesh.''

''You are far from an old man.'' Anne-Marie tapped his knee lightly with her cane. ''And I would never use such a vulgar expression. I believe,'' she said with dignity, ''that I told you I still had one or two dresses that looked well on me.''

''You said you'd knock my socks off.''

''Humph.'' The old woman rose with precise dignity, a smile lurking at the corner of her mouth again. ''I will indeed go dress.'' She gathered up the lacy shawl and the paperback she had placed on the bench and turned back to give Harris a brief, arch glance. ''*Ah, non,* you are far from old, *chéri.*''

Rachel smiled as the small, upright figure walked with measured steps up the graveled path to the main wing of the home. Harris, too, was watching her, a light in his eyes and a surprisingly gentle smile on his face. ''She must have been beautiful when she was young,'' Rachel said.

''She's beautiful now.'' Harris looked up at her, his face growing suddenly cold. ''This murder is not a game. I'm warning you. Leave it alone.'' He turned his chair abruptly and wheeled himself up the path with violent thrusts of his muscled arms.

Rachel stared after him, at a loss for words. After a moment she noticed the freckled aide helping a frail-looking woman make her way around the pond with a walker. She was watching Rachel with an anxious look on her face, but when she saw Rachel look, she turned to her elderly charge and pretended to be engrossed in what the woman was saying.

Without a word, Rachel made her way back to her truck and drove home. It was late. The sinking sun dazzled her with level beams of golden light that gilded the Columbia's broad waters. By now, she thought grimly, her mother had every right to be seriously annoyed with her.

She wondered who was right about Henry and his supposed son—her mother? Or Anne-Marie? She wondered, too, what stake Monsieur Harris McLoughlin from Ontario, Oregon, had in this affair.

CHAPTER

8

Her mother was waiting for her on the sofa with her suitcases by her feet, looking like someone waiting for a train. Peter purred on the back of the sofa beside her left shoulder, looking feline and picturesque. "I think we'd better get going," her mother said without irritation. "Aunt Catherine sounded a wee bit testy on the phone. She's doing a leg of lamb, and they dry out when they're overcooked, you know. Oh—and Sandy called."

Neither of them mentioned the fact that everything Catherine made was overcooked. The idea of blood made her queasy, so there was never a trace of pink in any meat that passed through heat at her hands. Her forte was bread. She could rival Joylinn for the quality of her cinnamon rolls and whole wheat loaves.

Rachel called Sandy before they left. It turned out that Bill had to be out of town, and Sandy wanted her to come over, watch old movies, and spend the night. Regretfully Rachel declined. It was true that she and Sandy didn't spend nearly as much time together as they had in the old days—back before marriage and career. But she would feel too guilty if she backed out of her mother's invitation. She hung up to find that her mother had already stowed her suitcases in Rachel's truck bed.

"Joshua and I took a little trip into Hood River this afternoon," her mother told her as they drove up the winding road that led south out of Blossom.

"So that's where he was."

"He said you're doing a great job and you didn't need him peering over your shoulder."

"Good thing I didn't have any questions for him that would have held up the job." Rachel winced at her peevish tone but couldn't help it. Her mother patted her knee.

"Good thing that you didn't." She smiled at her daughter. "But we didn't waste the day, dear. We stopped in at the county Hall of Records. Do you know they have a copy of every marriage certificate issued in the county somewhere in that office?"

"Henry's?" Rachel glanced at her quickly, then went back to negotiating the road. Curving sharply between stands of cherry trees, it was steep and rough—not one of the better maintained roads in the county. "Did you find a marriage certificate?"

"No." Her mother pursed her lips. "He certainly didn't get married in this county."

"If he got married at all." Rachel recounted Anne-Marie's story about Henry's military service to her.

"I suppose that could be true," her mother said thoughtfully. "He disappeared soon after we came back to Blossom, and I didn't know people very well then. I remember rumors about his absence but nothing specific. I'd never met Henry back then, and frankly I couldn't stand his father."

They had reached the stone pillars that marked the entrance to the orchard's driveway. Rachel turned onto the neatly graded gravel road. Uncle Jack might not be much of a conversationalist, Rachel thought as they wound through the well-pruned stands of trees, but he was a good orchardist. The ground between the trees was weed-free and clear of debris. Jack had introduced weeder geese into the management program back when she was about six. The noisy, aggressive birds had made her life miserable when she was little, but they kept the grass down beneath the trees and provided a change from turkey during the holidays every year.

Aunt Catherine met them at the door and hugged Deborah, enveloping her in her bony arms. "I'm so glad you're back." She scooped up one of the suitcases, handling it as if it was empty. "I know it's hard to stop working when there's daylight." This was directed at Rachel and constituted forgiveness for their tardy arrival.

"I'm really sorry." Rachel carried the other suitcase inside. "You know how I am about time." She genuinely liked her aunt, with her large lanky frame and easy, forgiving nature.

"Well, Jack's in the living room doing drinks. Herbert Southern dropped by." She rolled her eyes. "I hope they're not still talking politics. Good thing I have dinner as an excuse to stay in the kitchen."

After declining any help from Deborah on her first night home, she shooed them both into the living room.

"I was just telling Herbert how I want to sell off that back twenty acres of cherries. I bet you could use a drink, Debbie," Uncle Jack greeted them. As far as Rachel knew, he was the only person in the universe who called her mother Debbie. Dropping cubes of ice into a tall glass, he added gin and tonic water. The last golden light of the setting sun poured through the sash windows, turning the wide-plank oak floor a rich, honey-gold color. "I've been waiting until you got back to talk to you about it, but those trees have never paid their way. We spend more on spray and water than we're getting at the market." He squeezed a wedge of lime into the drink and handed it to Rachel's mother.

"Herbert here dropped by, so I invited him to stay. Just in case you had any questions for him. Figured I might as well run it by you now. You want one?" He brandished a tall glass at Rachel. "Sure seems funny to be mixing you a drink." He winked. "Just yesterday it was a Shirley Temple with a cherry in it."

"Thanks." Rachel took her drink, watching her mother from the corner of her eye. It was just like Uncle Jack to start off with orchard business the minute her mother walked in the door. "So do you have a buyer, Herbert?" she asked the realtor quietly. "Or did you just plan to list the acreage?"

Herbert cleared his throat and took a long swallow of his bourbon. "There's this man from Seattle. He's a developer. He's been looking around for a piece of property for a block of condos. We're talking something really nice here," Herbert went on quickly. "Nothing cheap and shoddy. These would be time-shares. Portland owners, most likely. Vacation folk. They ought to be big buyers down at the farmers market."

"Sounds good to me." Aunt Catherine leaned against the kitchen door frame, absently wiping her hands on her apron. "Tourists buy a lot of stuff at the market." She took fruit and some vegetables from her big kitchen garden to the local farmers market, where she shared a booth with a friend who produced a line of gourmet jams and jellies from local fruit. "I, for one, welcome them," she said decisively. "Rachel, honey, could you give me a hand with the salad?"

"Sure." Rachel picked up her drink, but hesitated. Everyone was looking at her mother, who was staring rather abstractedly at the gilded trees of the orchard spread out on the slope west of the house.

Jack cleared his throat. "I figure to use the money for that new spray equipment we need. Until those new apples start producing, we're a little tight."

"We all know Will would have said no to this." Her mother spoke at last, her eyes still on the gnarled branches of the old trees. "He was adamantly opposed to any sale of family property." For a moment she was silent, her eyes straying to the family photographs displayed on the wooden sideboard opposite the windows. In one of them, she, Will, and Rachel laughed from the bank of a stream as a very young Rachel proudly displayed the small trout she had caught.

"You are the one who is really carrying the burden of this place." She turned her attention on Jack at last. "I believe you care about it as much as Will did, even if the two of you didn't always agree on method. If you want to sell this acreage—if you think it benefits the orchard—then I won't stand in your way." She got to her feet, setting aside her nearly untouched gin and tonic. "Catherine, I'll help you with the salad. Rachel, you relax. You've put in a working day today, and I've just been lazing around." Giving her daughter a smile, she exited into the kitchen.

"Well, I guess you can talk to that developer man," Uncle Jack said a shade too heartily. "Another, Herbert?" He carried the realtor's glass and his own back to the sideboard. "Your mother has a good head on her shoulders," he said over his shoulder to Rachel.

Rachel wondered whom he was trying to convince.

"Oh, she made a good decision, all right. Very good decision." Herbert took the fresh drink Jack handed him and lifted it in a salute. "The real estate market is prime right now. Really prime. Might as well catch the wave, as they say." He took a swallow of his drink. "No point in passing up money when it's lying in the road."

"So how's that big deal of yours coming along?" Jack settled back into his easy chair, his glass balanced on his jeans-clad knee. "The one that was gonna buy you that Lincoln you want so bad."

For a moment Herbert hesitated, the glass poised at his lips. "Oh, it didn't work out." He took a gulp of his drink. "You know how things are in this business. On one minute, off the next." He waved a hand, but his eyes moved uneasily in Rachel's direction.

"Tough luck. Sounded like big money from those hints you kept dropping. Did the seller back out or the buyer?"

"Oh, things just didn't work out." Herbert picked up his drink again, put it down. "Look at the time. I got to get back to town."

"I thought you were gonna stay for dinner." Jack got

to his feet as Herbert rose. "Catherine already set a place."

" 'Fraid not this time." Herbert gave him a wide smile. "I forgot—I've got to see this client. Told him I'd stop by before eight."

"You'll miss a good dinner," Jack grumbled as the realtor retrieved his hat from the sofa arm where he'd perched it. "Why not see him in the morning?"

"He's going on vacation. Thanks for the drink," Herbert said heartily. "I'll bring you a formal offer from that developer tomorrow. He's chompin' at the bit. Catherine—I've got to go. Sorry I can't stay," he called through to the kitchen.

"You stop over another time." Aunt Catherine appeared in the doorway, wiping her hands on her apron, her expression mildly puzzled.

Rachel sipped her drink and watched Herbert make his exit without once looking in her direction.

"So what did you do to scare him off?" Uncle Jack gave her an exasperated look as Aunt Catherine disappeared into the kitchen once more. "He didn't even finish his bourbon. That's sure not like Herbert."

"I don't think it was me." Rachel shrugged. "What's this big deal that fell through, anyway?"

"He wouldn't say. But he was sure talking like he'd sold half of downtown Blossom the other night when we were playing poker over at Roger's." He chuckled. "Course, he'd had a few. Maybe he didn't want to be reminded. Lost his shirt that night, too."

"Dinner's ready," Aunt Catherine announced from the doorway, and they all trooped on into the dining room.

The big table looked odd with only the four of them sitting around it, even though Aunt Catherine had removed the extra leaves that had allowed it to seat seven family members comfortably. Meals were when she found herself missing her father the most, Rachel realized as she took her seat. His conversation had been the backbone of every mealtime—a mainstay of words and ideas that carried the conversation beyond the labors of the day. Tonight, however, talk centered briefly on her mother's visit—the health of family members and what new places she had visited, mostly—then moved on to the church rummage sale that Aunt Catherine ran every year. Lastly and predictably, they discussed the apple crop that was coming along nicely in spite of the dry summer. Rachel noticed that her mother was almost terse with her family news, and after that didn't say much. She picked at her dinner, a pensive, almost sad expression on her face. Rachel wondered if mealtimes didn't bring her father's absence home to her mother, too. Or maybe it was the sale he wouldn't have approved of.

The family dogs—a pair of Australian shepherds and Aunt Catherine's fox terrier—began to bark as Aunt Catherine was bringing a plate of oatmeal cookies to the table. "Maybe Herbert changed his mind and decided to come back for dessert." Her uncle tossed his napkin onto the table and went to the front door, yelling at the dogs to quiet down as he opened it. Rachel heard the murmur of male voices, and a moment later he ushered Jeff into the room.

"I was just passing by, so I thought I'd drop in and say hello. I'm just sort of reintroducing myself to folks around here." He said this with a straight face, his hat in his hands, but a gleam of laughter lurked in his eyes when he looked at Rachel.

"We heard you joined the Blossom Police. Sit down, sit down." Uncle Jack pulled out the chair across from Rachel. "Want some dinner? It's still warm. Well, have a few cookies," he said when Jeff declined with thanks. "They're Catherine's oatmeal crisps. I figure you put away a few when you were a kid." He gave Jeff a sly look.

"Well, I was over here enough." Jeff laughed. "I ate my share." He reached for one of the crispy rounds. "You never knew they were the real reason I hung around, did you?" He winked at Rachel.

"Any luck solving Henry Bassinger's murder?" Uncle

Jack helped himself to another cookie. "I heard you arrested that LA nephew of his."

"We just picked him up for questioning," Jeff said easily. "Routine."

"I remember that kid when he was little. Quiet, like Henry. Kind of sneaky, as I recall." Jack sipped at his coffee. "Nice brew, Cat. I like this new brand you're buying. Colombian beans, or something fancy like that," he told Jeff. "You're not in uniform tonight, huh?"

"I'm not officially on duty." Jeff glanced down at his jeans and chambray work shirt as if they surprised him.

"I forgot to bring in the eggs." Aunt Catherine spoke up suddenly. "Rachel, honey, would you go fetch them in? That pesky raccoon will get into them if I leave them out. Maybe you'd go with her and take the flashlight," she said to Jeff. "If you don't mind."

"Since when does it take two people to carry a dozen hens' eggs?" Jack raised his thick, ginger-colored brows. "Or are they layin' bowling balls now?"

"You know that henhouse door takes two hands to close," Aunt Catherine chided. "I don't want my eggs cracked all over the ground because Rachel was trying to latch the door while she juggled a flashlight and basket. And Jeff doesn't mind, do you, Jeff?"

"No, ma'am," he said politely. "I even have a flashlight in my truck."

"Oh, there's one on the shelf by the back door," Catherine said.

Silently Jeff escorted Rachel through the kitchen and out the back door. "This seems more like it," he said as he latched the screen door behind them. "I don't think I ever used the front door before."

"I guess that means my uncle has decided you're a grown-up." Or a stranger. "Do you think my aunt was subtle enough?" Rachel asked lightly.

"I think she just didn't want you to drop her eggs," Jeff said solemnly. "Since when have you had to use a flashlight to go out to the chicken house?"

"Since I couldn't carry a basket of eggs and shut a

door at the same time, I guess.'' Rachel laughed and rolled her eyes skyward at her aunt's transparent tactics. It was a beautiful summer night. Stars spangled the sky, crossed by the dusty gold band of the Milky Way. A sliver of moon hovered above the horizon, barely dimming the surrounding stars. She kept waiting for Jeff to slip his arm around her as they crossed the yard, but he walked silently beside her. Ducking in unison beneath the empty clothesline with clothespins like skinny roosting birds, Rachel felt a twinge of unease. The henhouse stood at the rear of the yard, beside the gate that led back to the big equipment and sorting sheds.

Halide yard lights lit the graveled space around the sheds, and warm yellow light spilled from the big sash windows of the tall old farmhouse, but beneath the branches of the huge old apple tree that shaded the henhouse, shadows reigned.

A hen squawked as Rachel pulled the door open, filling the air with the sound of fluttering wings and the dusty scent of feathers and old dry manure. The basket sat on a shelf beside the door, dimly illuminated by the light coming from the house. A dozen red and speckled hens blinked from their roosts. A tall, black-and-white rooster stretched his neck suddenly and crowed an ear-splitting fanfare. Rachel winced, grabbed the basket full of brown eggs, and retreated.

Something was wrong. Still isolated in silence, they walked side by side back across the yard to the yellow wash of kitchen glow. Below them, the sparse lights of Blossom twinkled. Rachel cleared her throat. ''Is it possible that Herbert Southern had some kind of agreement with Henry? My uncle says he was boasting about a big deal coming up, but tonight he acted almost scared when Uncle Jack mentioned it.''

''Not that I heard of.'' Jeff sat down on the edge of the wide porch steps. ''You trying to pin the murder on Sandy's dad to get this LA architect off?''

''What?'' Rachel gasped, stung by his tone. ''What is

eating you, Jeffrey Price? You've acted like a pissed-off teenager ever since we came out here.''

"I heard some interesting stories floating around town. How you and this rich architect were seeing each other.'' He enunciated each syllable very precisely. "Made me feel a bit used, to tell the truth. Guess I asked for it— made one too many assumptions.''

"Oh . . . God.'' Rachel flung herself away from the porch. "I can't believe it. Sometimes I *hate* this town. How *dare* you believe that kind of thing? How dare you?''

"Your landlady came to me. Seems she's worried that you might be in danger.'' Jeff's tone was cold. "Since he's spending nights there.''

"He passed out drunk on my sofa—once. What did you want me to do? Roll him down the stairs?'' Rachel hugged herself, cold suddenly. "I was going to tell you—''

"Were you?'' The faint light from the house turned his face to planes of stone. "I guess I told you enough. Like I said—my fault.'' He stood up.

"So say it.'' Rachel's hands were trembling, and she clasped them tightly together. "Ask me how I feel about Alex Cresswell. Ask me if I'm sleeping with him. Go on.'' She drew a shuddering breath. "Ask me, damn it!''

He turned his back on her and started around the side of the house.

"You're an idiot, Jeff Price,'' she whispered. She spun on her heel and ran for the kitchen door, realizing as she stumbled up the porch steps that she'd left the egg basket on the ground out front. And then she was crying, slipping through the kitchen, immensely grateful to find it empty.

A murmur of conversation came from the dining room as she slipped into the hall and along to the stairs. Jealous, she thought bitterly as she tiptoed up the stairs, stepping over the seventh one—the one that creaked to wake the dead. Narrow, possessive, and jealous—that's how Jeff was behaving.

She could have told him about Alex. Right away. Because she had nothing to hide. Rubbing the tears from her eyes, she went into her dark bedroom. The window was open, and the shade was up. With the lights off, she could see down into the yard. Jeff stood below her, his face turned up to her window, his expression hidden by the shadows cast by Aunt Catherine's trellised clematis. Rachel took a single step toward the window, then stopped.

Below, Jeff hunched his shoulders, turned on his heel, and vanished once more around the corner of the house. A few moments later, she heard the grumble of his truck engine and the crunch of wheels on gravel. "Idiot," she whispered, unsure which one of them she meant. Letting her breath out in a shuddering rush, she yanked the shade down and went back downstairs. "I'll do the dishes," she called through to the dining room as she went down the hall. "No arguments."

"Honey, you'll never get an argument from me about dishes." Aunt Catherine's chuckle followed her into the kitchen.

Rachel began to rinse the stacked dishes and load them into the dishwasher. It was a big commercial model that Uncle Jack had bought from a Portland liquidator many years ago. There was plenty of room for a big family's worth of dishes. Now she only managed to half fill the machine. As she placed the last glass in the rack, her mother stuck her head into the kitchen. "Jack and Catherine are going down to the new Baskin Robbins for ice cream. Do you want to come?"

"No thanks." Rachel closed the dishwasher door without looking at her. "I ate too many cookies to justify ice cream."

"The way you work, I wouldn't think you'd have to worry about calories." Her mother disappeared into the front room, but reappeared a moment later to boost herself up onto the counter. "I'm going to skip the calories, too. With more reason than you, young lady. Jeff took off without saying good night. That's not like him."

Rachel glanced up to find her mother's eyes full of knowing sympathy. She swallowed, her throat closing again. ''Well . . . we kind of had a fight.''

Her mother sat quietly, bumping her heels against the painted wooden drawers beneath her. ''How do you feel about him?'' she said at last, eyes fixed on the ancient mixer beneath its quilted cover.

''I . . . I'm not sure.'' Rachel measured detergent into the machine and turned it on. The roar of water and motor noise immediately put an end to anything except shouted conversation.

When her mother hopped off the counter and went out onto the back porch, Rachel followed. ''I left the eggs out front,'' she said. But there they were, the basket set neatly on the wooden table beside the door. She sighed. ''I think I blew it, Mom. I don't know if I can fix it. Jeff has a tough pride.''

''So do you, child of mine.'' Her mother sighed and sat down on the top step, hands clasped about her raised knee. In the soft light of stars and sliver moon, her face looked youthful and smooth, the lines etched by the years invisible. ''Try apologizing if it really matters?''

''I don't know.'' Rachel stared at the toes of her boots. ''I think it does.''

''Ironic conversation tonight.'' Her mother smiled gently.

''What do you mean?''

''Joshua asked me to marry him this afternoon.''

''What?'' Rachel sat down hard in the webbing deck chair behind her. ''That's crazy. You've only spent, what? A few hours with him?''

''We spent all of today together actually. He said we're too old to wait and play it safe. I think I agree with him.'' Her mother lifted her head, eyes on a private vista that Rachel couldn't share. The warm glow of yellow light seeping through the windows burnished the pure line of her throat.

She's young, Rachel thought with a jolt. The realization

shocked her. Parents were *old* by definition. "So what did you tell him?" she asked carefully.

"I told him I needed to talk to you. See how you felt about it."

Rachel looked away, unaccountably angry. *This is your choice, not mine,* she wanted to say. "Do you love him?" she asked after a moment.

Her mother remained silent for the space of a few heartbeats—a petite silhouette against the silent radiance of kitchen light. "Love is like a crocus," she said at last. "One day you're looking at bare ground. The next day you see a green shoot. Almost before you know it, the blossom opens. And to begin with, there was nothing but that muddy bare ground. I'm going to make some tea." She went back into the kitchen, and Rachel heard the sound of water running into the teakettle.

She went down the steps and around to the front of the old house. Her great-grandfather had built it when he planted the first trees. The lights of Blossom gleamed below, like an earthbound constellation. Suddenly they seemed enormously far away. Rachel turned on her heel and went back around to the kitchen door. "Mom?" she called through the screen door. "I think I'm going to go on home."

Her mother finished pouring steaming water into her small brown teapot. "It upsets you." She looked up, her eyes unexpectedly full of sympathy. "It would have to, I suppose."

"It's not that . . . Well, yes, it is." The scent of mint drifted to her on a breath of steamy air. "I . . . I'm not really that upset. It's a surprise. I guess I need to . . . think about it."

Her mother replaced the kettle carefully on the stove and came over to the screen door, not opening it, so that they looked at each other through a layer of rusty screening. "I understand," she said softly. "I really do. What I finally decide has as much to do with how you feel as it does with how I feel."

"That's not right."

"I think it is." Her mother nodded. "But remember one thing—your father was the most wonderful thing that ever happened in my life. Nothing and no one could ever change that."

"I didn't . . . I mean . . ." There was nothing more to say. Not tonight. "Good night," Rachel managed, her voice unexpectedly hoarse. "I'll call you tomorrow."

"I'll be here." Her mother leaned her hands on either side of the door, backed by light and framed by the peeling white trim of the frame. "I love you," she said. "Good night."

"Good night. Love you, too." Rachel fled into the darkness of the side yard, relieved that they didn't have to talk about this anymore tonight. She started her truck and pulled into the long gravel driveway that linked the O'Connor orchard with the county road.

Mrs. Meier.

It sounded . . . odd. Wrong? Rachel shook her head and turned the truck onto the dark asphalt road. Headlights briefly dazzled her as a pickup roared past. Uncle Jack and Aunt Catherine back from getting ice cream. She felt a flicker of relief that she had left before they had returned. Explanations would have been awkward.

The road meandered along the rim of the Gorge, dividing dark rows of fruit trees before it dropped sharply down toward Blossom. The buckled and sunken asphalt occupied all of Rachel's attention as she drove. Her headlights caught the gleam of small apples swelling among the carefully pruned branches. The gnarled trunks of the older trees cast writhing shadows ahead of her on the tight curves.

As she rounded another curve and began to drop down the side of the Gorge, movement in her rearview mirror caught her eye. A vehicle was following her—but without lights. Teenagers, she thought, out trying to give someone a bit of a scare. Deliberately she slowed, hoping her pursuer would get bored with the game and pass her. But the vehicle behind her slowed, too, maintaining its position precisely. Rachel fought down a prickle of apprehension.

A game, she told herself as she accelerated again. They're simply playing a game.

But she found herself constantly glancing in the rear-view mirror as they switchbacked down toward town, fighting the temptation to accelerate. This was not a safe road for speeding. With a surge of relief, she recognized the driveway of a neighboring orchard. One more bad curve and a dip, and then the road dropped straight into downtown Blossom.

As she accelerated into the curve, the car behind her suddenly leaped forward to pass, its engine roaring. Rachel caught a glimpse of a dark van as it hurtled by. Then, without warning, it cut directly in front of her. With a gasp, Rachel slammed on the brakes, twisting the wheel desperately. She missed the van's fender by a hair, then the truck struck the soft shoulder, and the wheel tried to tear itself out of her frantic grip. Rachel clung to it as the truck bounded and shuddered. It tilted suddenly and violently, and for one terrified moment Rachel thought it was going to roll over. But it merely bucked and shuddered down a steep slope, crashing into a tangle of limbs and trunks. With a final wrenching jolt, it stopped and stalled.

Silence. Rachel leaned her forehead against the cool plastic of the steering wheel, willing herself to stop trembling. Slowly the silenced crickets began to chirp again. Frogs creaked in their falsetto voices, and in the distance a cow bawled a long, sorrowful note. The Bakers' Jersey milk cow, Rachel thought absently. They must have weaned her calf finally.

After a time she felt steady enough to open the door and get out, although her knees still threatened to start quaking again. The chirp of crickets and the rustle of the apple leaves were the only sounds to mar the night. It seemed so *peaceful* after the violence of the past few moments. Rachel smothered an hysterical giggle. The truck had halted on the level, at the bottom of the sloped bank leading down from the road. It had come to rest in a grove of young apples, and miraculously she had managed to run over only a single slender trunk, although she had damaged several. If the trees had been older . . . She shivered, glad that she always wore her seat belt.

Headlights flooded the road above her, coming from the direction of the O'Connor orchard. Rachel fought down a moment of panic. Her attacker had gone on toward town, she told herself. The lights couldn't belong to him. But she flinched as the beam swept over her. If he had turned, would she have noticed? He could have doubled back through the field on the far side of the road. The access roads through the rows of trees weren't barricaded. She clutched the pickup's door, her heart pounding, as the car screeched to a halt.

"Rachel!" A hoarse shout cut through the murmur of leaf and insect. "Rachel, are you all right?"

Alex Cresswell. Relief swept over her, turning her knees to water. "I . . . I'm fine." She managed an impressively calm tone, considering. "I'm down here."

She heard footsteps on the bank, a grunt, and the sound of sliding. "My God, what happened?" Alex emerged from the darkness. "Did you lose control?"

"Someone . . . ran me off the road." This time she couldn't hold back the giggle. It sounded so melodramatic.

"You're kidding." Alex put his arm around her as her knees began to tremble in earnest. "You'd better sit down. I think you're in shock." His words sounded oddly muffled to Rachel, as if she had cotton in her ears. He was asking her something about the license number.

"I didn't even think about looking at it," she said breathlessly. The ground came up hard under her butt, and for a dizzy moment she thought she was going to faint.

"Put your head between your knees. Or better yet, lie flat." Alex was bending over her. "Why would someone run you off the road? Was the creep drunk?"

She did as he said, and it helped. "Henry," she mumbled with her forehead pressed against her knees. "It's because I've been asking about . . . about Henry. Or about his son. He wasn't a drunk driver. I guess it could have been a woman driving. The headlights were off, and I couldn't see anything. It was a van. Dark. I . . . I only got a glimpse, then I was too busy trying to stay on the road. . . ." She realized she was babbling and that Alex had drawn away, was staring at her with a strange expression.

"My uncle was a lifelong bachelor," he said in a tight voice. "He never had a son. Where did you hear that piece of crap?"

Rachel blinked, jolted out of her fog by his unexpected anger. "I . . . it's a rumor." She looked up at him as he towered over her. "It makes it less likely that you'd have killed your uncle, don't you see? Not if he didn't have a will. You wouldn't inherit if there was a son."

"There is no son. And he left the hotel to me in a will. He told me so, and he never lied to me. Never." Alex sucked in a ragged breath. "I'm sorry. I . . . I'm kind of tense right now. To put it mildly." He shook his head. "I have my cell phone with me." He turned his back on her. "I'll call the police," he said as he scrambled back up the bank.

"And a tow truck, please. I don't think you killed Henry," she called after him. "I never have."

He didn't answer, and she shrugged, getting cautiously to her feet to inspect her truck.

It was in remarkably good shape. The left headlight had shattered, and there was a minor dent in the front bumper where she had flattened the young tree. But other than that, from what she could see in the dark, the truck appeared to be undamaged. She finished her brief tour just as a black-and-white Blossom Police Department car pulled over on the bank in front of Alex's white rental car. The uniformed officer got out, leaving the lights twirling slowly, sending colored shadows sliding through the rows of trees.

It wasn't Jeff. Rachel felt a small guilty twinge of relief. The officer spoke briefly with Alex, then scrambled down the bank.

"You want to tell me what happened, Miz O'Connor?" The small, compact man gave the truck a cursory glance. "Mr. Cresswell said something about you getting run off the road. Not by him, I guess."

"By a dark van or panel truck," Rachel said. "I didn't get the license number or see the driver. He—or she—didn't have the lights on." She noticed that he had stopped short of the bottom of the bank so that he could look down at her.

"You didn't see anything that could identify this . . . uh, van?" He wasn't trying to hide his skepticism. Rachel peered at his badge but couldn't quite make out the name.

"No," she said. "I really didn't think about it. I was trying to stay on the road—or at least keep from rolling over."

The officer grunted. "I'll call in a description," he said dubiously. "Probably some kids out horsing around. By now they've hightailed it home, scared as the dickens." He gave her a sly look. "You seen Jeff tonight?"

"Yes, actually, I have." Rachel swallowed, her stomach suddenly tight. "Is a tow truck on its way?" she asked weakly.

"I called the sisters." He turned away, sweeping her truck with a disdainful sweep of his flashlight beam. "Gonna have some damage underneath."

She hoped not. Rachel turned her back on him, wondering how soon Jeff was going to hear about this—and what version he'd hear.

She was saved from her dark thoughts by the red pulse of the tow truck's rooftop light. Earlene was on tow duty tonight. She shoved the door open and leaned out to survey the scene, her usual unlit cigar bobbing at a jaunty angle in the corner of her mouth. "You ready, Lyle?" She directed the question solely to the officer.

Lyle waved assent. Earlene removed the cigar from her mouth just long enough to spit emphatically, replaced it, and proceeded to climb out and set out flares along the graveled shoulder in both directions. The wavering red light and drifting smoke gave the scene a hellish look of catastrophe that raised brief goose bumps on Rachel's arms.

With swift efficiency, Earlene backed the truck around so that its big towing arm faced the bank and the rear bumper of Rachel's truck. Leaving the engine idling, she hopped down and affixed the hooked cable to the truck's frame hitch. "Someone wanna steer?" she remarked to nobody in particular. "Be a hell of a lot easier."

"I will." Rachel climbed behind the wheel. She put the truck into neutral and released the brake, earning herself a terse nod of approval from the muscular Earlene. The truck jerked and shuddered as she started the winch, and slowly it began to back up the embankment. Once all four wheels were on solid ground again, Earlene shut off the winch and released the cable. "Start 'er up," she instructed Rachel. "Let's see what's broke."

Rachel started the engine, relieved as it purred to life.

"Hold it!" Earlene held up a restraining hand. As Rachel killed the engine, the stocky woman slid beneath the truck. A moment later, she was on her feet again. "You're leaking oil." She rolled her cigar to the other side of her mouth. "Banged up the oil filter, from what I can see. No big deal." She shrugged. "I'll haul it in, have it ready for you first thing in the morning."

"Thanks, Earlene." Rachel breathed a sigh of relief that the damage was minor. A new truck was not in her budget at the moment. Or major repair bills for that matter. Her loan payments were tough enough to meet some months.

"I should be done with it in a couple of hours." Earlene backed her truck swiftly around and hoisted Rachel's truck onto the tow beam. "Unless I get another call, anyway. That's twenty-five for the pull." She chewed on her cigar as she folded the bills Rachel handed her and stuffed them down the front of her grease-stained coveralls. "You gonna ride with me?"

"I'll give you a ride home," Alex spoke up. "No problem."

"So gimme a call if you need a lift over in the morning." Earlene winked and swung into the cab of her truck, giving Lyle a spare nod and ignoring Alex altogether. A moment later, the red taillights she'd affixed to Rachel's truck disappeared around the curve toward town.

"I have your statement." Lyle looked from the pad in

his hand to Alex, his eyebrows lifting suggestively. ''You want to drop by tomorrow sometime and look it over? When you get up?'' he drawled.

Rachel flushed. ''I'll be down first thing in the morning,'' she said coldly. ''I've got to be at work at dawn.''

''Sure thing.'' Lyle gave her what almost amounted to a leer as he pocketed his notebook. Still grinning, he headed for the parked police car up on the road.

''Jerk,'' Rachel said softly.

Alex was looking thoughtfully after the departing officer. ''You got some kind of vendetta with him?''

''Me? No.'' Rachel let her breath out in a gusty sigh. ''I never met the man before. I'm tired,'' she said, although it was a jittery kind of overwrought fatigue that didn't promise a good night's sleep. ''So what are you doing out here at this hour?'' she asked and immediately regretted her tone. ''I apologize,'' she amended as they climbed the bank to his rental car. ''It's none of my business, and I'm really glad you came by.''

''That's okay.'' He gave her a crooked smile. ''I was out for a drive.'' He shrugged. ''I drive or walk when I need to think.''

''So I hear.''

Alex gave her a brief enigmatic glance. ''Yeah. Well, I do think I need to start taking a witness along when I go. Or maybe I should just take up drinking. A bar is a nice acceptable and very public alibi.''

''Only if someone remembers you.'' Rachel climbed into the front seat of his rental. Staring into the darkness, she replayed the moment when the dark van sped past her, straining to recall a face, a glimpse of the driver. No good. She sighed and leaned back as they dropped down the hill and into Blossom.

Alex cleared his throat as he reached the street that led to her house. ''Are you sure you want to spend the night there by yourself tonight?'' He glanced into the rearview mirror, frowning. ''Someone knew where you were tonight. Maybe they know where you live, too.''

Rachel rubbed her arms, goose bumps rising again. That

thought hadn't occurred to her, but now it intruded with all its dark and ugly implications.

"Do you have somewhere else to go?" He was still frowning. "Do you want me to take you to the motel I'm staying in? They had plenty of vacancies when I left."

Blossom's only motel was run by Loretta and Dave Peterson, the biggest gossips in all of Hood River County. She opened her mouth to tell him to take her back to the orchard, then snapped her fingers. "Sandy! My friend," she explained. "She invited me to stay over there tonight anyway. It's almost on your way, if you don't mind taking me."

"Sure," he said.

He sounded so relieved. Rachel wondered if she should be insulted.

CHAPTER

9

"You certainly see a consistent architectural style in those little Oregon and Washington towns." Alex broke the silence as he pulled up to the curb in front of Sandy's house and parked. "They should give it a label."

"Northwest Rural?" Rachel suppressed a giggle, wondering just how close to shock she actually was.

"Ecotopian Modern, maybe. No—make it Ecotopia Classic, and save Modern for the houses with the greenhouse walls and indoor-outdoor tile."

"That's more California than Oregon." Rachel led him up the front walk. "Rains too much out here for indoor-outdoor anything."

"Well, I only spent summers up here, remember? Okay, fine. Northwest Rural." Alex laughed. "Maybe I should write a paper on it."

He had a warm and intimate laugh, and he smiled down at Rachel as she rang the doorbell. "How come you stick around here?" he asked. "You could do a lot more business in a more metropolitan area, you know."

"I know." Rachel sighed as she rang the bell again. "I thought about it."

"What about Los Angeles?"

"I thought people down there do astro-turf instead of landscaping," Rachel said with a straight face.

"Only in the Valley. Hey, you *have* to landscape down there. Water costs too much to waste on random watering." He tilted his head, his eyes unexpectedly serious. "You really are a talented designer. I checked out the references you gave my uncle. Those two places I visited were very original designs. I'm a junior partner with a very prestigious firm, you know. I could give you a lot of referrals and introduce you to some friends of mine— upscale contractors. They'd give you a lot of business. New and fresh plays well in LA, and your talent would at least get the appreciation it deserves. I bet folks around here think you're no different than the guys with the trailers full of lawn mowers, weed eaters, and fertilizers. Just somebody to mow the lawn and maybe prune the shrubs or plant a new arborvitae."

"Hey, I carry all that stuff in my truck." She laughed, but his words struck a chord. Mowing and pruning—that described a lot of her business. Not much different than what Julio did when he wasn't working for her. It was true—the kind of job she was doing for Dr. Meier didn't come along often. Not even in Hood River. Not yet. "I'll get more serious jobs," she said firmly. "Retirees are discovering Hood River and the Gorge. Wealthy Portland families are building weekend homes out here. Business is picking up."

"You sound defensive," Alex said mildly.

"I'm not . . ." She drew a quick breath and laughed. "All right, I am." Her uncle had made it clear that he didn't expect her business to succeed. It was an ongoing argument. "I like living here," she said. "If I moved to Portland, or Seattle, or San Francisco, I'd be facing a lot of established competition anyway."

"Unless you moved to Los Angeles and got referrals from me and my friends." Alex grinned at her.

"I just . . ." She could feel her cheeks warming. "I want to make it work *here*. Not somewhere else."

"Stubborn girl." He waggled an admonishing finger

at her. "That's not how you contribute to your IRA. I hope you change your mind." He lifted an eyebrow and nodded at the door. "I wonder if your friend's home."

"The lights are on." Rachel cupped her hands around her face to peer through the window, relieved at the change of subject—because his offer was a good one, and she was a fool to pass it up. Instant referrals in a city where people did indeed spend money on landscaping . . .

She didn't want to live in Los Angeles.

Squinting through the filmy lace curtain, Rachel made out an open magazine lying facedown on the sofa. A mug stood on the adjacent lamp table. "Maybe she went next door." She frowned, telling herself there was no reason to think anything was wrong—that she was still jittery from the accident. "I'm going to go see if she's at Doreen's." She marched back down the walk and around to Doreen's front gate.

"Maybe she ran to the store for a quart of milk," Alex said as he caught up with her. "Whew!" He whistled softly as Rachel opened the gate and ushered them both into Doreen's crowded front yard. "This place looks like a greenhouse on steroids. Now *here's* someone who could benefit from your design sense."

"I don't think she's worried so much about looks as about variety." Rachel climbed the three wooden steps to the porch, ducking pots of exuberant fuchsias, begonias, and trailing geraniums. The woman certainly had a green thumb. "She's really into herbs, and healing plants, and organic veggies. Ouch." She winced as she walked into a set of metal wind chimes hidden by an over-abundant spider plant. The silvery jangle reverberated through the evening hush—much louder than she would have expected. As she reached to still the wildly swinging metal tubes, the door opened.

"Who's out there?" Doreen peered through the screen. "Oh, Sandy's friend." Her tone thawed. "She's over here, if you're looking for her." The latch clicked, and she swung the door open. "Come in. We were just having tea and talking about you." She smiled at Rachel,

then turned her smile on Alex. "Hello." She offered
Alex a long-fingered hand. "I'm Doreen Baldwin."

He was staring fixedly at her. "I know you. I think
so, anyway." He blushed as he took her hand. "Sorry. I
just had one of those déjà vu moments. I'm Alex Cresswell. I just . . . were you a friend of my mother's? Martha
Bassinger? Martha Cresswell was her married name."

"I don't think so. Unless I cleaned house for her."
Doreen ushered them into a small living room that was
as lushly crowded with plants as the garden and porch.
"I've lived in Blossom for the last six years. Before that,
I was in Phoenix. Did you live in Phoenix?"

"No. And it wasn't in Blossom." Alex pursed his lips.

"Doreen keeps . . . kept house for your uncle," Rachel
said. "You probably saw her there."

"Oh, that's probably it." Alex shrugged again as he
glanced around the small room.

Houseplants crowded a long bookshelf at the big front
window. More spider plants dangled their offspring in
front of the side windows, and a banana tree in a tub
offered a long stem crowded with stubby green fingers
of young bananas. Richly patterned Oriental rugs nearly
covered the off-white carpet. Brocade cushions and
draped scarves added to the gypsy-tent atmosphere, along
with clustered candles and small primitive bits of pottery
and clay statuary. The house smelled of incense and,
faintly, cat box. A huge white Persian shaded with silver
stalked in from a back room, regarding them coolly from
huge green eyes. It yawned, then made a beeline for Alex
and anchored both front sets of claws in his trouser leg.

"Cats always love me," he muttered as he tried to
wrest his leg from the cat, who lashed her fluffy tail and
hung on harder.

"Chandi, behave yourself." Doreen scooped the big
cat into her arms and cradled her on her back, as if she
was an infant. "You are not being very nice." She
bumped her nose against the cat's forehead, which elic-
ited a velvet bat on her cheek. Laughing, Doreen dumped

the cat onto the shawl-draped sofa. "Cats." She rolled her eyes.

"They all torment me." Alex went over to examine the banana tree, ignoring the cat's continued glare. "Does the fruit get ripe?"

"I don't know." Doreen lifted her palms in a graceful gesture. "I ordered it from a newspaper ad. I paid a dollar for a six-inch start." She tilted her head, her eyes mischievous. "Come back in a couple of months. If they're ripe, you can have a sample." Her throaty tone and the gleam in her eyes made Alex blush like a teenager. In her youth, Doreen Baldwin would have been hard for any man to resist. Judging by Alex's reaction, it was still true.

"I . . . I just might do that," he stammered, and glanced about as if looking for an escape route.

"Rachel!" Sandy emerged suddenly from the bathroom. "I thought I heard your voice. Whatever are you doing here? I thought you were at the orchard."

"I was." Rachel noticed that Sandy's eyes were red, and her face looked puffy and freshly scrubbed, in spite of her bright, overly cheerful tone. "But I decided to come home after all." She hesitated, suddenly unwilling to mention the accident. A teakettle whistled from the kitchen, and Sandy started.

"Tea." Doreen put a comforting hand on Sandy's shoulder. "Would you like some?" Doreen acknowledged their nods and glided through the doorway into the neat green and white kitchen beyond. The cat stalked after her, giving Alex an arch feline glance that reminded Rachel strongly of her owner. "Sit down." Doreen's voice wafted from the kitchen. "Make yourselves at home."

"Interesting library." Alex had squatted in front of the bookcase. "*Culpeppers Complete Herbal, Healing Plants of North America, The Kitchen Herbalist, Magic and Medicine of Plants.*" He whistled. "Is she an herbal healer or a New Age shaman?" he asked Sandy.

"I like plants." Doreen swept back into the room carrying a black lacquer tray laden with tea things. Her hearing was certainly excellent. She gave the mildly embarrassed Alex a condescending smile. "The roadside plants we call weeds were once a part of many home medicine chests or kitchen larders. I was an ethnobotany major, working on my Ph.D. at one time."

"What happened?" Rachel couldn't help asking.

"I got pregnant." Doreen shrugged, her expression serene. "I had to quit and get a job. Medicinal plants still interest me, and I use some of them. End of lecture." She laughed and began to set out white porcelain cups with a blue dragon design on them. A wisp of steam curled from the spout of the matching teapot. "I brought out some gingersnaps, too." She set a plate of crisp brown cookies down beside the cups. "They've got candied angelica in them, and my homegrown ginger. Cream, anyone? I have honey." She pointed at a glass jar with a wooden dipper. "It's local. Alfalfa, I think."

"So what was it like, working for Henry?" Feeling a trifle awkward, Rachel picked up the teapot to pour as Doreen made no move to do so. "Did he tell you stories about the hotel, too?"

"Oh, he loved to talk about it." The older woman finally smiled. "I didn't mind. Cleaning is a lonely business most of the time."

"Did he ever mention getting married once? Or say anything about a son?" Rachel could feel Alex's glare.

"A son?" Doreen tilted her head. "Now that I think about it . . . he did say something."

"I told you—he was never married." Alex glared at Rachel. "He left home to play with a jazz band when he was in his twenties. He told me about it when I used to visit. He taught me how to play his trumpet and offered to pay for real lessons for me. My . . . my mother wouldn't let me do it. But he never got married. Or had a kid." He switched his glare to Doreen.

She lifted her shoulders in a graceful shrug. "More tea?" she asked Rachel.

"No, thank you." Annoyed by his outburst, Rachel reached for a cookie. The tea had an unpleasant bite beneath its minty taste. One of Doreen's herbs, no doubt. But the cookie was delicious. The chunks of angelica added a subtle and delicate flavor. "Did you try one of these, Sandy?"

"What?" Sandy, who had been staring morosely at the floor, jerked upright. "I'm sorry. I was . . . daydreaming."

"I just wondered if you wanted a cookie." Rachel pushed the plate at her, trying to catch her eye. But Sandy's eyes were glued to the teapot, and she didn't or wouldn't notice. "So do you mind if I stay over tonight?" Rachel asked cheerfully. "I don't feel like staying by myself."

Sandy raised her head at last, her brows creasing. "I guess so. Fine. But that doesn't sound like you. Is something wrong?"

Someone rattled the back doorknob, then knocked loudly on the wooden panels. Everyone turned toward the kitchen, and Doreen got swiftly to her feet. But not before Rachel glimpsed the bright glitter of anger in her gray eyes. She crossed the small kitchen in a few swift strides, unbolted the door, and opened it. Rachel casually picked up the teapot and carried it into the kitchen. Doreen held the door rigidly ajar, her body angled so as to hide her visitor from anyone in the kitchen.

"What are you thinking?" Her low whisper was barely audible. "Sandy's here."

A man said something, his voice low and unidentifiable.

Bill. The suspicion pierced her. Suddenly Sandy's red eyes and obvious distress made awful sense. Rachel set the teapot down on the counter and stepped quickly forward as Doreen began to close the door. "Hello," she said, breathless with anger, peering rudely over the older woman's shoulder. "I didn't expect . . ." And swallowed her words. Herbert Southern, Sandy's father, stood on the dark porch, his face pale. "I didn't expect to run into you twice in one night," she finished lamely. She owed Bill an apology for even *thinking* . . .

"You . . . you're okay?" He gave Doreen a brief look, then forced a smile as he faced Rachel. "I'm so glad. I came over here when Sandy wasn't home, hoping she had some news about you." His eyes narrowed. "You'd better call your mother. She's worried sick."

"What are you talking about?" Sandy stood in the doorway to the kitchen. "Hi, Dad. Were you looking for me? Why is Rachel's mom worried?"

"Rachel was forced off the road by a hit-and-run driver an hour ago." Herbert cast Doreen another brief glance. "She's damn lucky she wasn't killed."

"Forced off the road?" Sandy's hands flew to her mouth. "How awful! Rachel, why didn't you *say* anything?"

"Well, because I'm fine," Rachel said lightly. "I didn't want to upset everyone. How did you find out?" she asked Herbert anxiously.

"Jeff came roaring back to the farmhouse, looking for you. I'd run into Jack and Catherine while they were getting ice cream, and we were bringing back a grasshopper pie to share with you and your mother." He shook his head. "Jeff was pretty upset. I guess he heard it on his police radio, or the officer on duty called him or something."

Oh, great. Rachel closed her eyes briefly. The officer at the scene—Lyle—had probably been on his cell phone to Jeff before he'd rounded the first turn. "I'd better go call." Rachel glanced at Doreen. "May I use your phone?"

"Certainly." Doreen *tsk-tsked*. "Your poor mother. It's right here, dear." She pointed at the wall phone beside the spotless formica counter. "Would you like some tea, Mr. Southern?"

"I . . . uh . . . no, I'd better get on home." Herbert's glance veered between his daughter and Doreen. "I . . . I'm just glad that you're all right, Rachel. I was . . . I was worried. I'll just say good night."

"Good night, Dad."

"Good night, Mr. Southern," Doreen said coolly.

Rachel watched her friend's face as she dialed the orchard number. Sandy was staring after her father, her face white and pinched, hands clasped tightly in front of her. As Aunt Catherine answered the phone, and Rachel turned away, she caught Doreen staring at her.

The flare of rage in those intense gray eyes startled her. But Doreen turned away too quickly for Rachel to be sure she had really seen that anger.

"Hello?" Aunt Catherine answered, and Rachel had her hands full as she explained about the accident, that she was all right, and where she was, and why she hadn't called right away. She accepted her aunt's scolding humbly and managed to evade the questions about why she hadn't stayed at the orchard for the night as she had planned. Her mother was too relieved to be angry—which increased Rachel's guilt enormously. When she was finally able to satisfy everyone and get off the phone, it was late. She and Sandy and Alex took their leave, thanking Doreen for the tea and apologizing for monopolizing her evening. Doreen was gracious as she ushered them out, but Rachel had the feeling that anger still lurked behind the thin mask of her smile. As they once more crossed the cluttered living room, spotless without a single speck of dust or hint of disarray, Rachel's eye was caught by the bookcase.

Doreen saw her looking. "Is this what you noticed?" She swept up an oversized pack of cards that had been lying on a lace handkerchief, next to a framed picture of a young boy with a bright smile and dark, curly hair. "My nephew." She nodded at the photo. "And these are the Tarot." Her voice dropped, growing low and throaty as she slipped the cards from their box and fanned them out.

Like a carnival gypsy's tone, Rachel thought as she eyed the richly colored patterns on the backs of the cards. "I know what Tarot cards are. I've never seen anyone tell fortunes with them."

"They do not tell your fortune." Doreen sounded disdainful as she shuffled the cards. "Rather they give you a glimpse of your future. It is up to you to interpret that glimpse. Take one.'' She thrust the pack at Rachel.

For a moment, Rachel hesitated. Then she shrugged slightly and picked a card. Staring at the man hanging, bound and blindfolded, by one ankle, she swallowed. ''Let me guess.'' Her voice sounded shaky. ''Death?''

''Not necessarily.'' Doreen's eyes were hooded as she slipped the cards back into their box. ''It can mean change. It can mean danger, too. Perhaps . . .'' She raised her head suddenly, her eyes catching Rachel's, holding them with piercing intensity. ''Perhaps you should stop what you are doing,'' she said softly.

''What is that?'' Rachel whispered.

''I have no idea.'' Doreen smiled and turned away to put the cards back on their shelf. ''But it might be best to consider if you truly seek change. That is the cards' message.''

''I have a theory that Tarot and astrology and all that kind of stuff are primitive forms of psychoanalysis,'' Alex mused. ''Sort of a magical Rorschach test.'' He winked at Rachel. ''So now you get to delve into what kinds of changes might scare you. Moving to LA?''

''Who would want to live in Los Angeles?'' Sandy yawned. ''Right now, any card Doreen drew would suggest sleep to me.''

With a chorus of thank-you's, they exited, then heard the lock click behind them. The night had turned cool, and Rachel wrapped her arms around herself as they walked through the herb- and blossom-scented jungle of the front yard.

''I didn't know you were interested in Tarot,'' Alex said as they reached Sandy's front walk.

''I'm not.'' At the far end of the block, Rachel spied a car that looked like Herbert Southern's Jeep Cherokee parked behind a screen of overgrown lilacs.

''Then how come you were looking at the cards?''

''I wasn't.'' Rachel glanced up at him. ''I was looking at the bookshelf.''

''What about the bookshelf?'' Sandy asked sleepily.

"And what about the accident? Why would somebody run you off the road, Rachel?"

"There was a book missing from the bookshelf."

"So?" Alex shrugged impatiently. "She was reading it."

"Maybe." Rachel frowned. "It wasn't lying around. Nothing is out of place in that house, if you noticed."

"Maybe she loaned it to someone."

"Maybe." But in that meticulously ordered room there had been that single space, like a missing tooth, and a tiny line of tawny summer dust to mark its position— as if Doreen had hastily removed it, without even taking the time to dust the spot with her hand or rearrange the books to hide the space.

What had been shelved there? Something she didn't want them to see? Something she had pulled out quickly, when she realized they were coming up her walk?

Or had she removed the book because Sandy was at the door? Now they had reached Sandy's front door. Alex looked up at the star-filled sky as Sandy unlocked the door and pushed it open.

"I guess I should go on home." He looked at Rachel. "I could stay, if you two want some company."

"I think we'll be fine. We'll be asleep before we have time to worry about anything." She smiled up at him, "Doreen made you blush."

"She scares me." He grinned crookedly. "She's a sexy lady."

"She's *old*," Sandy said sleepily.

Rachel and Alex exchanged glances. "I should get old like that," Rachel murmured.

"You'll do better." He winked. "You have better bones. I guess I'll be going, then. Could I invite you to have dinner with me?" he asked wistfully.

"Some evening."

"Some evening, it is." The tall architect bowed formally, gave her another wink, then turned and headed for his car.

"I thought you and Jeff had a thing going." Sandy

glanced after him. "I mean . . . he's from *Los Angeles*."

"I don't have a 'thing' going with either Jeff or Alex."
Rachel took her friend firmly by the arm and steered her
into the house. "Jeff and I went steady in high school.
This is now. And Alex is nice. Period. Now, tell me
what's eating you," she went on quickly before Sandy
could pursue the subject. "And don't tell me 'nothing.' "
Closing and locking the door, she leaned theatrically
against it, arms spread to block all escape. She was trying
to elicit a smile, but Sandy merely slumped onto the
floral-print sofa, her shoulders drooping as she squeezed
her clasped hands between jeans-clad knees.

"I don't know . . ." Her lower lip trembled. "I don't
know if I should . . ."

"Sandy, what's *wrong*?" Rachel abandoned her pose
and sat down beside her friend. "Tell me, girl." She took
Sandy's ice-cold hands in hers. "It sure seems like you
need to tell somebody, and I'm right here. Oh, Sandy."
Her voice faltered. "It's not Bill, is it?"

"Oh, no!" Some animation returned to Sandy's face,
and she pulled her hands from Rachel's. "How can
you even *think* that?" Reproach thrilled in her tone. "I
mean . . . oh . . . Rachel." Tears welled up in her eyes
and spilled over. "I'm afraid even to tell Bill. He's
so . . . *upright* about everything. And I might be wrong.
What if he heard? What if he found out that I'd been
going around accusing him . . . saying . . ."

"Whoa, girl. Just slow down a minute." Rachel got
up and hurried into the bathroom. She returned a moment
later with a damp washcloth and a handful of tissues and
handed them to Sandy. "Accusing whom? Of what? Just
start at the beginning, okay?"

"You have to promise." Sandy blotted at her eyes,
succeeding only in smearing her mascara into a raccoon-
like mask. "You have to promise not to tell anyone. *Anyone,* okay?"

"Okay, I promise. Here, let me." Rachel retrieved the
washcloth and wiped away the worst of the smears.

"It's Dad." Sandy gulped. "Something's terribly wrong."

"He's sick?" Rachel felt a chill of apprehension. He had certainly looked bad enough tonight.

"No, not that." Sandy shook her head, her blond hair tumbling around her face. "Although I keep worrying that he's going to have a heart attack. That's how Grandpa died, and Dad looks so bad. I know he's not sleeping, and I don't think he's eating well. It's just tearing him up."

"What is?" Rachel struggled to keep the impatience out of her voice.

"Henry Bassinger's murder." Sandy looked around fearfully, as if the walls might have sprouted ears. "He . . . he's involved in it somehow. But he didn't kill Mr. Bassinger. You can't think that!" She stared at Rachel, a hint of horror in her wide eyes. "Dad wouldn't hurt a fly. But what if he was *there*? What if they had an argument or something and . . . I mean, everyone knows that Henry had been acting strange lately. Maybe he just fell off that old walkway. But if it comes out—that Dad was there—maybe a jury would think . . ." Words failed her. She closed her eyes, dissolving once more into tears.

"Whatever makes you think that your dad might have been there?" Rachel soothed, wiping her eyes. "The police must have asked him about that by now. And why do you think he was involved with Henry at all? Henry wouldn't sell that property." But even as Rachel spoke, she was remembering her uncle's questions about that big deal of Herbert's, and his reaction. And Henry had flaunted a new source of financing to Alex during their fight.

"I . . . heard him on the phone one afternoon. When I dropped by the office. He was talking to Henry. I heard him call him by name. They were arguing, and I heard Dad say . . . something like 'I own a share of it. You can't do this.' Or something like that. Dad hung up as soon as he realized I'd come in, and I didn't say anything." She pressed the dissolving tissue to her face, her shoulders shaking. "He dropped by the bank the other morning," she spoke through her fingers. "He . . . he told me . . . he was home that afternoon. When Henry was killed. He said he was working on the computer. I guess that's what he told Jeff—the police." Sandy raised an anguished, tear-streaked face. "He wasn't," she whispered. "I stopped by to drop off a pair of pants I'd mended. Because his secretary said he'd gone home for lunch. But he wasn't there. And . . . and when I was processing checks from the day before, I found one. From Dad's account. Made out to Henry Bassinger. Rachel, it was for ten thousand dollars."

So that was where the money had come from in his account? "What did you do with that check?" Rachel touched Sandy's shoulder.

"I . . . I tore it up." Sandy clenched the sodden remnants of tissue in her fist. "Only they're going to find out sooner or later, because the money was already in Henry's account, and he'd written checks on it. So I couldn't change the numbers. But maybe they won't find it. Or maybe they'll think it was some kind of mistake."

"Oh, Sandy." Rachel got up and went to get another tissue, glad to escape briefly. *You have to promise not to tell* . . . Herbert and Henry had perhaps had some kind of a deal that didn't include Alex. What if Henry had changed his mind—decided to back out altogether?

In his younger days, Herbert Southern had had an explosive temper. He had mellowed over the years, but that temper might still lie dormant, like a volcano, ready to explode under the proper stimulus. Rachel returned with a fresh tissue. "I'm going to make us some cocoa, and then we both need to go to bed. It's after one A.M. Did you tell Doreen?" she asked as Sandy blew her nose.

"No." She shook her head. "But Doreen started asking me if something was bothering me—like you did—and I lost it." She tried to smile. "Doreen is so nice. She said she noticed that Dad looked poorly when he was over here for the party, and she wanted to give me some herb tea for him. I left it over there, I guess."

"Yes, Doreen is nice," Rachel said. She went on into the kitchen and put a pan of milk to heat on the stove. Getting the can of cocoa down from the shelf and scooping sugar out of the can, she wondered if Herbert Southern was sleeping with Doreen Baldwin. Sandy's mother had died years ago. It seemed awfully likely.

Sandy had stolen a check from the bank and had changed the bank's records to hide the transaction. And *she* had promised not to tell anyone. Rachel stirred the cocoa as it heated, staring at the patterns of tawny foam on the surface of the milk, not really seeing it. Herbert Southern hadn't been home when Henry Bassinger had died.

She had promised not to tell.

CHAPTER

10

A new teal blue Mazda Miata partially blocked the entrance to the turnaround in front of Dr. Meier's house the next morning. Rachel yawned, wishing she had stopped at The Bread Box for a cup of Joylinn's coffee. Apparently Sandy only drank decaf. Earlene had offered her a grease-stained mug of something that she called coffee when Rachel had retrieved her truck that morning, but Rachel had declined politely. She had made the mistake of drinking the sisters' coffee once before. She suspected they used the stuff to clean engine parts.

Now she eyed the offending car with sleepy irritation. "I'll go get this thing moved, Julio." She got out and yawned. "I'm too tired to lug the tools an extra fifty feet. Why don't you finish flagging the last of the sprinklers in the back garden."

As Julio hurried off—grinning—with his handful of flags, Rachel climbed the wide front steps. She stifled another yawn. It wasn't quite seven A.M.—but Dr. Meier got up early to go jogging. Her mother had always been an early riser, too. Rachel frowned and walked around to the French doors that opened into the kitchen. If Dr.

Meier was up, she reasoned, he'd most likely be making coffee.

A dark-haired woman in an apricot silk bathrobe stood with her back to the windows, scooping coffee beans into an electric grinder. She whirled around as Rachel tapped on the glass, clutching the robe at her throat. "My God, you frightened me." She shoved the French doors open so hard that Rachel had to skip back out of the way. "You must be the gardener. Next time ring the damn bell."

"Sorry," Rachel said. The woman's tousled hair and bleary eyes suggested that morning wasn't her best time of day.. "There's a green car blocking the driveway. We need to unload equipment."

"We have to talk." The woman pushed her hand through her thick hair. "Alonzo nearly quit yesterday. He said you were utterly uncooperative. You need to keep in mind that we're putting on *the* wedding of Portland's social scene, and I will not—will *not*—tolerate your getting in Alonzo's way. It was incredible luck that he was available at all. I've assured him that you'll cooperate fully with him in the future." The threat hung in the air like a thundercloud.

Rachel felt herself bristling like her aunt's terrier, and forced a smile onto her face. "I'm sorry. I can't do what he asked." So this was Dr. Meier's daughter? She had a tawny, sulky sort of beauty, but her manner left a lot to be desired. "Mr. Zwycaffer wanted me to make design changes—but that kind of request would have to be approved by Dr. Meier."

"*I'm* approving it." His daughter began to grind coffee beans, making conversation nearly impossible.

"I'm sorry." Rachel raised her voice. "I can't do that. My contract won't let me."

"That's ridiculous." The woman spun around, the grinder in her hands. "My father isn't home, and Alonzo will be here in an hour. If you don't agree to do what he wants, he'll quit. And if he does . . ." She stabbed a polished nail at Rachel. "You're fired." She turned back to making coffee.

End of discussion. Rachel nodded politely and went out to see if Eduardo and Jorges had arrived.

They had. The three men stood at the edge of the deck, eyes riveted on the huge kitchen windows, faces sharing a look of appreciation. Dr. Meier's daughter—her silk robe barely covering her thighs—was exquisitely visible. As Rachel closed the French doors with just a hint of a slam, all three swiveled to face her. Eduardo and Jorges ducked their heads and greeted her in Spanish.

She led them across the slope, explaining the job, which Julio translated for his friends. He enjoyed his role as translator. Eduardo and Jorges were both older than he. Julio didn't quite strut as he pointed out the flags they had put in to mark the layout of the pipes. The two men nodded, familiar with this task since they worked in the orchards. Without wasting any time, they collected their narrow-bladed trenching spades and got to work, with a minimum of talk and a maximum of effort. She got an honest day's work from them, she thought with satisfaction. And she didn't have to look over their shoulders every minute, either.

She and Julio began to dig the water feature. Once dug, she'd line it with heavy plastic, then add the rocks and the pump. The soil where they were digging was rocky, but they didn't encounter any solid basalt, for which she said a small prayer of thanks. If they had, Alonzo would have had his way, and the water feature would have had to move. You can't trench for water lines through solid stone.

As if her thoughts had conjured Alonzo, the Zwycaffers rolled into the driveway. Rachel straightened with a sigh, wishing vainly that Dr. Meier would pull in behind them. If he was out running, he must be training for a marathon.

It suddenly occurred to her that he might be out having breakfast with her mother. "Take a break," she called, laying aside her shovel. "I'll be right back." Squaring her shoulders, she marched across the yard, reaching the deck just as Elaine and the Zwycaffers emerged from the kitchen.

"I will bring the roses out from Portland. Since you insist on roses." Alonzo sounded irritable. "If we trim them with glitter and white organdy and go for the camp look, they will work, I suppose. Ferns are much more elegant."

"What about some tuberose?" Elaine looked happy and excited, her eyes gleaming as she waved a coffee mug. "I was lying in bed last night just visualizing, you know? And I thought—tuberose. Tall white spikes of elegant, creamy blossom. Perfect!"

"No." Alonzo's face began to take on a stubborn look. "Roses are bad enough. This changes the dynamic—shifts the balance away from the effect I am trying to achieve."

"Don't get yourself excited, dear." Jayne's gentle reminder carried the merest thread of warning, but Alonzo blinked at her, as if she'd poked him with a pin.

"Well . . . perhaps I shall consider it." He nodded, his face as puckered as if he was sucking on an unripe lemon. "But I will have to think. I must *feel* it."

"I'm sure it will work." Elaine clasped her hands and sighed. "I just know it will be lovely." She caught sight of Rachel, and her expression chilled. "Yes?"

"No!" Alonzo looked past her, his smile fracturing like glass. "Look at that . . . pit! I asked for a terrace there—for the buffet. I will *not* work with a *swamp* in the middle of my party. No!" He stomped his foot.

"Now, Alonzo," his wife began, "we were going to—"

"No." He pointed an accusing finger at Elaine. "Roses, tuberoses—they are bad enough. You told me the landscape would be as we discussed."

"I . . . did. It will!" She gave Rachel a panicked, furious glare. "She . . ."

The familiar roar of the MG's engine sounded from the drive. With a surge of relief, Rachel watched the small blue car dart up the curving driveway and pull up by the front deck in a scatter of gravel.

Her mother got out of the passenger seat. She saw Rachel on the deck and waved gaily. Her face was flushed and happy, and her eyes sparkled as she took Dr. Meier's hand and ran up the steps with him. Both of them were dressed in jogging shorts and T-shirts.

"Elaine, dear, you're finally up." Dr. Meier kissed his daughter's cheek. "And I see you've met Rachel."

"This . . . *person* is going to cost me my wedding." Elaine crossed her arms, her eyes flashing. "She demands your rubber stamp on every little thing I ask her to do."

"Well, I don't generally use a rubber stamp. Perhaps I'd better hear the story." In spite of his mild tone, Dr. Meier looked annoyed. Rachel's mother hung tactfully in the background, apparently fascinated by a planter full of portulaca. Elaine shot Rachel a sizzling look, then turned back to her father.

"Alonzo merely asked for a patio for the buffet tables and the wine fountain. Is that so much?"

"So where does he want this patio to go?" Dr. Meier kept the smile on his face.

"There!" She flung out her hand in a dramatic gesture. "Where they're digging that . . . that *pit*."

Dr. Meier looked over the tops of his glasses. "That's the water feature, I believe. For my blue herons."

"What? Dad, you're kidding." Elaine rolled her eyes. "I mean . . . really. Put your pond in later. That's the only plane on this . . . this *mountainside* where we can put the buffet."

"And the wine fountain." Dr. Meier cleared his throat. "Does Alonzo usually demand that his clients landscape for him?"

"Of course not, Daddy. *Really*." Elaine let out an exasperated breath. "But since you're landscaping anyway . . . I mean, it's just a little thing. You can always put in the pond or whatever after the wedding. I want it so much."

Dr. Meier glanced sideways at Deborah, who looked

interested and mildly amused. He shook his head and made a face. "I'm sorry, my dear," he said to his daughter. "You'll just have to instruct your Alonzo to put his buffet and wine fountain somewhere else."

"There *isn't* anywhere else. You can't do this to me." Elaine's voice rose into something that was almost a wail. "He'll quit, and it was such a *coup* getting him. Oh, this will mess up everything."

"This is my home," Dr. Meier said firmly. "I'm willing to let you use it, my dear. I'm willing to pay for most of your fine wedding, but this is my home. I've dreamed about it for years."

"That's so unfair. You can put in your stupid pond later." Elaine stomped one slender foot. "Father, you're being so selfish!"

That earned her a look from Dr. Meier that apparently went right past her. Rachel coughed and turned away to cover an embarrassing urge to giggle. Even Jayne, who was close enough to overhear, raised a smooth British eyebrow. Only Alonzo, arms crossed in a stony pout, seemed oblivious. Her mother studied the portulaca blooming in the deck planters. Dr. Meier cleared his throat.

"Now that that's settled, I'd like you to meet Deborah O'Connor. Deborah, my charming daughter Elaine," he said with only the merest hint of irony in his voice. "Elaine, this is Deborah O'Connor. She is a kindred soul—something I never expected to find again in this lifetime." His voice grew tender, and he put his arm around Rachel's mother as their eyes met. "I've asked her to marry me."

"You . . . you've *what*?" Words seemed to fail Elaine briefly. Rachel looked at her mother and received a lopsided smile that glowed with warmth in spite of her apologetic expression.

"This is . . . this is crazy." Elaine found her voice at last, twin spots of color glowing on her cheeks. "I mean, you haven't . . . I've never even *met* you." She looked at Deborah for the first time, her expression a mixture of alarm and surprise, as if Rachel's mother had just that moment materialized from thin air. "I mean . . . I have a wedding to do, and . . . Daddy, this is a major life decision. Not something to just . . . to just leap into like this."

"You seem to have coped just fine with your daughter's leap," Dr. Meier said dryly. "I'm too old to contemplate the wisdom of my choices." He tucked Deborah's arm firmly into his. "I love this woman, and that's all that needs to be said."

"Elaine, I'm so glad to meet you." Smiling, Deborah extended a hand. "And I apologize for this bit of theatrics." She gave Dr. Meier an exasperated look. "You love doing this kind of thing, don't you?"

"Proposing to beautiful women in public?" Dr. Meier murmured with a grin. "Damn right."

"I . . . I'm glad to meet you." Elaine touched Deborah's hand and dropped it as if it had burned her. Her eyes widened as she registered Deborah's youthful face and athletic figure, and the color drained slowly from her face. "Daddy, we *have* to talk." She gave Deborah a brief perfunctory smile. "Right away." Turning on her heel, she stalked back into the house.

"Go talk to her," her mother murmured to Dr. Meier. "Joshua, that was mean."

"Introducing you to her? Because you're prettier?" Dr. Meier smiled, but a hint of sadness lurked at the corners of his eyes. "I'm sorry about her behavior, Deborah. I'm afraid I let it matter too much that she was my wife's child, after she died. It's my fault." He turned to Rachel. "Deborah told me that this is hard for you. You and your father were very close. What your mother and I have . . . it'll never take the place of what Ruth, my wife, and I shared—or what Deborah and your father shared. This is something different, and if anything, it will keep the memory of those first loves of ours bright and new forever. I hope you can understand this."

Rachel swallowed, an unexpected lump in her throat. "I'm trying. I think I really can." She looked away from Dr. Meier's smiling face to her mother's eyes. There were tears there. Tears of joy? "It's going to take me a little while to get used to it, that's all." She swallowed again, willing the lump to go away.

"Thank you, sweetheart." Her mother took her hands and kissed her lightly on the cheek. "For understanding."

"We're going to fly to Vegas. For one of those disreputable Vegas weddings." Dr. Meier cast a grinning glance after his vanished daughter. "Too bad my granddaughter didn't have the same idea." He chuckled. "Then we're off to San Francisco for a few nights for our honeymoon. Would you like to come along?" He tilted his head, one eyebrow raised. "Or would you settle for pictures?"

"What about all this?" Rachel gestured at the house.

"Oh, we'd just make Elaine nervous if we hung around. And she'd drive me crazy. This way, she can come to terms with the marriage in her own time. She doesn't need me in her way while she's getting ready for this social orgy anyway." He cast a shrewd glance at the graded slope. "Our contract stands as written," he said. "I'll make that clear to my daughter."

"Thank you," Rachel said, feeling more than a little breathless. She wasn't sure she was taking this any better than Elaine, if the truth be told.

"One thing." Deborah stepped forward, her expression serious. "I want you to promise me you'll leave the investigation of Henry's death to Jeff and the Blossom Police. You might have been killed last night."

"The driver just meant to scare me," Rachel said with more confidence than she felt. "Really."

"Maybe. Jeff was furious, by the way."

Rachel crossed her arms, telling herself he was being unreasonable. That she didn't feel guilty. "I'm leaving the whole thing alone," she said. "Honest."

"I hope so." Her mother narrowed her eyes, as she had when Rachel had been little and protesting that she was too sick to go to school. "I'm really worried about you, Rachel." She gripped her daughter's hand. "I'll make you a deal. Actually it was Joshua's idea." She and Dr. Meier exchanged a brief smile. "According to a Portland club owner friend of his, Henry lived in San Francisco while he was playing with bands. If he got married—it might have been there."

"Or on the road," Dr. Meier cautioned. "They toured most of the time."

"If you promise— I mean *promise*—to keep out of trouble and stick to landscaping while we're gone, we'll check the records."

"It'll be fun playing detective." Dr. Meier squeezed Deborah's hand and smiled down at her. "All right, love. I'll go talk to my daughter." He kissed her, made a show of squaring his shoulders, and vanished into the house.

"I did tell Joshua that my answer depended on you." Her mother sat down on the wooden bench beside Rachel. "He's acting as if everything is settled, but it isn't yet." She laughed. "He didn't get to be Chief of Medicine without learning to dominate where he can." She gave Rachel a rueful smile and squeezed her hand.

"That's all right." Rachel looked down at her mother and smiled. "You should have seen Elaine's face when she realized you could be her sister."

"That's ridiculous! I'm more than a decade older than she!"

"Nobody's going to guess that from looking at you." Rachel grinned. "Ha! I made you blush."

Deborah sighed. "Poor girl."

"Her?" Rachel rolled her eyes. "Miss Spoiled Rotten? Save your sympathy, Mom."

"You don't understand, dear," her mother said gently. "Sometimes I feel a bit guilty, you know—that I've robbed you of your Jewish identity living out here."

"That's silly. I grew up knowing I was Jewish. Well, half Jewish."

"Oh, we celebrated Chanukah and Passover and the High Holy Days. But we had Christmas with your cousins, and you hunted Easter eggs with them." She gave

Rachel a rueful smile. "You've never lived in any community other than Blossom."

"So?"

"So Elaine isn't having the wedding out here because she wants to, dear. She's married to a prominent lawyer, who is very active in the Portland Jewish community. And her daughter is pregnant by and marrying, no less, a rather socially unacceptable boy, I gather, who is Catholic. If she did the wedding in the city, she'd be listening for all the whispers and counting heads to see who didn't come."

"Oh." Rachel nodded. "Out here, she can blame the distance."

"And tell herself everything is fine."

"Well, I still don't feel a whole lot of sympathy for her."

Her mother smiled and kissed her forehead. "You're not required to, sweetheart."

Out front a car engine roared. A moment later, the teal Miata tore down the long driveway, raising clouds of dust. "Uh-oh." Deborah got quickly to her feet and hurried into the house. After a minute or two, Rachel followed her. A jazz piece was playing softly on the stereo, and she recognized it with a jolt. Pausing, she listened to the intricate notes of a trumpet solo. "Dr. Meier? Dr. Meier!" She hurried through the empty kitchen and burst into the living room beyond. Her mother and Dr. Meier started guiltily apart from a rather close embrace on the sofa.

"Goodness, child, didn't anyone ever teach you any manners?" Her mother fanned herself, flushed and laughing, her hair in tousled wisps about her face. "Next time knock first before you crash in."

"I thought only teenagers necked on the sofa," Rachel said dryly.

"Who said we're not teenagers?" Dr. Meier's eyes twinkled. "Don't let appearances fool you."

"Who is that again?" Rachel pointed to the impressive CD and tape player against the wall. "The trumpet player, I mean. You told me once, but I've forgotten."

"Clyde Montaine?" Dr. Meier walked over and picked up the CD case from the top of the stereo. "He really only showed up at the major clubs a couple of years ago. This is his first CD." He handed her the case.

Rachel looked at the jacket shot of the lanky grinning man in a blazer worn over a Hawaiian shirt and blue jeans. Dark-haired, with high cheekbones, he looked vaguely familiar. Posed in front of an urban tenement, he cradled the polished brass of his trumpet lovingly. His gray eyes danced with secret mischief. "Nice-looking guy." She handed the CD back to Dr. Meier. "Clyde Montaine . . ." The name didn't mean anything, and she couldn't remember where she'd seen him. "Henry played this CD over and over again."

"Maybe he was a fan." Her mother spoke up. "I played *Abbey Road* until the grooves wore out, back when I was in college."

"*Abbey Road?*" Rachel looked at her blankly.

"The Beatles, dear." Her mother rolled her eyes. "What's this generation coming to? Anyway, my point is that fans do that kind of thing."

"Maybe," Rachel said slowly. "But Henry wasn't any teenager. And I don't mean he played it once or twice a day. He'd played this CD over and over again, until I think I've got every note memorized."

"So what do you think?" Dr. Meier perched on the arm of the sofa. "It meant something to him? Montaine's too young to have been playing the clubs when Henry did."

"I'd sure like to ask him if he knows Henry," Rachel said thoughtfully.

"You promised." Her mother leaped to her feet. "Rachel Anne O'Connor, you *promised* you'd quit sticking your nose into Henry's death. And you expect me to just go off and leave you here to get yourself shot or run off a cliff? Ha!" Her mother crossed her arms and glared at Rachel.

"Now calm down, Deborah," Dr. Meier soothed.

"Rachel does happen to be a grown woman in her twenties."

"You just got done saying that chronology doesn't count." Deborah glowered at the two of them alternately. "Twenty-five going on thirteen is more like it."

"Even if Clyde Montaine was playing in a local club—which I doubt—what kind of danger is there in talking in public to some musician who might or might not know Henry?" Dr. Meier asked. "Personally I think that accident was just that—an accident."

"Me, too," Rachel said quickly. "I mean, if someone was trying to hurt me, he could have run me into some pretty big trees anywhere on the way home. In fact, that's about the only place you could run off the road and not go head-on into an apple tree."

"Humph." Her mother eyed her suspiciously. "Jeff certainly seemed to take it seriously."

"Well . . . you know what happened just before. Maybe he thought I ran off the road because I was angry." She felt a twinge of guilt, but that might be true. She never had called him to let him know that she was all right. She'd been waiting for him to call, she admitted to herself. They were playing a silly game, outwaiting each other. She resolved to call him first thing after work.

"I know you, child of mine." Her mother looked doubtful, but she was smiling. "Remember—I don't look up any marriage records unless you behave yourself."

"Mom, how can I do anything *but* behave myself?" Rachel laughed and kissed her cheek. "I have to have this yard landscaped and ready for a wedding in a few weeks, remember?"

"You heard her." A smile lurked at the corners of Dr. Meier's mouth. "That's a promise—so the trip is on, lady. Don't you dare try to back out on me now, or you'll find out just how stubborn I really am."

"Don't count on winning in that category," Rachel drawled. She picked up the CD. "May I borrow this?" she asked Dr. Meier. "The case, at least?"

"Take the CD, too." He retrieved it carefully from the

player and inserted it into its case. "He's worth listening to."

"Thanks." Rachel headed for the kitchen door. "You two behave," she said severely.

They didn't answer. She decided not to look back as she exited. It was still going to take some getting used to, she thought grimly. Her mother and Dr. Meier. Shaking her head, she glanced at the CD in her hand, then stowed it carefully in the glove box of her truck. Harvey was just rolling up the driveway in his backhoe, his grinning son behind him in the dump truck. Back to digging, she told herself. The excitement was over.

For the moment, at least.

CHAPTER

11

Rachel and Julio and the crew had the Meier property to themselves for the rest of the morning. Harvey placed the boulders that defined the planting areas and departed to another job. Jorges and Eduardo dug steadily and neatly, extending the grid of trenches for water and electricity across the staked outlines of beds and paths. The small pond was turning out to be a relatively easy dig. No rock outcrops appeared, to Rachel's relief.

"Let's break," she told Julio, pushing damp hair from her face. They had made more progress than she had expected, considering the rocky nature of the terrain. "I'm going to go into town to pick up the valves and sprinkler heads." She hosed off her spade beneath a tap mounted on the deck. "You three can keep working on the trenches after lunch."

"Sí, señorita." Julio got his lunch cooler from the truck bed, then glanced apprehensively at the driveway. "If *la señora* returns—what then?"

"It's okay, Julio." She patted his shoulder. He had been withdrawn and quiet all morning. "You don't speak English," she said firmly. *"Comprendes?"*

"No, señorita. No hablo inglés. No comprendo." He

lifted his hands palms up, his expression slack and stupid. "She will believe, *señorita*," he said. For a moment anger glittered in his eyes, then he ducked his head and carried his cooler over to the shade, where Eduardo and Jorges were unpacking their own lunches.

She suspected that the police—Jeff or someone else—had been out to question Julio and his sister again. He wouldn't admit it, but he was obviously afraid. She felt a brief surge of anger as she climbed into her truck. The breeze from the window dried her sweaty T-shirt as she drove down the hill and into Blossom. The Blossom Feed and Seed stood at the far end of town—three brick silos and the original buildings, constructed of pegged, adz-hewn beams and frow-split cedar shakes. *Feed and Fertilizer and Orchard Supplies* had been painted on the plank walls decades ago. The faded black and silver letters could still be read from the highway.

Rachel backed her truck up to the loading dock beside a muddy black Dodge panel truck. Nobody occupied the cracked vinyl of the front seat. Rachel eyed it as she got out of her pickup, remembering the dark shape hurtling past her last night. Slowly she walked around to the far side of the van. There, on the right front fender, was a tiny streak of white paint. Thoughtfully she touched the shallow dent in the metal.

"Yo, Rachel." A stocky young man in a T-shirt, jeans, and red logger's suspenders waved cheerfully from the loading dock, where he was maneuvering a hand truck full of grain sacks. "What do you need today? Give me a minute to get this feed loaded, and I'll be right with you."

She had gone to school with Brian Ferrel. His father, Andy, owned Blossom Feed and Seed, and was concluding his third term as Blossom's mayor. "I'm here to see if I can pick up my order," Rachel told him. "I know I said I'd pick it up tomorrow, but I've got a good crew."

"I had it ready last night." Brian grinned at her as he opened the back of the Dodge van and began to toss in the eighty-pound sacks. He made it look as if they weighed about five pounds, and muscles bulged on his shoulders.

"Who owns this?" She nodded at the van. "Do you know?"

"The Youth Farm. I guess they got a flock of sheep now." Brian frowned. "Sis lives over that way, and it makes her real nervous—all those druggie and gang kids next door. I sure don't like it much—nothin' more than a sheep fence between them and her."

"They've never caused any trouble, have they?" Rachel asked thoughtfully. The Youth Farm was an experimental project—designed to help teenagers who had been arrested for nonviolent crimes by putting them onto a working farm. It got positive press in Portland, but a lot of the local residents were less than enthusiastic about its presence.

"Just 'cause nothin's happened doesn't mean it won't," Brian said darkly. He slammed the van's door. "Lester Warren says they stole a bunch of stuff from his barn—his place backs right up on the property."

"Doesn't Lester blame every lamb he loses during lambing on the coyotes?" Rachel asked innocently. "He sure has a lot of coyotes up there."

"Well . . . yeah. Lester likes to lay blame." Brian grinned at her. "No, I guess they've behaved themselves out there. So far. I'll get your stuff loaded."

"Thanks, Brian." Rachel waved and climbed the old timber steps up to the loading dock, where she picked her way through the maze of stacked salt blocks, spray tanks, feed sacks, and racked tools that crowded the narrow walkway. Inside, the store was even more cluttered. She squeezed down an aisle crammed with boxes of electric fencing supplies, ear tags, grafting equipment, and rat poison. Sacks of pasture seed mixes and bins of loose seed stood against the wall at the end of the aisle. It was truly a rural feed store—supply central for the area agriculture.

Andy Ferrel stood behind the wooden counter, scowling at a young man who was accompanied by a lounging youth dressed in jeans, Doc Marten boots, and a scuffed leather jacket. The sulky teenager looked up as Rachel approached. He had acne and a round, juvenile face that looked very young beneath his close buzz cut. As he sighted Rachel he stiffened, his pale eyes widening.

"Excuse me," Rachel said.

He bolted for the door, knocking a stack of steel pet bowls from a shelf as he dashed past her. She staggered back amid the clattering avalanche as he dashed through the door and out onto the loading dock.

"Hey." The man, clad in jeans and a *Save the Whales* T-shirt, stared after the vanished teen, his expression incredulous. "Cass? Hey, Cass!" he yelled. "Get back in here." Then he shook his head, his young face perplexed. "What got into him?"

"Looks like you got a prison break," Andy drawled.

"Not Cass." Still shaking his head, the young man handed the check he'd been writing to Andy. "He's only got two weeks to go and he's out. I'll pick up those pans. I'm sorry."

"Leave 'em be." Andy shoved the check into the register. "Better go get your kid before he hurts someone."

"He won't." The young man's lips tightened. "Cass isn't a violent kid."

"What's he doin' in jail, then, huh?"

"He got arrested for drugs. He's off them." The man pocketed his receipt and started to leave.

"Excuse me." Rachel intercepted him at the door. "I'm Rachel O'Connor." She held out a hand. "I've got a local landscape business."

For an instant he regarded her warily. "Glad to meet you. I'm Willis Bard. A counselor at the Youth Farm." He returned her handshake. "I apologize for Cass. Are you okay?"

"I'm fine," she said. "I think I scared him."

"You? How come?" He edged toward the door. "I hope he's waiting at the van," he muttered.

"I'd like to talk to you." She walked with him.

"Sure. Actually I was going to call you." He sounded

mildly embarrassed. "I saw your truck parked outside the hardware store the other day and wrote down the number."

"Really?" She smiled. "You need some work done?"

"Well, no, not quite. I wanted to talk to you about our apprentice program." He craned his neck to peer at the van parked at the far end of the loading dock. "We're always trying to get local businesses to hire our kids— teach them a marketable skill. We offer some subsidy money. The kids we place are motivated and reliable." He had the grace to look sheepish. "Not that you've gotten much of an example of that this morning. Damn. He's not in the van." He looked up and down the street, his expression openly worried now.

"I think I may know why he ran," Rachel said slowly.

"I thought you were kidding." He was giving her his full attention now. "Do you know him?"

"I'm not sure. Maybe." She nodded at the van. "Was somebody using it last night? After eight-thirty?"

"I can check." His expression chilled. "Is there a problem?"

"I'm afraid maybe there is. I'll show you." She led him down to the parking strip and pointed out the faint scrape of white paint on the panel truck's fender. "A dark van or panel truck forced me off the road last night. I couldn't get a license number—the driver didn't have any lights on. But the van brushed my truck." She showed him her truck's dented fender and again pointed to the streak of white paint on the van.

"I'll check it out." Willis looked grim. "Nobody can use any vehicle without signing out and signing in again. And the kids can't use it without being accompanied by a member of the staff." He let his breath out in a long sigh. "You think Cass was in the van, huh? And that's why he ran?"

"It could be." Rachel met his unhappy gaze, feeling sorry for the man. "No damage was done. I'm not going to press charges or anything. I just want to know."

"I'll take a look at the log. Do you have a card? In

case I can't find the note I made of your number?''

She handed him one. He shook his head again, shoulders slumping. "Cass is one of our success stories. He came out of a bad home, got into drugs and the gangs, and got arrested a couple of times. But here—it was like he never really believed there was any way for him to have a real job and a real life. He *wanted* to make it. Damn," he said softly. "If I don't find him, I'll have to go report him missing." He looked up and down the street. "I think I'll walk around town for a while and see if I spot him. If he takes off, he's back to square one. Damn," he said again with feeling.

"I hope you find him. I'd like to talk to him," Rachel said.

"I'll find him," Willis said grimly. "When I do, I'll call you."

"And I'll call you about your apprentice program. I'd be willing to hire one of your kids, part-time, when I have the work."

"Thanks." He gave her a startled look. "We could sure use the help. Cass has been working with an LA architect off and on for the last year, learning drafting. This guy works for one of the big LA firms. He says Cass is talented. Stupid kid." He clenched his fists. "He can't throw this chance away."

"An architect?" Rachel raised her eyebrows. "Do you remember his name?"

"Sure. Alex Cresswell. Really nice guy. He's teaching a couple of kids—mostly over the Internet, but he's in town once in a while. Listen, I've got to go. I'll call you." He lifted a hand to her, then strode off down the street, turning his head as he scanned side streets and driveways for his runaway.

Rachel looked after him, frowning. She had almost been willing to believe that last night's accident had been just that—a kid who managed to sneak out of the Farm in one of their vehicles and had hit her accidentally, maybe while horsing around.

But he worked for Alex Cresswell, who had offered his services to the school.

Thoughtfully she checked over the supplies that Brian had loaded into her truck. When she went inside to pay Andy, he took her check with a grunt. "It was a bad day for Blossom when they opened that prison farm," he grumbled as he handed her her receipt. "One of those kids is gonna kill somebody one day."

Rachel left the feed store, frowning, and wondering if she still had Alex's phone number. As she was about to climb into her truck, a Blossom police car zoomed off the road in a tight turn and screeched to a halt beside her. Jeff leaped out, his face stormy.

"Am I under arrest?" Rachel asked lightly.

"If I could figure out a reason." He didn't smile. "I hope you finally called your mother. She was worried sick."

"I didn't know you'd heard anything until Herbert showed up at Sandy's house." She sighed. "I didn't want to worry Mom. That's why I didn't call right away. How did you hear?"

"Lyle called me." Jeff's lips were tight. "It's a small town, in case you've forgotten."

"No, I have not forgotten." Rachel raised an eyebrow, swallowing a sudden surge of irritation. "Nice to know that the Blossom Police Force is keeping such a close eye on my private life. Listen, I've got to get back to work." She started to get into the truck but stopped as Jeff touched her arm.

"Wait, okay?" He took a deep breath. "Lyle was being a jerk," he said through clenched teeth. "You know, I stopped to apologize." He looked away. "I don't think I'm doing much of a job."

"You never did apologize very well." Rachel leaned against the truck door. "You're about as bad at it as I am."

"That bad?"

Suddenly she began to giggle, and then they were both grinning at each other, equally at a loss for words. "I'm

sorry,'' they said in unison, which made them grin some
more.

"I was going to ask you . . . but you're probably too
busy . . .'' Jeff sounded as shy as she felt. "I've got two
days off. Want to go into Portland for dinner?''

"Are you giving up on Henry's case?'' Rachel asked
in dismay.

"I'm not handling it anymore.'' He looked away, a
muscle jumping in his jaw.

"Not handling it?'' Rachel blinked. "Why not? Who
is?''

"Lyle.'' He wouldn't meet her eyes. "The chief heard
some rumors around town and thought . . . I was talking
about the case too much.''

"My fault,'' Rachel whispered.

"I think Lyle sort of put a bug in his ear about you
and Cresswell. And you and me.''

"There *isn't* anything . . . Oh, Jeff.'' Rachel touched
his arm, her chest constricting. "I'm so sorry.''

"Not your fault.'' Jeff let his breath out in a long sigh.
"Lyle's been bent out of shape since I signed on here.
So he got what he wanted. He's in charge. And we found
Henry's will, by the way. He leaves everything to his
son.''

"His son!'' Rachel nodded. "Mom was right. So who
is this mystery kid?''

"He'd be an adult now.'' Jeff sounded irritable. "And
we don't have a clue. It's like the old man wanted to
make us all guess. But it sure isn't Alex.''

"Which makes it less likely that Alex murdered him,
Jeff.'' Rachel lifted her hands, palms up.

"We also found his prints all over the house after that
break-in.''

"Well, he was staying there.''

"Some of the places we found them were pretty unusual for a casual visitor. Like locked desk drawers. It
was him, all right.'' He nodded sharply. "Maybe he figured that he could find the will and destroy it. He must
have just about put his hand on it.''

"Maybe he just wanted to read it. A lot of his money is tied up in the project after all," Rachel reminded him. "I gather he and Henry didn't have anything written down yet." Which was pretty trusting of Alex, she thought. But then, Alex had apparently thought a lot of his uncle. "Did anyone else inherit anything?"

"Doreen, actually." Jeff frowned. "I mentioned that to Lyle, but he's not taking it very seriously. Henry named her as beneficiary of his life insurance policy. He was carrying a pretty substantial policy, too, so she should be comfortable for the rest of her life." He gave Rachel a sideways look. "Lyle is looking hard at your kid, too."

"Julio? That's crazy!"

"I sure couldn't find a lot of reasons to suspect him— but he was there. Lyle's going to pin this on somebody."

"No wonder Julio looked worried today." Rachel clenched her fists briefly. "And what about Doreen? She inherited. And she sure doesn't seem like your basic domestic hired help to me."

"Well . . . I gather that she cleans for a lot of widowers and bachelors."

"Doing more than cleaning, you mean?" Rachel wondered if she cleaned house for Sandy's father.

"She's a pretty striking woman."

"She has a nice house—and doesn't seem to work all that hard," Rachel mused.

"Like I said, I brought the subject up with Lyle." Jeff shrugged.

And Lyle wasn't interested in her. "Let's go into town tonight." Rachel seized his hand. "Forget Lyle. I bet he couldn't find his way out of a sack."

"All right." Jeff gave her a lopsided smile. "Warren Zevon is playing at one of the little music clubs downtown tonight. I haven't heard him in years."

"That would be great." Rachel didn't hesitate. "As long as I can get back to work on Dr. Meier's yard on time tomorrow morning."

"We'll manage." This time his smile reached his eyes. "What time?"

"I'll quit at five," Rachel promised. "We're ahead of schedule."

"Leave at six? That'll just give us time for a fast dinner. He doesn't play until eight-thirty."

"I take it you don't have to obey the speed limit if you're a member of Blossom's Finest?" Rachel drawled, trying to elicit a chuckle. "Or were you planning on grabbing a drive-through hamburger on the way?"

"It's not that long a drive to Portland," Jeff said innocently.

"Ha." She laughed. "See you at six."

"By the way, did Henry pay you in cash?" Jeff leaned through the open window as she started the engine.

"Henry didn't pay me at all until he gave me that check the day he died." Rachel rested her crossed arms on the steering wheel. "Why?"

"He made regular cash withdrawals from his account on the fifteenth of every month—five hundred dollars. That left his account pretty low most of the time." He frowned thoughtfully. "If he was spending the money on groceries and clothes, you sure couldn't see the evidence in his closet or kitchen. I think his clothes must have come from the thrift store in Hood River, from the look of them. And I sure haven't heard any rumors about any secret wild living. No sign of drugs or alcohol at all."

"If he ever left that hotel, it was news to me." Rachel shook her head. "He even had the Blossom supermarket deliver, and it's only a fifteen-minute drive away. As far as drinking, he'd go into town and drink Scotch at a bar about once a week." She shrugged. "He always had the Taxi Sisters drive him."

"The Dew Drop." Jeff nodded. "That roadside dive on the old highway, out toward Hood River. He drank Dewars. The bartender said he was a regular—used to talk about opening up the hotel, having the Portland paper out for the gala, inviting the governor. Blue sky, the bartender said. He never listened much. But he did say that in the last few weeks, he'd been talking about money, investors, that sort of thing. He told me he'd even started to wonder if the old guy was on to something finally. Last time he was in, he was boasting about investors fighting over the chance to give him money. The barkeep said the numbers sounded real.''

"He hinted to Alex that he had another source of money.''

"Well, it's Lyle's problem now.'' Jeff's face closed once more. "He made it clear to me that he doesn't need a lot of help just now.'' He turned away.

"Jeff?'' Rachel touched his arm, but there were no words. "See you at six, then.''

He nodded and strode back to his car, his posture stiff. Jeff had been a fierce competitor in high school, pushing for a 4.0 average, a presence in any sport he competed in. It had been his own drive that pushed him to excel—his mother's indifference had shocked Rachel the first time she had encountered it. Maybe it was because of that indifference that he worked so hard to be the best. Rachel sighed and put the truck into gear.

His removal from the investigation had to hurt. A lot.

She drove back to the Meier house, thinking over the information Jeff had given her. Dr. Meier's car was in the driveway, as was his daughter's glittering teal Miata. Deborah sat on the deck steps, her arms crossed on her knees, her profile stony. Raised voices echoed from inside the house.

"I decided they should work this out without me.'' She turned a bleak smile on Rachel as she reached the deck. "I think they scared your employees. They were eating lunch when the yelling started. They dropped everything and went back to digging. Didn't want to be witnesses, I suppose. . . .''

"What are they arguing over?'' Rachel glanced toward the house.

"Guess.'' Her mother stood. "Could you give me a quick ride into town? I'm going to go back out to the orchard. I'll get one of the Taxi Sisters to take me.''

"Mom . . ." Rachel paused, at a loss for words for the second time within the hour. "Do you want this?" she said finally. "You and Joshua, I mean?"

"This is the first time you've used his given name," she said softly. "Oh, Rachel, I want it more than you know."

"Then you can't go back to the orchard. Don't leave Joshua to deal with his spoiled-brat daughter by himself. Is that fair?"

"She's his daughter." Her mother looked away. "She's right. I don't have any rights here."

"She said that to you?" Rachel clenched her fists. "And you're going to walk away and help her convince Joshua that you don't really care, that he really should forget you, be a nice single parent who is only interested in his daughter's desires? She's jealous." Rachel snorted. "What did you expect? She's only been the center of his universe for the last twenty-some years. And here's this stranger moving in to steal a big chunk of Daddy's attention. I mean, come on . . ." She trailed off as she saw a spark of amusement ignite in her mother's eye. "Okay, so I've been describing myself." She smiled sheepishly.

"Well, I don't think you ever saw yourself as the center of the universe." Her mother's eyes twinkled. "That would be a bit tough to pull off, living in the middle of the rather diverse family you grew up with. You're right." She tossed her hair back over her shoulders, her face determined. "I don't know why I was willing to let this woman tell me what I can or can't do. Joshua matters. I want to marry him. I want to share the rest of my life with him." She met her daughter's eyes, a trace of defiance on her own face.

"*Mazel tov*," Rachel said softly.

Her mother smiled, bent down to kiss her swiftly on the forehead, then turned on her heel and marched into the house. A moment later, the shouting ceased. Shaking her head, Rachel went down the deck steps and around the side of the house to see how her crew was getting on. Her mother could hold her own just fine. She'd been the mediator in a wrangling household all her life—one of those people who could stop a verbal brawl without ever raising her voice.

But a small ember of anger smoldered in her chest against this spoiled woman who put herself before her father's happiness. *I hope it rains on her fancy wedding,* she thought, and then rolled her eyes at this bit of childishness.

The trenches were nearly complete. Piles of dug-out rock marked the courses like cairns marking a trail. She nodded, pleased. Julio did a good job of being crew boss, in spite of his age. She never needed to show him something twice, and he took the initiative to do things on his own. It made him a valuable employee.

Rachel found the three men out at the lower end of the property, digging secondary irrigation lines. Julio looked up as she approached, his expression fearful. *"Que pasa?"* she asked, jerking her head toward the house.

"La señora." He shrugged. "She yells. I say *no hablo inglés*, and I go dig." He looked quickly at the house and away. As always when he was upset, his accent had thickened. "The *hombre* comes—the *loco* one. They all yell. They drive away. She throws tools." He looked at his feet. "I did not do it, *señorita.*"

"She threw tools?" For the first time, Rachel noticed the rusty stain on his shirtsleeve. "At you?" Her jaw dropped as he nodded hesitantly. "What kind of tools?"

His eyes flickered down to the rake.

"Julio, let me see." Rachel took his arm and gently pushed up the sleeve of his chamois work shirt.

A tine of the rake had gashed his upper arm. It wasn't deep—more of an abrasion than a cut—but dried blood crusted it, and he was developing a nasty bruise. "Come on." Rachel beckoned sharply.

He got to his feet apprehensively, eyes shifting from the house to her face.

"We need to clean this up and put something on it. That rake was dirty." She marched up the steps to the deck. "You won't get into trouble," she assured him. "*She* threw the rake at you." But he didn't seem reassured. He still seemed unsure of his status, even though he was in the country legally.

Rachel led him into the kitchen without knocking. He stared at the gleaming tile and glittering array of pots and pans nervously.

"Go wash your arm." Rachel pointed him toward the big double sink and handed him the bottle of antibacterial soap that stood beside it. The house was quiet, and she wondered if everybody had left. "I'll get the first-aid kit from the truck." She marched around to the front of the house. The doctor's car was gone, although the teal Miata still stood where it had been parked.

Rachel grabbed the first-aid box from her truck box and went back inside. As she smeared the scrape with antibiotic ointment, she heard the muffled sound of weeping coming from the living room. "How's your arm?" she asked as she put the ointment away. "Can you bend it?"

"Oh, *sí*." He flexed it to demonstrate and almost managed to hide the wince it cost him.

Yeah, sure. "Take the rest of the day off." Rachel shook her head as he started to protest. "Don't worry, I'll pay you for your time anyway." *And bill it directly to Elaine*, she thought grimly. "We'll finish up and start laying pipe tomorrow. Go tell Eduardo and Jorges." As he disappeared through the French doors, she turned on her heel and marched into the living room.

Elaine Meier Levine curled on the sofa where Rachel had surprised her mother and Dr. Meier, her face buried against a brocade pillow, weeping softly and deeply. Rachel stopped indecisively for a moment, then marched across the rich Oriental carpet. "Mrs. Levine, I have to talk to you."

Elaine jolted upright with a startled gasp. "At least knock before you walk in," she said without force. Sniffling, she wiped damp hair back from her puffy, tear-stained face. "What do you *want*? Oh, no, I don't even have a tissue." She gave up fumbling in her pocket, tears overflowing again.

"Hold on." Rachel went back into the kitchen, returning a moment later with a couple of paper towels. Elaine made a face, but immediately wiped her eyes and blew her nose.

"So what *do* you want?" she asked petulantly. "Dad isn't here. He left with that . . . with that . . ."

"With my mother," Rachel interrupted briskly.

"Oh. Yes." Elaine gave her a startled look, then actually blushed. "I didn't mean . . . I'm sure . . . She seems like a very nice lady, but . . ." Tears welled in her eyes again. "I can't believe this. It's like he doesn't care anymore. Here I am with this *wedding,* and he runs off to go play. Everything's a muddy mess, and he won't buy turf—which is *your* fault, and Alonzo quit, and everybody will talk about it, and Sam is going to be furious. Oh, God . . ." She buried her face in her hands again, her shoulders quivering. "I can't believe she got pregnant. She was on the *pill*. She *told* me. And with *him*. How could she? How *could* she?"

Aha. Rachel felt an unexpected twinge of pity. "You hit my assistant with a rake. He's injured."

"Oh, no." Elaine jumped up off the sofa, her eyes wide with alarm. "I didn't. I mean, I didn't mean to." Her face had paled. "It just sort of . . . sort of *bounced*. It was his fault. He shouldn't have come up on the deck. I mean . . . he scared me."

"Oh, come *off* it," Rachel snapped. "He's a teenager, for Pete's sake. He wasn't even going to show me what you did—he's so afraid of making trouble."

"I . . . I'm sorry. Oh, God, if Sam knew about this . . . What's *happening* to me?" She spun around, clutching her tangled hair, her voice shrill. "Everything's falling apart. First Brianna, now Dad, and *Alonzo* . . . Oh, God, what am I going to do?"

"Have the wedding." Rachel shrugged. "Why don't you get a local caterer?"

"Everybody expects Alonzo. I mean . . . *everybody* who is anybody uses him."

"So be different. Surprise folks. Maybe you'll impress them."

"With a wedding from CostCo?"

"We don't have a CostCo in Blossom," Rachel said pleasantly. "But I know a woman who does incredible wedding cakes and puts on some really impressive events. You should go take a look at her portfolio." She pulled out one of Joylinn's cards and dropped it on the sofa beside Elaine. "She's very original—probably quite different from what your Portland friends expect. Why not go talk to her? Of course, she may already be booked for that weekend." She turned away without waiting to see if Elaine had picked up the card. "In any case, the yard should look quite nice by the date you set. And I don't *think* my assistant plans to press charges."

That shook Elaine all over again. She did, after all, have a lawyer for a husband. Rachel left the woman standing in the middle of the living room, still sniffling, but with a thoughtful pout on her tear-stained face.

Julio was waiting with Eduardo and Jorges. The two men agreed to show up early in the morning, then departed in Eduardo's aged Mustang. From the stiffness with which he climbed into her truck, Rachel guessed that Julio's arm was hurting him quite a bit. "Here." She handed him a couple of extra-strength aspirin. "These might help. See how you feel tomorrow."

"I will be fine for work," he said stoically. He downed the aspirin, his young face worried. "*La señora*, she is not mad?"

"*She* hit *you,*" Rachel said grimly. "You get to be mad, not her." Actually she was feeling a bit shaky herself. She didn't do confrontations well.

"The policeman—he comes to *mi hermana* last night. He ask if I need money. If I bet. She says they will arrest me."

"They won't," Rachel said forcefully. "You didn't do anything."

He nodded politely, but his eyes were bright with fear.

CHAPTER

12

The phone rang while Rachel was in the shower. For a moment she contemplated grabbing a towel in case it was Jeff, but decided that was what machines were for, and besides, she didn't have time to clean up the water before he showed up—if she slopped out into the kitchen to answer and it wasn't him.

A message from a prospective client had waited on her machine when she arrived home. Still angry at Elaine, Rachel had called back—and had spent over an hour answering questions and providing references. Rachel had decided that she should probably bid that one high. The client was obviously going to micromanage every step of the way. But . . . it was a big job.

If she got it.

Rachel grabbed her towel and stepped out of the shower. It was 6:05. Good thing Jeff was always late—at least he had been, back in high school. Drying herself briskly, she began to dress. She had opted for black stretch pants, a long sea-green silk tunic, and an embroidered vest. The ensemble gave her stocky frame some semblance of elegance anyway, and it didn't take long to get dressed.

The answering machine was blinking furiously when she finally paid attention to it. Three messages. Three? She let out an annoyed breath. The phone must have rung nonstop while she was in the shower. Glancing at her watch again, she debated between makeup and listening to messages, decided that she'd rather not have Jeff watch her put her makeup on, and one of the messages was probably from him telling her he was on his way in any case.

So she was putting on the finishing touches of mascara when he knocked at the door. Peter leaped down from the sofa back with a yowl and stalked over to sit squarely in front of the door, lashing his tail. "Coming," Rachel called. She gave one last careful swipe to her eyelashes, tossed the mascara back into the drawer, and hurried to open the door.

"Your attack cat is glaring at me." Jeff walked over and leaned down to scratch Peter's head. To Rachel's surprise, her cat arched his back in pleasure and began to purr like a buzz saw.

"Wow. You do have a way with cats." She smiled and shook her head. "Usually he scratches people who touch him without an invitation."

"Maybe I was a cat in my last life." He grinned. He was trying hard, but shadows lurked in his eyes.

"We'd better get going or we really will be eating at a burger joint." But as she started for the door with him, the blinking answering machine caught her eye. "Oh, wait. I'd better check these." She sighed and hit the message button, betting that at least one was from her prospective client.

"Mademoiselle O'Connor, this is Anne-Marie Celestine DeRochers-Smith."

"Wow." Jeff's eyebrows rose. "That is some name."

"Quebecois. Joylinn's grandmama."

"I am calling you in regard to your question about the possibility of a secret marriage by Monsieur Bassinger, the younger. I had a conversation with another resident here, a very charming woman whose daughter owns a florist shop in Hood River, and who was a—shall we say—intimate friend of Monsieur Henry's father." She cleared her throat delicately. "According to her, I was misinformed. The young Henry did indeed run away to play with a jazz band and married a woman of—shall we say—less than desirable origins. *Le papa* was beside himself, of course, and eventually prevailed upon young Henry to come home. He intended to have the marriage annulled. Madame, my friend, did not know for certain if this event was accomplished. Please feel free to call me if you have any questions. Ah, yes: Monsieur McLoughlin entreats me to convey his good wishes. You have made the impression on him." The old woman's voice tinkled with amusement. *"Au revoir, ma petite."*

"McLoughlin." Jeff regarded the machine thoughtfully. "That name sounds familiar."

"He lives at the home—an old guy in a wheelchair." Rachel held up her hand as her mother's voice emerged from the machine.

"We're off, my dear. Las Vegas, ho. Actually Joshua was pretty upset by today's little episode. He says he's not coming back here until after the wedding, but he'll calm down. I'll call you, dear. Take care. And . . . thanks for understanding. Love you."

"What's that all about?"

"Mom's getting married," Rachel said. "Tell you in the car."

"Miss O'Connor." A man's voice spoke. "This is Willis Bard. The van was signed out by one of the staff the night you had your accident. But it turns out that that particular person didn't take it out after all. I'll get back to you."

"I found the van that ran me off the road. I think." Rachel rewound the machine, not quite willing to meet Jeff's gaze. "I just sort of happened onto it. At the feed store. I'm not really poking around in this anymore."

"It doesn't matter at this point." Jeff sighed. "So what did you find out?"

"I'm pretty sure that the van belonged to the Youth

Farm, and that a boy named Cass was in it or driving it.''

"I'll tell Lyle." Jeff frowned. "I don't know if he'll pay much attention. He's made up his mind that if the murderer wasn't Cresswell, then it had to be your kid."

Rachel bit her lip. "Jeff—I got you taken off this case. It's my fault for poking around, and I'm sorry. I was worried about Julio, I guess, and . . ."

"Hush." Jeff put his arm around her. "Lyle would have made trouble for me somehow. Don't blame yourself too much."

But she did. Smothering a sigh, she went down the stairs with him, holding hands. Mrs. Frey was watching them. Rachel smiled and didn't mind at all as she climbed into Jeff's truck.

"Maybe this friend of Anne-Marie's knows who Henry married."

"I don't think Lyle is going to follow up on this line of investigation. So I think I just might drop by the home tomorrow. On my own time." Jeff pulled into the left lane and roared around a big double semi rig, pulling sharply back into the outer lane. "Just for a friendly chat."

Jeff wasn't going to stop working on this case, because justice mattered to him. Rachel brushed his leg with her fingertips. "I'm proud of you," she said.

"Why?" He looked startled.

"I just am."

Shaking his head, a crooked smile on his lips, he negotiated the evening traffic. "Politics is always going to be my downfall," he said after a while. "That's why I decided to apply to small towns rather than go for a big-city police force. For all the good it did me." He laughed shortly. "But Henry was just a harmless recluse who never hurt anyone. I want to find out who pushed him off that walkway." He gave her a sideways glance. "So what do you want to check out in Portland?"

"Me?" Rachel arched her eyebrows innocently. "I just thought we were going to listen to Zevon. But . . .

we might ask around, see if any jazz fans know this guy." She pulled out the CD that Dr. Meier had loaned her.

"Clyde Montaine." Jeff craned his neck to read the jacket. "Who's he?"

"A new rising star in the world of jazz musicians, I gather." She regarded the CD thoughtfully. "Henry played this album every single day. It must mean something."

"You think he's the mystery son?" Jeff pursed his lips. "He looks a little like Henry. Not a lot."

"He looks like he's about the right age." She slipped the CD back into her shoulder bag.

"Just because Henry played jazz for a while doesn't mean his son turned into a jazz musician," Jeff murmured.

"Probably not," Rachel conceded.

"But we might as well ask around. I agree with you. As long as we really do listen to Zevon," he said severely. "I demand that much."

"I promise. I like him, too, remember?" Rachel settled back in the seat and grinned at him. "So where are we going to eat dinner?"

"McDonald's," he said with a straight face. "So tell me about your mother getting married. That's a surprise, isn't it?"

"To put it mildly." Rachel told him the whole story of Dr. Meier and discovered that she was starting to feel okay about it. Her mother had sounded so *young* on the phone, so full of excitement. Rachel wondered how much loneliness she had hidden during the years since her father had died.

In Portland, Jeff took her to a small Thai restaurant on the southeast side of town and introduced her to Thai curry. It was spicy, but she had shared lunch with Julio often enough to have developed a fair tolerance for hot peppers.

"I got introduced to all kinds of ethnic food down in

LA,'' Jeff told her. ''There's a lot of good food in that town, I'll give it that.''

He told her about the move and about life in an inner-city high school. It sounded grim to Rachel, in spite of his anecdotes. He told her a little bit about his time with the Los Angeles Police Department. ''Politics,'' he said. ''Like I told you. I can't seem to keep my mouth shut.'' He grimaced. ''I get steamed and shoot my mouth off, and then I find out I made an enemy out of somebody I can't make an enemy out of. So then I'm more pissed off, and I lose my temper faster, and I just keep digging the hole deeper.'' He sighed. ''But I'm not doing so well here, either, so I don't know. Maybe I'm in the wrong profession.''

''You're not.''

He smiled, shook his head, and fell silent as he paid the bill and ushered her out onto the sidewalk.

Portland had its share of nightlife, Rachel thought, as she eyed the restaurants, bars, and clubs spilling light and strolling patrons onto the sidewalks. After Blossom, it felt like a major metropolis. She fought a twinge of claustrophobia as they walked the four blocks to the small club where Zevon was playing.

It was early, and something funky and familiar blared on the sound system. Most of the tables in the club were already full, as was the bar at one side of the dimly lit room. On the small corner stage, power lamps glowed like red and green jewels on the amps and speakers. Rachel and Jeff took the last empty table—a tiny thing the size of a phone book.

The waitress came around to take their drink orders. ''There's a cover,'' she said. '' 'Cause we got a live band tonight. Five bucks each.'' She idly flipped one of the half dozen gold rings in her ear as Jeff pulled out his wallet.

''We can be PC, and I can pay for my share,'' Rachel offered with a smile.

''Next date, you can pay for both of us.'' Jeff ordered

a glass of stout, and Rachel decided on red wine. "Good luck," Jeff murmured under his breath.

"You've become a wine connoisseur in California, as well as a gourmet?"

"You can't live in California without getting to drink good wine once in a while." He got up suddenly and threaded his way through the increasing crowd to the bar. People were trickling into the club in a steady stream as it got closer to the time Zevon was supposed to play. They ordered their drinks at the bar and clustered along the walls and sides of the room. It was getting warmer by the moment, the air thick with cigarette smoke and the humid scent of bodies, perfume, and sweat. Rachel thought about taking off her vest but decided she'd probably walk off and forget it if she did.

"Here." Jeff slid into his seat just as a burly man made a hopeful move toward it. "This might help." He opened a black-and-white tabloid paper that featured downtown entertainment and events on the tabletop in front of them, just as their waitress arrived with their drinks.

"You lookin' for something in there?" She popped gum as she whisked down two cocktail napkins and set Jeff's tall beer glass and Rachel's wine down in front of them. "I know who's playin' where around here." She looked to be about eighteen, Rachel decided, although she had to be twenty-one in order to serve liquor. Her blond hair was cropped short and moussed into rumpled spikes, which with her thin, fine-boned face gave her a waiflike air.

"Actually, I was wondering if a particular jazz musician ever played in Portland." Rachel got out the CD, guessing that this girl wouldn't know anybody who wasn't a member of a current techno band.

The waitress picked up the CD and turned it over casually. "I know Clyde. Sure, he plays here. All the time." She shifted her gum to the other side of her mouth and handed the CD back to Rachel. "He's playin' right now. In this posh restaurant at the old railroad station. They just started havin' music there. This lawyer friend of mine asked me to go, but I had to work. It's one of those fancy places with tablecloths, a rose in a vase. You know. Rich people and lawyers go there.''

"I see." Rachel hid a smile at the waitress's evaluation of the restaurant, then turned to Jeff, eyebrows rising.

"Want to go to Reno tonight?'' he murmured. "Put a little of that luck out on the roulette table?'' But excitement glinted in his eyes, for all his laconic tone.

"He's in Portland all the time. If you ask me, he's got a wife stashed out in Beaverton. Or a girlfriend. Bet you.''

"Where is this restaurant?'' Jeff asked thoughtfully.

"Across Burnside.'' She pointed vaguely north. "Look for the clock tower. You can't miss it. There's all these fancy new apartments along the river now. That's where my lawyer friend lives. Since he was divorced. Pays a whole lot of rent.'' She shook her head so that her multiple earrings jingled. "Place flooded last year. His fancy carpet got all wet—boy did it *stink*. And you can hear the guy next door hiccough. You know, my place is better. It maybe doesn't have a deck and a gas barbecue, but, hey, it was a mansion once. Six units now—but the walls are *solid*. I can turn the stereo up way loud, and nobody bangs except old Mrs. Murphy, and she bangs even when I'm not making any noise. She's just nuts.'' She shrugged and popped her gum again. "You leavin'? You want your cover back? I'm not supposed to—but, hey, we're making tons of money tonight.''

"We might as well stay.'' Jeff gave Rachel a wistful look. "We probably won't get a chance to talk to Montaine until he's through with his set. We could listen to Zevon for a while and then wander over.''

"He breaks about ten.'' Their waitress snagged two empty glasses from the next table. "I know because my boyfriend's a real fan. We go see him every time he's in town. Bores me.'' The glasses clinked as she balanced them in one hand. "Me, I like KMFDM. Now, there's a hot group.''

Rachel shook her head as the girl swayed away between the now crowded tables, her fistful of empty glasses held high. "We really lucked out to find him here. I wonder when he got into town."

"We'll ask him. So your mom is really getting married." Jeff took a swallow of beer. "You know, I'm glad. She always seemed a little out of place, even in the middle of your big family."

Rachel gave him a startled look, studying him with new appreciation. It was something she hadn't realized herself until recently—how different her college-educated, New York-raised mother was from her mostly high school-educated farmer in-laws. "She worked at fitting in." Rachel studied her wine thoughtfully. "I hope this is really good for her."

All conversation ended as Zevon walked onto the tiny stage. The audience burst into applause as he settled himself, then quieted as he swung into his opening set. Jeff grinned throughout, sometimes mouthing the words, having a great time. But it was he who touched her arm when the break came. "Nearly ten," he said over the rising tide of conversation around them. "We'd better go."

He might claim that this was Lyle's case, but solving it mattered to him. She held his hand as they found their way to the old Union Station. Bright new condominiums and apartments lined the bank of the Willamette River in a solid row with decks and neatly landscaped brick paths. Floodlights lit the clock tower of the classic old railway station. Light and music spilled from the doorway to the restaurant at the south end of the station.

They entered, and Rachel had to smile because it matched their waitress's description so perfectly. Patrons sat at the white-draped tables sipping drinks or eating late dinners, lit by flickering candle jars that turned the roses in their vases a dark crimson. They were mostly older couples, well dressed, mixed with a fair number of younger, junior-executive-type men with even younger dates. An elegantly dressed hostess ushered them to a table near the back.

The tall man in the subdued spotlight raised his trumpet and launched into the familiar solo that had played so often in Henry's hotel. Rachel leaned her elbows on the table as the waiter departed with their order, watching the musician's rapt concentration as his long fingers coaxed the soaring notes from the trumpet. He looked more like Alex than Henry, she decided, which proved nothing, but excitement gathered in her stomach as he concluded his piece and bowed his head to polite but enthusiastic applause.

Jeff leaned toward the waiter as the man set down their drinks. "Could you give a message to Mr. Montaine for me?" he asked the young man with an easy smile. "We're friends of his father, in town for the evening. We'd love to buy him a drink. Jeff and Rachel."

"I'll tell him." The young man took the ten Jeff held and deftly tucked it away. "I don't promise anything." He shrugged. "He kind of keeps to himself, you know? Quiet guy."

"That's fine." Jeff ran his finger thoughtfully around the rim of his beer glass as the waiter departed. "Think he'll come out?"

"Depends, I guess." She wrinkled her nose, watching the back of the restaurant.

About the time she was ready to give up, a tall figure appeared near the waiters' station, threading his way through the tables with athletic grace, stopping to reply to comments with an easy smile. He didn't have Henry's blocky stature. Rather, he was tall, with a leaner build than Alex. His skin had a golden cast to it, and his curly dark hair dramatized his gray eyes.

Gray eyes . . . Rachel frowned as the nebulous connection slipped away from her. Something about those eyes . . . Then he was at the table, smiling down at them, the tension in his shoulders denying the relaxed expression on his face. His eyes went from one to the other of them, and there was no smile in their steel-gray depths.

"What's this about my daddy?" Montaine drawled in a soft, Southern accent. He pulled out a chair and sat down, turning to thank the waiter, who had appeared with a tall glass of iced tea. "I don't know y'all." He turned back to them, his eyes hooded as he sipped his tea. "Was this your idea of how to get me to come sit with you?" He gave them a quick grin. "You coulda just asked."

"Actually, we're hoping that we do know your father—even if we don't know you." Jeff lifted his untasted beer, set it down again. "We're looking for Henry Bassinger's son."

"Well, that's me." Montaine shrugged, drank some of his tea, then leaned his crossed arms on the table. "I use my aunt's name, 'cause she raised me. But I guess I could call m'self Clyde Bassinger. If I wanted to. I don't. What happened? Did the old boy die and leave me money?"

"Actually, he did." Jeff nodded. "Did you see much of your father?"

"See much of him?" Anger glinted in the musician's eyes. "I never saw nothin' of him. I know his name—my mama told me once. He never wasted his time on us. I guess his family didn't like him getting married to some bayou babe. Mama told me once that his daddy offered to give her money if she'd divorce him. She told him to go to hell—said she'd keep the name, even if that's all she got."

"What's your mother's name? Where does she live?" Rachel leaned forward eagerly.

"I dunno where she is." He shrugged. "New Orleans, last I heard. She gets around." He gave her a bland smile. "I grew up with my aunt Evangeline in Live Oak, Louisiana. Evangeline Montaine. Mama's boyfriends didn't want a snot-nosed kid underfoot. So my aunt Evangeline just kind of took me over. That's why I use her name. It seemed right. Mama's name is Darlene—Ballou to start with, then Bassinger. Dunno what she goes by now." He shrugged again. "She might be dead for all I know."

His manner was easy and open, but there was a shuttered quality to his gray eyes. Whatever was going on in his head, Rachel thought, he wasn't sharing it.

"So what's this about my long-lost daddy leavin' me money?" Montaine turned to Jeff. "Were you shittin' me, or is that for real?"

"He died a few days ago." Jeff kept his eyes on Montaine's face. "He was murdered."

"What?" Color drained from Montaine's face, leaving it a sickly, sallow hue. "Do ya . . . do you know who did it?"

"Not yet," Jeff said evenly. "We will. But he left you the hotel he owned. The property should be worth quite a lot of money. You'll have to prove you're his son, of course."

"Oh . . . I got my birth certificate." Montaine looked away, his face tight. "That's so crazy, you know? Him dyin' and me in town a couple days later. You know, every time I played here, I thought about seein' him— used to run it through my head like a movie. Changed the plot every time. Sometimes I figured I'd just say 'Hi, Dad.' Sometimes I meant to walk up to him and deck him. Dunno which I really would've done." He lifted his shoulders in a jerky shrug. "Never will now, I guess."

"So you weren't in town on Tuesday?"

"Not even in the state." Montaine swiveled sharply back to face Jeff. "I didn't have no gig here until tonight. Portland's a hick town. Nah. I hung out in San Fran— where I had my last gig. They got a nightlife there. Drove up yesterday. We stopped in one o' those casino towns out on the coast. Hey." He grinned. "I picked up a few hundred playin' blackjack. Not bad."

"You got people who can say you were in San Francisco on Tuesday?"

"You a cop?" Montaine said harshly.

Jeff opened his wallet and proffered his badge.

"Blossom Po-lice." Montaine drawled out each syllable. "Yeah, I got friends who'll say where I was. I'll give you their numbers if you want. We was partyin' at this pool hall over in Oakland. Then we sort of went out cruisin', you know?" He looked back at the stage, then got quickly to his feet. "I'd give 'em to you now—the numbers—but I got to get back to work. After the gig, okay?" He gave them a broad smile. "I'll buy you a drink. Since I guess I'm a wealthy man now, huh?"

"I think he's lying." Rachel watched him disappear through a doorway near the waiters' station. "About something, anyway."

"Me, too," Jeff said thoughtfully.

"I think he already knew Henry was dead." Rachel got to her feet. "Be back in a second." She headed for the women's rest room near the swinging doors through which Montaine had vanished. When she emerged a few moments later, she heard a familiar voice. Montaine. She stood aside as a busboy bumped through with a tray of dirty dishes, then peeped through the crack between the door and the wall. A public phone booth was mounted on the wall in the short hallway. Clyde Montaine leaned against the wall with his back to her, talking on the phone.

"You, me, and Sal, okay? Over at Sammy's in Oakland. Yeah. We picked up some girls and split. Okay. Yeah, we're square now. What? You want it in writing or something? Okay. See you."

Rachel ducked away as a waiter bustled from the kitchen with a tray of sandwich plates. By the time Montaine pushed through the doors, she was making her way nonchalantly back to their table.

"He doesn't have an alibi," she murmured to Jeff as she slid into her seat. "He was on the phone back there, setting one up with his friends, from the sound of things."

"Eavesdroppers never hear anything good about themselves," Jeff said. "Nice job. Did you get any names?"

"Sal." She shrugged. "Busy place. I couldn't listen very long."

"Well, now I understand why he couldn't give us any numbers until after the rest of the set." At that moment, the spot came back on, and Montaine stepped into its brilliance.

He might be lying, but he was one heck of a trumpet player, Rachel decided. No wonder Dr. Meier had spoken so highly of him. He and his band improvised on each other, spinning into a wild jam that earned frenzied clapping at its conclusion. All too soon, it seemed, he was bowing to applause, his face gleaming with sweat, a triumphant light in his face.

"He really gets into his music, doesn't he?" Jeff murmured as they made their way to the back of the restaurant. "I'd call that passion."

Montaine was waiting for them at the swinging doors. "Here." He handed them a sheet of hotel paper. "Call Sal, or Donny, or Sanders. They'll tell you where I was. The legal part of the night, anyway." He flashed them a grin and a wink. "You all come listen again, okay? As long as you tell me another rich relative died and left me money." With a wave he strolled through the swinging doors. They had been dismissed. So much for buying them a drink.

"Sal." Jeff looked at Rachel, who shrugged. He tapped the sheet of hotel paper. "The Benson. Nice place to stay."

"Expensive." Rachel nodded. Maybe very expensive for a man who had only one album out yet and made his money playing restaurants and small clubs. She followed Jeff out to the parking lot.

It was late. There were few cars in the lot, and patrons leaving the restaurant were rapidly thinning the numbers. One car caught Rachel's eye. A rented Toyota Camry gleamed in the light from the halide streetlamps, parked near the rear door of the restaurant. One of the busboys lounged against the wall near it, smoking and watching it. "Look." Rachel pulled Jeff along the sidewalk. "Isn't that Alex's car?"

The busboy gave them a challenging glare as they approached, took a last drag on his cigarette, and tossed it into the gutter.

"It's not Cresswell's." Jeff shook his head. "Cresswell's car has black leather upholstery. This is brown."

"Oh," Rachel said, relieved.

"It belongs to the jazz guy. What's-his-name . . . Montaine." The busboy kept his eyes on them. "I'm keepin' an eye on it for him. You talk to him about it."

"Maybe the whole family rents white Toyotas." Jeff looked at the hotel parking tag hanging from the rearview mirror. It had been issued by the Benson. He looked at Rachel. "Your kid saw a white Camry parked in the bushes on Tuesday," he said softly. "I didn't ask him if he noticed the color of the seats." He took Rachel's arm as they headed back to his truck. "I think I'll do just that," he said. "First thing in the morning." He gave her a sideways glance. "What say we head back and see if we can catch the end of Zevon's gig, huh?"

CHAPTER

1 3

They made it back to the club in time to hear Zevon end his last set, but to Jeff's disappointment he didn't manage to speak to the musician.

The highway was nearly empty on the way back to Blossom, traveled mostly by long-haul truckers pulling single, double, and even triple trailers. They made good time, but it was already in the wee hours by the time Jeff pulled into Rachel's driveway. "It was fun," Jeff murmured and leaned across the seat to kiss her.

The kiss went on for a long time, and when they finally parted, more than a little breathlessly, Jeff's eyes never left her face. Invite him in? Rachel hesitated. She was tempted—but her feelings about Jeff were still unsettled. A lace curtain panel moved in Mrs. Frey's downstairs window, and Rachel smiled grimly. "The woman never sleeps," she murmured, and gave Jeff a chaste kiss on the side of the mouth. "Time for me to say good night like a good little girl and go upstairs."

"The old girl's probably enjoying the show." Jeff leaned forward again, but when Rachel opened the door to get out, he sighed and got out, too. "All right," he grumbled. "We'll be good. Just as well, I suppose. I want to talk to Peron about that car first thing in the morning.'' He gave her a crooked smile. ''I don't really expect to pick up where we left off in high school,'' he said softly. ''You're not stuck with me, you know.''

''I'm not stuck with you at all.'' Rachel paused at the foot of the stairs, aware of the warmth radiating from his body. She was tempted to invite him in and let Mrs. Frey say what she wanted.

She shook her head. ''I think . . . you still scare me a little,'' she whispered.

''Do I?'' He touched her chin with a fingertip. ''Why?'' he whispered.

''I don't know.'' She shook her head, thinking of her mother's deep grief after her father died, not sure she even knew what she meant. ''Good night,'' she murmured instead, then fled up the stairs, heart hammering, feeling that she had just revealed a lot more than she had intended to. Peter waited on the landing, tail lashing, obviously annoyed at her late return. She unlocked her door and followed him as he stalked inside, discovering that she was afraid to look back at Jeff. As she closed the door, she heard his truck rumble to life, and a moment later tires crunched on the gravel.

Rachel let out a gusty breath. ''So how do I sort this out, cat? I'm not even sure how I feel.''

Peter leaped onto the back of the sofa, ignoring her, and began to sharpen his claws on the fabric.

''Hey! Knock it off!'' She shooed him off the sofa, then went on into the kitchen to apologize for her late return with a treat of canned tuna.

He glowered at her, obviously not ready to forgive anything yet, but he ate the tuna. Rachel stumbled off to bed while he was still licking the plate, dropped her clothes in a heap at the foot of the bed, and was asleep before her head hit the pillow. She didn't even twitch when Peter knocked the empty tuna can off the counter and began playing soccer with it on the linoleum floor.

Morning came all too early—made even earlier by Peter's clawed kneading of her bare arm. Revenge for her desertion of him last night? Rachel stumbled out of bed, yawning, and headed for the bathroom. The tuna can was waiting for her in the short hallway between bedroom and kitchen. Rachel picked it up, gave Peter a bleary glare, and made the coffee extra strong. It didn't help much.

Julio gave her a knowing and amused look as he climbed into her truck. Rachel half expected him to suggest a bowl of *Menudo*—a spicy soup with the power to cure hangovers, according to local legend—but he kept his thoughts to himself. Rachel yawned all the way to Dr. Meier's house, hoping that she wouldn't have to start the day off with another confrontation.

But her fears proved to be groundless. The driveway was empty, and the dark, locked house had an abandoned look to it. Rachel wondered briefly if Elaine had decided to give up on the wedding after all. Rachel decided she couldn't get that lucky. Eduardo and Jorges pulled in a few moments later, and she set them to finishing the trenching, while she and Julio began to lay out the pipe. The peace and quiet were an unexpected blessing. Julio even seemed more relaxed today.

With no interruptions, the four of them managed to get the water system tested and operational by noon. Eduardo and Jorges had a lot of experience working on irrigation systems, and she blessed them both for it. Plumbing was the bane of the landscape business as far as she was concerned. She had long ago decided that she suffered from bad plumbing karma. But for once, when they tested the system, they had only a minor leak or two. She gave her crew full credit for that success and told them she'd buy lunch in celebration.

The offer was a bit self-serving since she hadn't had time to pack any food this morning anyway. She figured she'd worked hard enough to justify anything up to and including one of the cheeseburgers-with-everything from the Homestyle Cafe. Eduardo and Jorges were enthusiastic, and Julio had the limitless appetite of a teenager, so Rachel left them filling in trenches while she drove into town to get their burgers.

The usual lunchtime crowd filled the cafe's formica-topped booths and tables. Rachel spotted Sandy's father in the corner booth near the kitchen, which was odd. Most days he occupied his usual table out in the middle of the floor, where he could greet everyone who came in. The waitresses held the table for him at lunchtime. Today he sat with his back to the room, staring moodily into his coffee mug. Rachel thought about what Sandy had told her, and hesitated.

He turned abruptly, as if he'd felt her gaze on him, gave her a brief uninviting nod, then went back to his coffee. Surprised and a little stung, Rachel marched over to the counter to place her order.

"Hey, I heard you and Jeff Price had a hot date in Portland last night." Carolyn, the counter waitress, gave her a knowing wink as she scribbled Rachel's order on her pad. "Never knew you were such a fast worker, girl."

"News sure travels fast in this town."

"Well, my hubby jogs with Lyle Waters in the morning." She made a face. "One of those men things. Anyway, Lyle is on the force, too."

"I've met him," Rachel said dryly.

"Yeah. Well, he told Ronnie about it. You want fries with those burgers?"

"Just a green salad for me." Rachel frowned, wondering what exactly Lyle had had to say and why he seemed to be taking such an interest. "We just went into town to listen to music. It was just a date, you know?" She wondered why she sounded so defensive.

"Sure, honey." Carolyn was grinning. "That's why you're ordering the salad, right?" She patted her thickening waist, which seriously strained the seams of her pink gingham uniform. "Hey, once you're married, you don't have to starve yourself anymore. I'll put your order up." She stuck it onto the revolving wheel mounted on the pass-through counter between kitchen and dining area. "So tell me about the murder. I hear you found the old man's body." Her blue eyes glittered with curiosity. "That big-city nephew of his did it, didn't he? I never trust a man who wears an earring. Is he gay?"

"I have no idea who might have murdered Henry. And no, Henry's nephew isn't gay." She glanced at her watch. "Uh . . . I've got an errand to run. I'll be back in ten minutes, okay?"

"I guess." Carolyn pouted. "Chuck's slow this morning," she yelled back over her shoulder. A violent clatter of pots and pans answered her from the kitchen.

Rachel escaped with relief. Carolyn was one of Blossom's premier gossips—and prone to misquotes. Sometimes Rachel wondered if the misquotes were less due to a poor memory than an attempt to liven up a bit of dull news. She and Carolyn had never been particular friends in high school. Blond and popular, Carolyn had moved in different circles, although they had shared a team report on the Aswan Dam for Global History once. Rachel had done all the research. Carolyn had contributed a couple of *National Geographic* photos of the pyramids for her share.

As she passed the booths, Rachel noticed that Herbert Southern had also left. A dollar bill lay on the formica next to his half-filled coffee cup. Deep in thought, Rachel walked the two blocks to The Bread Box. She and Julio had long ago agreed that the best dessert in town was one of Joylinn's Double Chocolate Hazelnut Brownies. She pushed the door open, sniffing hungrily. Her stomach informed her that if she didn't immediately eat one of the fresh cinnamon rolls that perfumed the air, she would certainly die of starvation before she could bring lunch back to her crew.

"Hi, Rachel." Joylinn's voice came from the kitchen, seeming to float on a wave of cinnamon and baking bread. "Be right with you."

"Do you have ESP, or did you recognize the sound of my stomach growling?" Rachel called back. She perched on one of the wooden stools in front of the bakery's small espresso bar and planted her elbows on the marble countertop, willing herself not to stare at a pile of cheese Danish.

"Here." Joylinn deposited a tray of fresh cinnamon rolls on the counter, plucked a fat one from the center, and slid it onto a paper plate. "Wouldn't want my best friend to expire of hunger right here in front of me." She set the plate down with a flourish in front of Rachel.

"Temptress." Rachel grabbed the roll and took a big bite before conscience could intervene. Still warm from the oven, fragrant with yeast and cinnamon, it evoked rolled eyes and a heartfelt sigh of appreciation. "Nobody does these like you." She took another huge bite.

"I hope I didn't just spoil your lunch." Joylinn was laughing.

"I wish." Rachel finished the roll in ravenous haste, then wiped her fingers on the napkin. "I'll skip the brownie I was going to have for dessert," she said virtuously.

"My dear, you are not at all fat." Joylinn plopped down on the stool beside her and brushed damp wisps of hair back from her face. "Solid and muscular, but certainly not fat."

"Solid and muscular are nice terms when applied to a draft horse." Rachel found herself staring at the tray of rolls and looked away. "I gave your name to the daughter of one of my clients, by the way. She's doing a wedding."

"Elaine Levine?" Joylinn nodded. "She told me you sent her. Thank you very much. I think." She grinned and wrinkled her nose. "She spent an hour and a half here complaining about the trials and tribulations of putting on a wedding in a hick town like this—and then telling me everything that *had* to be done just so. She made it sound as if the guests were going to recoil in horror, fling their plates on the ground in disgust, and stampede for their cars if any single detail wasn't perfect."

"Uh-oh." Rachel widened her eyes. "What have I done to you?"

"Actually you've done me a huge favor." Joylinn sobered. "It's going to be a very big wedding, and she wants an elaborate buffet." She grinned. "I think I impressed her. I have a feeling that she expected some truck-stop waitress type who was going to suggest chicken, hot dogs, and potato salad. On paper plates."

"Uh-oh, speaking of truck stops . . ." Rachel glanced at her watch. "I'd better go get our burgers before they get cold. I'm so glad Elaine actually hired you."

"Well, I have a feeling that she's not going to be a lot of fun to work with, but oh well." She shrugged. "It would be nice to only have wonderful clients. Here." She reached into the display case beside the coffee bar and slipped four huge hazelnut brownies into a sack. "On the house. A little thank-you present."

"Oh, wow." Rachel sniffed the rich, chocolaty aroma rising from the bag, then closed it tightly. "I don't know if I can trust myself. . . ."

"I'll tell Julio I gave you four." Joylinn grinned. "You'd better make sure he gets his share."

"Oh, I will." Rachel sighed and patted her waistline. "I have *some* ethics." She waved and left the bakery, wanting to whistle. How wonderful for Joylinn. In spite of her smiles and cheerful manner, the bakery was just barely paying the bills. The catering job might bring her some future business, even if most of the guests were from Portland.

Rachel ducked into the Homestyle Cafe, paid for her burgers, and carried the big Styrofoam boxes out to her truck. The scent of grilled meat made her stomach growl in earnest, in spite of the cinnamon roll. She stowed the food on the seat and was about to climb behind the wheel, when a small, furtive figure emerged from the narrow alley between the Homestyle and the Springtime Dry Cleaning and Laundry.

Cass.

Rachel leaned on the open door of her truck as he

approached. He moved hesitantly, as if he expected her to leap at him. When he reached her, he scuffed his feet for a moment, his eyes on the pavement between them. He was wearing sagging stonewashed jeans and an oversized black T-shirt instead of the Youth Farm uniform of work jeans and a knit shirt. "I gotta talk to you," he mumbled, his eyes still on his feet. "I don't think Willis will let me come back unless I do. I . . . I'm sorry. I wasn't tryin' to hurt you—I was just supposed to scare you. That's why I waited till we got to that place where there were only those puny trees. We'd been workin' down there, weedin' for the guy who owns 'em, and I knew they were too small to really bang up your truck or anything. It was just a prank, you know?"

"So it *was* you." Rachel regarded his shorn head, wondering if his remorse was genuine or an act. "How come you're apologizing? I thought you ran off."

"I did. But I got to thinking—it was stupid, running." He lifted his head at last, and his gray eyes were clear and angry. "I done a lot of stupid stuff in my life—like runnin' you off the road. But, hey—you gotta quit someday. Willis is the first really decent guy I've known. He wanted to help me—no price tag, nothin'—and I blew it off. It'll be back to the detention center when they catch me, and I'll never see Willis again, and even if I did, he'd—" He broke off, a muscle twitching in his jaw, and looked away. "I want to go back. I figure he could maybe fix it for me, if I told you I was sorry. And if you said it was okay, that you weren't gonna go to the cops or sue the Farm or anything . . . then maybe." He shrugged and met her eyes again. "I guess I really am sorry. For doin' it. I mean, you could be as nice as Willis. I don't know."

"Thanks." If this kid wasn't sincere, he was the best actor she'd seen in a long time. "Why don't I give you a ride back to the Farm, and we can see Willis and whoever we need to talk to together?"

He nodded, a tentative smile softening his face.

"One thing, though—who paid you to scare me?"

"Well . . . yeah." He looked away. "I guess I . . ." He

fell silent, his eyes fixed on something down the block behind her. "I gotta go," he muttered. "I'll see you."

"Hey! Wait!" Rachel took a couple of futile steps after him as he vanished down the alley again. He ran like a scared cat. No way she was going to catch him.

She turned to look down the block. A few people meandered along the sidewalk, shopping or just strolling. Nobody she knew. But as she started to get into her truck, Alex Cresswell emerged from the drugstore and hurried off down the sidewalk without even glancing in her direction. Alex? He volunteered at the Farm, worked with Cass. As she turned her truck around and headed back through town toward Dr. Meier's house, she passed Herbert Southern, hurrying along the sidewalk in the same direction Alex had taken. He returned her wave, his expression preoccupied and faintly troubled, but as she slowed and rolled her window down, he turned and abruptly entered the video store.

He sure didn't want to talk to her today. Rachel drove slowly back to the job, no longer hungry, wishing she had brought Willis Bard's phone number with her. She was half tempted to swing by her apartment and get it—call him and tell him she'd just talked to his runaway. She glanced at her watch and decided to let it go until after they finished for the day. Right now she owed her crew their lunch. Cass was obviously hanging around town.

To her surprise and alarm, one of Blossom's two police cars stood in Meier's driveway. Relieved, she recognized Jeff, standing with Julio near the kitchen deck. Julio gripped his rake, his face pale as he answered Jeff's questions. Both men looked up as she approached.

"Julio says he didn't get close enough to see if the Toyota's seats were brown or black." Jeff was frowning. "What's eating him?"

Julio eyed her mutely, betrayed by his white-knuckled grip on the rake handle.

"Lyle has been hassling Julio and his family." Rachel set the burger containers and the six-pack of Coke she'd picked up down on the deck. "Can you get him to back off?"

"I'll try." Jeff didn't sound hopeful.

"Lunch," Rachel told Julio, nodding at the food. "Go eat." She snapped two Cokes out of the plastic rings. "Here." Handing one of the cans to Jeff, she watched Julio vanish quickly around the corner of the house. "His family was on the wrong side down in Guatemala," she said slowly. "He won't talk about it, but I think his sister is all he has left. I think anyone in a uniform scares him."

"Got it." Jeff nodded. "I'll do my best to back Lyle off." He glanced wistfully at her burger as she peeked at her lunch. "That looks like a Homestyle burger. Let me get my dry, stale, peanut butter sandwich out of the car, and I'll eat with you."

"Don't look so martyred. Since you bought me dinner last night, I'll share with you." Rachel punched his arm lightly. "They're big enough for two, and Joylinn already fed me a cinnamon roll, so I'm not really hungry."

"Lucky you."

"She gave me brownies for dessert, too."

"Her hazelnut wonders? Now, I really think you shouldn't eat any of those," he said virtuously. "Just to help out a friend, I'll eat your share. Remove the temptation, shall we say."

"Over my dead body." She snatched the bag away from him as he began to open it. "I might let you have one—if you behave."

"I don't know if I can behave. I've never tried." He sat down beside her on the deck steps and snagged a chunk of tomato from her salad. "You should have gotten the fries."

"I had an odd encounter on the way back here," Rachel said abruptly. She told Jeff about Cass's confession to her on the street. "I'm sure someone paid him to run me off the road, and I think he was about to tell me who it was, but then he saw something and bolted. Maybe the person who had paid him?" She nibbled at her burger. "Alex Cresswell came out of the drugstore a moment

later. Willis Bard told me he volunteers at the Farm—
teaching kids how to use CAD machines. And I saw Herbert Southern down the block. He could have been close
enough for Cass to spot."

Jeff frowned at his half of the burger. "I don't think
Herbert is involved in this. But it's possible. The rumor
that he just lost some kind of big deal is certainly going
around."

Rachel put down her share of burger, her hunger evap-
orating, wondering if she should tell Jeff about Herbert's
check. "I think it's possible that Herbert's involved," she
said slowly.

"What do you know?" Jeff narrowed his eyes.

"Nothing." She had promised Sandy. Jeff gave her a
narrow stare but went back to eating his burger with no
further comment.

"Just like I remember," he mumbled around a mouthful of burger. "Guess who showed up in town today,"
he said abruptly.

Rachel shook her head, her mouth too full to even
attempt speech.

"Clyde Montaine." Jeff wiped his fingers and nodded
as she raised her eyebrows. "I kid you not. He showed
up to see Henry's lawyer, birth certificate in hand." He
finished his burger and wiped his fingers on a paper napkin from the bag. "I'll tell you something else, too—his
alibi fell apart like a wet tissue."

"Well, we knew it would." Rachel stifled a small pang
of regret as the last of her burger vanished. "You
checked with his friends?"

"A buddy of mine works out of Oakland now. He sort
of unofficially checked out the three guys. And guess
what—one is familiar downtown. He deals crack.
Doesn't get busted very often, but my buddy made it
clear that he could become the center of a lot of precinct
attention. He was the soul of cooperation after that—said
that Montaine didn't show for their regular pool night,
but it was no big deal. Lots of times he's on the road."

"So he could have been up here." Rachel folded her

napkin into a small, neat square and nested it in the empty burger box. "He could have gotten a room in Portland and driven out here."

"Could be." He crumpled his own trash and jammed it into the box. "He's got a record, too. Assault and battery. I guess he gets a bit rowdy after he's had a couple of drinks. And we got the report back from the lab. The DNA test on the scrapings from under Henry's fingernails matches Alex's profile. Now he says the old boy got hysterical and he grabbed his arms to calm him down." He frowned. "You know, I think I believe him."

"That's new, isn't it?"

"A lot of people mentioned Henry's unpredictable behavior, and everything we have against Cresswell is purely circumstantial. Although Lyle is going to bring him in. He hasn't found enough to arrest your kid, and he wants to wrap this up fast. To impress the chief." Jeff's frown deepened. "I don't know. There are too many people involved. I'm not sure it's as simple as it looks." He got to his feet, picked up the bag of trash. "Thanks for the lunch." He offered Rachel a hand and pulled her to her feet. "I'll see if I can find a way to repay you."

"I'll hold you to that promise." She smiled at him, aware of Eduardo and Jorges eating their lunch and openly observing. "Later," she said firmly.

"Later." He sighed. "I'm on my way out to the Farm to have a talk with this Bard person." Jeff touched her face lightly. "Dinner tonight? Will that do as a repayment?"

"You could come over, and I'll cook," she suggested. "I don't think I can handle another late night. And it's a chance to show off." She smiled. "Bring a bottle of white wine."

"You're on. Seven?" He smiled, caught her hand, raised it to his lips for a courtly kiss that made her crew grin, then turned and headed for his car, taking the bag of trash with him.

•   •   •

Rachel started checking out local nurseries while Julio and the crew finished backfilling the irrigation trenches. There wasn't much available locally. Not as much as she had hoped. The Rhinehoffers had the biggest selection. They carried a lot of native species, but they didn't have the curly willow she needed, and the huckleberry plants they had left in stock were too small for what she wanted.

"Sorry," Daren told her with a shrug. "A Portland landscaper came out here to do a place in Hood River. He just about bought us out."

She and Julio would have to spend a couple of days with her trailer, visiting the Willamette Valley nurseries. Rachel sighed, although she'd expected this. It would have been nice to save a couple more days. Still—the place would look great when they were finished, she reassured herself as she drove back to Dr. Meier's house. It would be a unity of contrasts—the herbaceous lawn, the water, shrub banks, all leading the eye to the taller plantings. Open space would balance the dense plantings, with some nice boulders to add interest.

Feeling good about their progress in spite of her minor setback, she dropped the silent Julio at his sister's house at the end of the day. Then she headed directly for the Blossom Super Giant, work clothes and all. It was already past five, and if she wanted to do anything fancy in the way of supper, she needed to get it started now. Pushing the wire cart through the small cross between country store and suburban supermarket, she picked out mushrooms, red and yellow sweet peppers, and a package of chicken breasts. A bunch of fresh parsley and rosemary went into the cart, along with some raspberry and orange sherbet. She stopped next at Joylinn's to buy a round loaf of crusty sourdough and a bag of plain shortbread cookies.

"I want to run the wedding menu past you," Joylinn told her as she wrapped the bread and rang up Rachel's purchases. "I told Elaine I'd have it for her by Monday, and now I'm getting cold feet."

"Don't. You're so creative." Rachel took the packages, resisting the temptation to sample just one piece of shortbread. "She'll be thrilled—I'll bet on it. But I'll be happy to look at it anyway."

"Great." Joylinn smiled. "We had a record day today, too. I guess some of the Hood River sailboarders liked my sandwiches and spread the word. I did a lot of box lunches today." She handed Rachel her change. "I feel like The Bread Box is really going to make it."

"Of course it will." Rachel laughed. "After all, I personally do my best to support it. As much as my waistline can stand." Joylinn laughed and turned to greet a new customer, and Rachel left, smiling. Joylinn had worked hard to make this bakery succeed. She deserved to make it if anyone did.

At home, Peter greeted her with yowling complaints about imminent starvation. Rachel fed him, then sent him firmly outside after he made a sneaky grab for the chicken breasts on the counter. One eye on the clock, Rachel sliced onions, minced garlic, and began to sauté the breasts with the vegetables. As the chicken browned, she added fresh rosemary, a pinch of thyme, and pepper. White wine sizzled as she poured it in. With a sigh of relief, she covered the pan, turned it down to simmer, set a pan of water on to heat for pasta, and bolted for the bedroom. She had lettuce in the fridge, and it wouldn't take more than a few minutes to slice the peppers and a tomato for a simple salad. She was going to make it, she decided as she tossed her clothes into a pile behind the door and hopped into the shower.

She kept listening for the doorbell as she toweled dry and put on black tights and a magenta tunic whose cut flattered her stocky build. Jeff was late as usual. For once she was glad as she finished applying minimal makeup and struggled with her unruly hair. He still hadn't arrived when she decided that there was nothing to be done but leave it alone, and went to check on the chicken. It was done, and the water was simmering in the pasta pot. She debated starting the linguini, then decided to play it safe and wait until he arrived. She turned off the chicken and began to assemble a simple salad.

By half past the hour, she was starting to get worried. Jeff was habitually late, yes—but by no more than a few minutes. But then again, she reminded herself as she shook a jar full of vinaigrette dressing vigorously, he had a job that was full of unexpected delays. The chicken would keep—a bit of a wait would improve it. If he was going to be very late, he'd call her, she told herself. Rachel picked up the article on native grasses in the backyard landscape that she'd been intending to read for a week now and settled into the cushions piled in the corner of the sofa beneath the reading lamp.

She tried not to watch the clock.

It was nearly nine P.M. when someone finally knocked on the door. Rachel flung her magazine aside and hurried to open it, firmly quelling a small spurt of irritation that he hadn't called. His drawn face banished her anger as he brushed past her into the room. "The kid you think ran you off the road was named Cassidy Petrovka, right?"

"I . . . I didn't ask Willis for his last name." Rachel took Jeff's hand. It was cold. Clammy. "What happened?"

"He's dead." Jeff turned away abruptly. "I could use a drink right now."

"Dead, how? How about a glass of wine?" Rachel hurried into the kitchen and poured him a glass of the gewürztraminer she'd used to cook the chicken.

He gulped it as if it was a shot of whiskey, then blinked, and his eyes seemed to focus on her for the first time. "Car accident," he said. "He stole a car. The state cops tried to pick him up, and I guess he panicked when he saw the lights. He took an off-ramp too fast, lost control, and flipped the car. It burned." He looked toward the kitchen again.

Rachel took his glass without a word and emptied the bottle into it. She had another bottle in the refrigerator. She got it out, trying to banish the images that kept forming in her head. "Was . . . was anyone else hurt?" She picked up a glass for herself and carried it and the bottle back into the living room. Jeff shook his head.

"A trucker on the ramp managed to keep his rig from jackknifing—God knows how. A couple of cars got banged up as people tried to get out of the way, but no real injuries," he said thickly. "Just the kid. He was heading east. I guess he figured he had somewhere to run. It's my fault." He emptied the second glass of wine. "I told Lyle we ought to pick him up for questioning. Lyle vetoed it. Said the administrator told him the van wasn't off the Farm property that night. Somebody lied." He clutched the glass so hard that Rachel expected the stem to snap. "If we'd pulled him in, he'd be down at the station right now."

"No." Rachel stared into her empty glass. "If it's anybody's fault, it's mine." She shuddered.

"It's not your fault." Jeff put the glass down and took her hand. "You told me about your encounter with him. What more could you do?"

"I could have called Willis Bard right then—as soon as Cass ran. I was so worried about my bloody *schedule*." Rachel closed her eyes and drew a deep breath. "Sandy made me promise not to tell, and it didn't seem all that important. But . . . this . . . changes things." Her voice shook. "Sandy overheard Herbert and Henry discussing a business deal. It sounded to her as if her dad was buying the hotel. Later she came across a check at the bank from Herbert's account. It was made out to Henry. It was a big check, and . . ." She hesitated, then spoke firmly. "He lied about being home at the time of Henry's death and asked Sandy to back him up. I should have told you, Jeff." Rachel buried her face in her hands. "But Sandy's—"

"You should have. But you're not a cop, sweetheart." He patted her shoulder gently, then pulled her against him. "You didn't know. Hell, *I* didn't seriously consider Herbert as a suspect."

"But you do now?"

"I do now," he said grimly. "I wonder where he was this afternoon—*after* you saw him on the street. What time was that exactly?"

"It was about one-fifteen, give or take five minutes." Rachel bit her lip. "I checked my watch in The Bread Box because I had to pick up those burgers."

"Don't blame yourself, okay?" Jeff lifted her chin until she had to meet his eyes. "You told me about it, remember? I'm the one who gets the blame, if anyone does. But even if you'd called Bard right away, there's no reason to think that events wouldn't have worked out just the same. Cass would have had even more of a reason to steal Doreen Baldwin's car and—"

"Doreen's car?" Rachel frowned.

"Does that mean something?"

"I don't know," she said slowly. "I mean . . . I could be wrong, but I think Herbert's having an affair with Doreen."

Jeff's eyes narrowed, but he didn't say anything.

"If Cass knew Herbert, then maybe he knew about Doreen—where she parked her car—something like that. Did he steal it from in front of her house?"

"In back, actually." Jeff frowned at the blank wall. "She walked downtown—she cleans for Camilla and Catherine Rodriguez who have the florist shop. They live upstairs, and I guess she cleans there on Saturday afternoons, because that's when they do the farmers market in Hood River." He got to his feet. "Mind if I use the phone? I want to talk to Lyle."

"Go ahead." Rachel picked up the wineglasses and bottle and headed for the kitchen. "I'll finish getting dinner ready. I think we both need to eat."

CHAPTER

14

Dinner was a quiet affair. Jeff praised the chicken, but he didn't eat much—although he drank more wine. Blaming himself. Rachel wondered what would have happened if she had chased Cass, caught up with him eventually. Would he have given her a name? Would that have kept him safe? He could have at least gone back to the Farm instead of stealing a car and trying to flee. For that matter—why Doreen's? Her house was clear across town from The Bread Box. Even if he knew her, why not take one closer? People didn't lock their cars in Blossom.

There were too many unanswered questions.

"We got the toxicology report back on Henry." Jeff spoke up after a lengthy silence. His voice was thick, and he was beginning to slur his consonants. "Funny. They found . . . alkaloids. At . . . atropine."

"Atropine?" Rachel deftly snagged the wine bottle as he reached for it. "Why was Henry taking that?"

"His doc says he wasn't." Jeff emptied his glass and contemplated his half-eaten dinner blearily. "I'm sorry. This is really good. I'm just not hungry, I guess."

"Do you mean he was poisoned?"

"Maybe." Jeff shook his head. "Didn't kill him. Th'fall did. Cran . . . cranial hemorrhage." He laughed unevenly. "Joke's on the poisoner, huh? He coulda' waited anoth . . . another day." He gave her a sheepish look. "I think I drank too much."

Too much wine and too little sleep, from the look of him. "What kind of poison?" she asked.

"Dunno yet." He rose unsteadily and picked up his plate. "The lab's running some more tests. Lyle thinks Alex drugged him, then got mad and tossed the old guy over the cliff. The chief thinks so, too. Stupid. Lemme help you with the dishes." He nearly dropped the plate. "I better call the Sisters. Don' want to get busted for a DUI."

"You sure would be driving under the influence." Rachel laughed, but her heart ached. He looked exhausted. "Why don't you stay here? You can use my bed."

He put his arms around her, swayed against her, and for a moment Rachel could feel his muscles trembling with fatigue. Eyes closed, he brushed her hair lightly with his cheek. "I want to stay sometime," he murmured. "A lot. But not like this. Okay?"

"Okay." She kissed him gently. "I'll take you home. You drank all the wine. I'm sober."

In spite of his protests, she coaxed him down to her truck and got him into the passenger seat. She remembered the route to the old Ferren house. It wasn't as bad as she remembered, although the roof of the tiny cottage sagged, and it had obviously received very little care for a long time. Weathered plank shutters were fastened back against the clapboard walls that had long since had any trace of their original paint. The wooden porch was about ready to fall off, but the weedy yard had been mowed, the overgrown bushes trimmed, and the tiny house had an incredible view of the Columbia River far below.

"What a neat place to live."

"You think so?" Jeff gave her a doubtful look as he climbed unsteadily from the truck. "It's a shack, but I've been fixing it up some. I like the location mostly. I figured it might put you off.''

"Why? I bet the view is fantastic.''

"It is.'' He smiled, and some of the tight lines in his face relaxed briefly. "The old man who owns the property is thinking about selling. Five acres. I might try to buy it—if I decide to stay here.''

If. That single syllable carried a lot of echoes. This was a man who didn't compromise on what he perceived as right and wrong. Rachel took his arm and climbed the rickety porch steps with him. The single room inside was clean, the walls and ceiling freshly painted. A faded Oriental carpet covered the floor. Not much furniture, she noted. A futon sofa, a stereo system, and a small table of pale wood, with two matching chairs. The kitchen occupied the back of the room, and a couple of doors implied bedroom and bathroom. At least it had indoor plumbing.

"Thanks for the ride.'' He faced her in the doorway and kissed her lightly.

"I'll pick you up in the morning.'' She was obviously being dismissed. "What time?''

"You don't need to.''

"I have your truck. What time?'' For a moment she held his stare. Then he shrugged, gave her a faint grin, and looked away.

"I'm off. Lyle figures the case is over.'' Bitterness tinged his words. "Come by whenever. I'll be working here somewhere.''

"Henry's funeral is at two. I'm going, so I'll pick you up before that.''

"I'll pass.'' He didn't meet her eyes.

"No, you won't,'' she said gently. "You're part of this community, whether you think you are or not. And we want to see who *doesn't* show up.''

"Okay.'' He still wouldn't meet her eyes. "Whatever you say.''

She touched his cheek, then left, stabbed by complex and undecipherable pain. All the way home she found

herself remembering her father and her mother, laughing
together as they worked in the orchard, played cards, or
just went shopping. She wondered if her mother and Dr.
Meier were married yet and where they were.

She slept in the next morning. It was Sunday. Julio and
his sister, devout Catholics, went to Hood River to hear
mass. This morning, however, the phone got her out of
bed early.

"Hi, kiddo." Her mother's cheerful voice came over
the line. "Congratulate us, love. We did it. And I . . . I'm
so happy."

"Oh, Mom, I'm so happy, too." A lump rose in Rachel's throat. When had she last heard such *joy* in her
mother's voice? "I'm so glad!"

"I feel bad that we bolted off the way we did," her
mother went on cheerfully. "Well, no, I don't really feel
bad about anything. But it did save us a lot of headaches.
How's Elaine doing, by the way?"

"Oh, she's okay. She hired Joylinn to cater after that
Alonzo creep quit. I bet the wedding will be the talk of
Portland—just because it isn't what people expect.
Mom?" She hesitated. "I really am glad, you know."

"I know," her mother said softly. "Thank you. And
guess what?" she went on brightly. "We have a little
surprise for you. We checked marriage records for Las
Vegas, as long as we were here."

"Henry got married there," Rachel said breathlessly.

"You got it." Dr. Meier got on the line now. "What
a job! This really is the marriage capital of the universe.
But we found it. March 14, 1975. Henry Bassinger and
Darlene Ballou. She was from Louisiana."

"Clyde Montaine told us that. He *is* Henry's son."
Quickly Rachel caught them up on the events of the past
thirty-six hours, leaving out Cass's death. "Jeff said
Montaine showed up to meet with Henry's lawyer."

"Things are getting complicated fast," Dr. Meier said
thoughtfully. "Maybe we'd better come home. From

what your mother tells me, you could use someone to keep you out of trouble.''

"Don't come back on my account." Rachel smiled, filled with warmth by the genuine concern in his voice. "Enjoy San Francisco. I'm behaving myself. Really." Time enough later to tell them about Cass.

The phone call left her filled with elation for her mother's newfound happiness, mixed with an odd sadness. The feeling defied easy analysis and left her too restless to spend her free hours on housework or catching up on paperwork. A low-pressure system from the coast had moved in overnight, bringing a few high clouds and cooler temperatures, along with a flow of ocean air up the Gorge. She decided to do a few errands in town before she picked Jeff up. A packed lunch from The Bread Box would be just the thing after last night. Joylinn kept the bakery open on Sundays for the tourists and weekend sailboarders.

Blossom drowsed on summer Sundays. A few tourists strolled the streets, eyeing the old wooden storefronts and the derelict feed mill at the edge of town. They were—as yet—genuinely old, rather than artful restorations. The tourists mostly looked doubtful. But the outdoor tables on the small deck Joylinn had added to her bakery were full of couples in trendy leisure wear and Portland families sightseeing with small children. Rachel leaned against the edge of the crowded espresso bar, waiting to place her order while Joylinn dashed around with plates of rolls, salads, and sandwiches. Her assistant, Celia, worked the espresso machine nonstop. Business was definitely good this morning.

As she waited for a lull, she noticed Willis Bard sitting at the far end of the bar, his eyes fixed on his espresso cup. Rachel made her way over to him. "I'm sorry about Cass," she said.

He jumped as if she had poked him with a pin, then looked up. Quick anger leaped into his eyes, then they dulled, and he looked down at his untouched coffee again. "Not your fault, I guess," he said in a low voice.

"Or no more your fault than ours. The ones you lose are tough."

"He came to talk to me." Rachel sat down on the vacant stool next to him. "He apologized. He said he wasn't going to throw his chance away—because of you."

"But he did." Willis didn't look up at her. "In spades."

"I think . . . someone scared him," Rachel said slowly. "I think that's why he ran. I'm pretty sure that someone paid him to run me off the road. I think he saw that person, panicked, and took off."

Willis raised his head to stare at her incredulously. "I checked the van log," he said. "It was checked out to one of our staff. She said she changed her mind and didn't use it."

"Cass admitted it." She met his gaze, watched him think about it. Slow color grew in his cheeks, and he looked away finally.

"I'll talk to Anne—the woman who checked it out," he said slowly. "And I'll ask around. If the van went out, *somebody* saw it." He gave her a brief sideways glance. "If somebody caused that boy's death . . ." His hands clenched into fists, and he stood up abruptly. "I'm going to go talk to Anne right now." He looked at Rachel directly this time. "If I find anything out, do you want to know?"

"Yes. Very much. Right away, please."

"Okay." He nodded briskly. "I think our local police have written his death off. I sure haven't." He tossed a couple of bills down on the counter, turned on his heel, and strode out of the bakery.

Rachel went back to the counter, where she ordered lunches for two from the harried Joylinn. "Not right now," she assured her friend. "I'll stop by later—is eleven-thirty okay?"

"Bless you, girl." Joylinn gave her a quick grin. "I'll make 'em special. If this keeps up, I'm going to have to hire more help!" She whisked away to take the order of a middle-aged couple in matching Lands' End short sets at a nearby table.

Smiling, Rachel left the bakery, feeling virtuous as she passed the decimated display trays of rolls and pastries. Outside she dropped a quarter in the corner pay phone and dialed Jeff's number. She glanced at her watch as the phone rang. Nearly ten o'clock. Even with a bad hangover, he should be up.

"Hello?" He picked it up on the seventh ring.

"I was about to give up. Don't tell me you were still asleep!"

"I was under the sink cleaning out the trap, thank you." He didn't sound too bad. "Actually, I've been up for a couple of hours."

"You do better after too much wine than I do." Rachel laughed.

"I went running this morning. After the first half-mile, I decided I'd live." A smile sounded in his voice. "What's up?"

She outlined her lunch plans.

"I think I'll be ready for food by then," he said. "After the funeral I think I'm going to need some private time."

"Could you handle a little company?"

"Yes," he said quietly. "I could."

"I'll see you at noon, then." Slowly Rachel replaced the receiver. Jeff was too hard on himself. He always had been. As she got back into her truck, she noticed the dent on the fender. Talking to Willis had made her think about the incident, she supposed. It looked ugly, marring the pristine new-car perfection of the truck. On a whim, she turned left and drove down to the gas station run by the Taxi Sisters.

Earlene was pumping gas this morning. She nodded to Rachel as she pulled in, topped off the new, forest-green Jeep Cherokee she was filling, twisted the cap back on, and disappeared into the grimy concrete-block building with the credit card the driver handed her. A moment later she emerged, handed card and credit slip to the man for his signature, then stuffed the slip into her pocket as she sauntered over to Rachel.

"Whatever happened to cash?" She shifted the unlighted stub of her perennial cigar over to the other side of her mouth. "Now it's all plastic. The big-city folk afraid of catching a disease from it or somethin'?" She shook her head. "We got to pay the companies to handle their damn cards. Roberta says we got to, or everybody'll go to the Chevron station outside o' Hood River. Hell, maybe she's right." She shrugged her linebacker shoulders. "We sure got plenty o' business. But if they want to ride in my cab, they pay cash. I don't care what Roberta says." She drew a remarkably gentle finger across the shallow dent in the truck's end. "So you ready to get that dent taken care of?"

"Yep." Rachel nodded. "The truck looks so *nice* otherwise. Can you tell me about how much it's going to run?"

"Four hundred. Maybe less, if I find a deal on a used fender at the yard. Might be tough, new as this baby is." Earlene examined the dent more closely. "Bodywork takes a lot of time—costs a bundle."

Rachel did some quick mental calculations and blessed Dr. Meier for the size and scale of his landscape plans. "Go ahead." She nodded decisively. "After all, this truck is advertising."

"I'll make it shine for you, honey." Earlene's cigar bobbed emphatically. "You won't know you got dinged. Be glad it was minor." She jerked her head toward the rear of the lot. Rachel followed her gaze. A twisted heap of burned and blackened metal had been a car once. Rachel shuddered.

"Yeah, he messed up good, didn't he?" She shook her head, her expression grim. "Lot o' kids go bad these days. A couple of good lickings early on would've straightened out most of 'em, I bet. But, shoot, he was pretty young to get offed like that. Wonder who did it." She shrugged. "Hell, maybe they were after the Baldwin woman and didn't mean to get the kid at all. She better watch her back.''

"What?'' Rachel stared at her. "What are you saying? I thought Cass lost control on the freeway and flipped the car.''

"Oh, he lost control all right.'' She squatted to peer at Rachel's dented fender. '' 'Berta noticed it right off when she started poking around in the mess. Somebody cut a speed-sensor cable on a wheel. Take a high-speed turn, the wheels don't straighten out. I guess that's what happened. So he run right into that concrete divider and . . . blooey.''

Cass had been murdered. Or had somebody meant to kill Doreen? And if so, why? "Did you . . . did you call the police?''

"Talked to Lyle. Didn't make his day, I don't think. First he said it happened in the crash. Uh-uh.'' She spat onto the oil-stained asphalt. "Not when it was cut clean, it didn't. Now he's making it out to be some sort of drug revenge thing.'' She shrugged. "Whoever did it knew their way around a car. I bet none of those punks out at that fancy farm can change oil. But, hey—those kids are all gang. He's probably right. I sure didn't vote for havin' that Youth Farm in the backyard, I'll tell you. Dunno who did.'' She stood, wincing and rubbing her knees. "Bet it was the Hood River folks. They didn't want it in their backyard, so they figured they'd dump it on us. It'll come in less than three hundred. I don't have to get you a new fender.''

"Thanks,'' Rachel said faintly. Another murder. She swallowed, wondering if Jeff knew about this. "How long is it going to take to fix it?'' She forced her mind back to the matter at hand. "I'm in the middle of a big job and I need it every day.''

"You bring it in after work, I'll have it for you by morning. I don't sleep much anymore.'' Earlene moved off in the direction of the office. "Roberta c'n handle any tow calls. Might have to drive it with primer for a day or so. That okay?''

"No problem," Rachel said, wanting only to get to a phone. They settled on Wednesday evening, and Rachel used the station phone to call Jeff while Earlene went out to pump more gas. But this time Jeff didn't answer. The machine picked up on the third ring, and she hung up without leaving a message. She'd be seeing him soon enough, she thought. On her way back to the truck, she shuddered as she passed the twisted ruin that had been Doreen's Acura.

If someone had meant to kill Cass, how would the killer have known which car he'd steal?

Who would want to kill Doreen and why?

Not Sandy's father. Herbert wouldn't do something like this. Rachel started the engine but didn't pull out of the station lot right away. It was beginning to feel to her that the events surrounding Henry Bassinger's death formed a coherent picture—only she wasn't looking at it right.

"You havin' trouble?" Earlene paused beside the truck on her way back to the office with another despised credit card.

"I'm hunting for a missing puzzle piece," Rachel said. "I think I know where to look for it." Earlene gave her a perplexed look and stomped off to run the card through the machine.

"I guess you can't turn back the clock," Rachel said out loud to herself as she pulled out into Blossom's sparse Sunday-morning traffic. "But sometimes you can take a peek at yesterday."

Doreen Baldwin was out in her yard when Rachel pulled up in front of Sandy's house. She was watering the ranks of potted herbs that lined her porch, singing some hymn to herself. "You'll have to pardon me." She smiled over the fence at Rachel. "I'm not really the religious sort, but Sunday mornings just feel kind of holy to me. Sandy's not home, honey. She and Bill went shopping."

"Oh." Rachel stopped, disappointed. Sandy never went anywhere on Sunday before noon.

"You look like you're troubled." Doreen peered at her, lips pursed. "Can I help you out?"

"Oh, it's okay." She eyed the narrow strip of grass between Doreen's fence and the street. "I'm sorry about your car. I never noticed it. You must have parked it in back."

"Sure did. There's a concrete patch where a garage used to be. Fell down in an ice storm a few years back." Doreen nodded and sighed. "It was a really nice car—only three years old. But mostly I'm sorry for the boy who stole it. My insurance will pay for the car." She smiled, her face once more hinting at what must have been stunning beauty when she was younger.

"I'm surprised he'd steal a car in broad daylight around here. There are houses all along the street."

"I guess I left the keys in it when I brought the groceries in." She clucked her tongue ruefully. "Stupid of me. Had my hands full and forgot. I guess I just don't worry about car thieves in Blossom. You sure there's nothing I can help you with?"

Rachel sighed and glanced at her watch. "I was going to ask Sandy to come with me over to the Bassinger Hotel. I've got to pick up some tools I left there and I guess . . . I just don't want to go there by myself." She made a face. "Doreen, you cleaned for Henry. Did you ever notice a really thick red leather photo album lying around? He had it out once when I was there, and he said something about ghosts living in it." She smiled at the older woman. "It occurred to me that there might be a picture of his wife in it."

"His wife!" Doreen arched her eyebrows. "Do you really believe that tale? That Henry got married way back when?" She laughed. "He liked to tease, honey. In fact . . ." She glanced at Rachel slyly. "I got this feeling that he was . . . you know . . . queer."

"Oh, he was married all right." Rachel nodded. "In Las Vegas."

"Well, maybe and maybe not." She laughed again and shook her head. "I hear some young fellow already showed up to say he's Henry's long-lost son. Me, I bet old Henry's laughin' at all this, wherever he is." She brushed loam from her trim jeans. "I'm fixing to go in and have some lemonade. You want to join me? You know . . ." She frowned. "I think I do remember seeing that album once. That's right. I noticed it mostly 'cause the leather was all gray with mildew. But when I offered to clean it up, Henry told me not to bother. It was maybe a couple of years ago." She was moving toward the porch as she spoke.

Rachel glanced at Sandy's empty house and followed. She still had time to get out to the hotel, pick up the toolbox she'd left there, and maybe have a quick look for the album. Doreen wasn't about to lose a guest for lemonade by remembering the whereabouts of the album too quickly.

And she might let something slip. Something that might suggest a connection between Cass and her car and somebody with murder on their mind.

Doreen sat her down on the sofa where she and Sandy had sat on Thursday night, then disappeared into the kitchen. The refrigerator door slammed, and ice tinkled against glass. "He was looking at it in the lounge," she called through the kitchen door. "But he didn't keep it there, I know. It's probably out in the gazebo. I'm sure I'd have dusted it if it was lying around. But I told him on my first day out there that no way was I going to hike out there to clean that place. Not unless God gave me wings." Doreen appeared in the doorway with a laden tray. "Don't you go out there looking for it, young lady. I heard they let that nephew of his out on bail. We don't want to find you at the bottom of the Gorge, too. We don't need two murders."

"We've already had two murders." Rachel gratefully accepted the tall, ice-filled glass that Doreen handed her. "The boy who stole your car was murdered, too. Someone fixed the car to crash."

"Oh, mercy." Doreen clasped her hands to her throat.

"That's *awful*. What if . . . what if he'd abandoned it and I'd driven it? Oh, my lord!"

If she was faking her alarm and surprise, she was doing a good job. Rachel sipped her lemonade. "There's a woman out at a nursing home near here who says she met Darlene Ballou in San Francisco, back when she and Henry were first married. I'm going to go talk to her."

"Darlene who? You mean there really *is* a wife?" Doreen sat forward on the wing-back chair across from the sofa, her expression bright with curiosity. "I surely didn't believe it. So what do you think? Did this mystery wife come into town and do him in?" Her eyes glittered. "Wouldn't someone have seen her? And why would she murder him?"

"Maybe she lived around here." Rachel sipped her lemonade. "She could have moved here right after Henry came back." The drink was strongly flavored with mint and had a slightly bitter herb taste.

"White ginseng," Doreen said, noticing her expression. "The Chinese use it for all kinds of tonic reasons. It's a very powerful herb—if a wee bit bitter." She smiled wryly. "I'll get you some milk if you'd rather not finish it."

"Oh, it's fine." Rachel took a large swallow. "His son Clyde is the more likely suspect," she went on.

"Well, he'll inherit a nice piece of real estate. If he's who he says he is." Doreen finished her own lemonade, her composure unruffled, and refilled both glasses from the glass pitcher she'd set on the coffee table. "I bet that nephew of his thought he was gonna get that place. Joke's on him." She shook her head. "He's family, too. That's awful."

"If you believe Alex did it. You know, you have a bit of a Southern accent." Rachel sipped politely at her fresh glass of lemonade. The ginseng wasn't so bad once you got used to it. "I never noticed it before."

"I worked in New Orleans—N'Aw-lee-ans—for a while. Cleaning hotel rooms." Doreen's eyes were sharp in spite of her easy smile. "I pick up accents easy."

"Well, I guess I'd better go get the rest of my tools." Rachel glanced at her watch again, debating. Jeff would be furious if she went to the hotel by herself.

How dangerous could it be? she reasoned as she carried her empty lemonade glass into the kitchen. If she saw any sign that anyone was there, she'd leave instantly. And why would anyone be there now? The police had plenty of time to search for whatever they were looking for.

Doreen offered her a bottle of lemonade to take with her, but Rachel declined with thanks.

"Do you want me to come along?" Doreen asked as she walked Rachel to her truck. "I'm off this afternoon."

"No, thanks." Rachel gave her a smile as she climbed into the cab. "I was just being a sissy. I'll be fine."

She hoped so anyway. As she drove away, she glanced in her rearview mirror to find Doreen standing at the curb, watching her drive out of sight.

CHAPTER

15

The old hotel had an oddly spooky feel to it. Only a few days had passed since Henry's death, but already the place felt abandoned. Derelict. Leaves drifted in a small shoal against the stone curb that edged the parking lot, and a loose shutter banged in the breeze. It was as if the old hotel mourned the passing of its former owner.

Nerves, Rachel told herself as she got out of the truck. The summer afternoon resonated with bird trills, the squawk of jays, and a background insect hum that never stopped. A squirrel chattered angrily at her as she crossed the needle-strewn asphalt to the walk that circled the building. She had a key. It opened the lounge door in back. Henry had let her stow her tools in an empty closet between the lounge and the dining room, since the outbuildings were mostly roofless ruins. She had laid a plastic tarp down over the wide, hand-milled fir planks of the floor. It must have once held china, chairs, or maybe bulky suitcases or trunks brought by guests.

The heavy French doors creaked as she swung them open. The lounge gaped cavernously, full of shadow. Rachel stepped inside, the hair on the back of her neck prickling. She caught a whiff of old dead ashes from the

big stone fireplace and heard the tiny rodent scuttle of a
mouse along one wall. As she moved into the center of
the room, the walls seemed to waver and shift. All of a
sudden, the room was full of light. Men and women sat
in the chairs and sofas, laughing, drinking, chatting with
each other as flames leaped in the fireplace and a mus-
tached bartender mixed drinks in a silver shaker.

The image came and went in a blink of time. Rachel
gasped as she backed into the oak bar. She spun, her heart
pounding as something moved in the shadows. Recognizing her reflection in the mirror behind the bar, she
laughed weakly, her heart still beating fast. Again, something moved at the edge of her vision, but when she
whirled to face it, she saw . . . nothing.

Icy fear trickled down her spine. Something was happening to her. The floor tilted suddenly under her feet,
and she clutched the bar for support, her head beginning
to throb. *Allergy,* she thought. *You're allergic to Doreen's ginseng.* Forcing herself to ignore the increasing
headache, feeling slightly better, she took a deep breath
and looked around. The album would be in the lounge,
Doreen had said. Or the gazebo. She started looking—
opening drawers in the antique escritoire that stood
against the wall, searching the high shelves in the closet
where she kept her tools, investigating the shelves behind
the bar, opening every cupboard and drawer she could
discover. Her headache diminished, although she found
herself squinting in the dimming light. *Cloudy,* she
thought vaguely. *It's going to rain.*

She found dust, cobwebs, and the occasional abandoned mouse nest. Nothing more. Opening the tap in the
sink behind the bar until the water ran clear from the
rusty pipes, she drank handfuls of cold water. It tasted
wonderful, hot as she was. Her skin burned, as if she'd
been out in the sun too long, and she wondered if she
was developing hives from the ginseng. Her head began
to hurt again, and she struggled to think clearly.

The gazebo. The album was in the gazebo, and she

had to hurry. There was a reason she had to hurry, but she couldn't recall it at the moment. Shadows moved at the edges of her vision, stalking her as she fled the lounge. It wasn't cloudy—but the sun seemed so feeble—as if it was winter, not summer. Panting, struggling with an unreasonable fear that wanted to seize her by the throat, she held tightly to the stone wall that edged the terrace, facing the walkway to the gazebo. *A panic attack,* she thought with brief surprise. *I'm having a panic attack.* . . . Someone—perhaps the police—had strung yellow plastic tape across the opening. She tugged at it, her hands unaccountably shaking. It broke like cobwebs, and she nearly fell backward.

Something . . . something was wrong.

She pushed sweat-damp hair from her forehead, trying to think, trying to remember something important. Lemonade, she thought, but whatever it was that she was trying to remember, it slipped away, dissolving like mist. Something was back *there.* Behind her. The sudden certainty burned her like whiplash, and she lurched forward onto the plank walk. The boards seemed to undulate beneath her feet, but she ran, pursued by shadows.

Halfway to the gazebo, she stumbled and fell to her knees. The waterfall tumbled over the lip of the Gorge wall here, misting her face and hands with clammy spray. Far, far below, water churned to foam around wet, gray rocks. This was where Henry fell.

Shivering, Rachel couldn't move. The roots of firs and cedars above her pried slowly, imperceptibly, at the stone piers that supported the plank walk. She could feel the pressure, feel the stones slowly giving way. With a cry, she scrambled to her feet and ran, her feet thudding a panicked drumbeat on the weathered planks.

With a cry, she burst through the open door of the gazebo, trembling with relief. Filmed with cold sweat, her stomach clenched with nausea, she stared around the octagonal stone structure. Cracks webbed the mortar in the polished stone slabs of the floor, and she imagined that she could see them widening, feel the stones tilting beneath her feet as the whole structure cracked and slid a thousand feet down to the river in a deadly avalanche of stone and wood . . .

Stop it! Rachel clenched her fists until her nails bit her palms, concentrating on the pain. *Get a grip,* she told herself. It seemed a little lighter now, as if the clouds were thinning. Only there weren't any clouds, were there? The album. She remembered now—she was looking for pictures. Red leather. Full of Henry's ghosts.

Fighting down the terror, she forced herself to look around the sparsely furnished room. A heavily carved leather-and-wood chair stood near one of the windows that overlooked the river, flanked by a reading lamp. A small writing desk was near the door. That, a carved chest, and a sofa upholstered in leather across from the empty fireplace made up the rest of the furnishings. The leather upholstery was cracked and stained, and mouse droppings lay scattered across the open front of the writing desk.

Rachel stumbled to it first, pulling open the drawers with jerky haste. She found nothing but a pile of yellowed stationery in one drawer and a clutter of well-thumbed paperback mysteries in another. Stiff-legged, she crossed to the chest, unsteady on a floor that rolled with the slow surge of the ocean. *Hurry,* she thought numbly. *Then go call Jeff for help.* She watched a hand that felt disembodied reach out to lift the heavy lid of the chest.

The album was there.

Rachel tugged the heavy leather volume out of the drawer, laid it on the writing desk. The rich crimson leather had darkened with age to the color of old blood, and Rachel's stomach heaved again as she opened the cover. Forcing herself to concentrate, she turned the pages slowly, scanning the faded black-and-white images.

She recognized Henry's father from Historical Society photos, assumed that the others in those pictures were probably family members. Then there were pictures of

couples or small groups posed in front of the new hotel.
Guests? She pursed her lips in a soundless whistle, her
head almost clear again. The gardens had indeed been
wonderful—a fairyland of lawn, stone-paved walks, private nooks, and dozens of exotic plantings. She felt a
pang of regret for the ravages of neglect and time that
had decimated the more delicate species and blurred the
carefully laid-out landscape beneath years of fallen leaves
and accumulated soil.

She turned another page and stopped. So far the photos
on each page had been meticulously laid out, names and
dates inscribed beneath each picture in the same spidery
hand. This page differed. The lines of script didn't seem
to correspond with the photographs. The page held several pictures, crammed together, crookedly aligned, some
overlapping the others. In one, Henry lifted a trumpet in
a murky room that might have been a club or a bar. In
another he laughed at the camera, a dark-haired young
woman on his arm. In the center, superimposed on the
surrounding photos, he held a bundled infant in his arms,
his expression almost defiantly proud, the dark-haired
woman hovering behind him.

Rachel bent to peer at the woman, squinting because
the light was fading again. The woman was stunning—
her delicate heart-shaped face framed by wings of glossy
dark hair, her huge eyes accentuated by deft makeup, her
Cupid's bow of a mouth shaping a demure and knowing
smile. *Darlene* had been scrawled across one corner of
the photo in Henry's familiar jagged hand.

Oh, yes, Darlene Ballou had been a beautiful woman.
Doreen Baldwin still was. Rachel straightened, closing
the album with trembling fingers. There had been a picture . . . She pressed her palms against her throbbing temples, trying to bring the memory into focus. A picture in
Doreen's living room . . . A child.

Clyde Montaine as a child. No wonder he had looked
familiar.

Clutching the heavy album, Rachel stumbled toward
the door. But the floor tilted suddenly, and she dropped

the album, crying out as she clutched a windowsill to
keep from falling. Deeply overhung to keep out the rain,
the window had no glass. Clutching the frame, leaning
out over the sill, she found herself staring up at the cliff-
side greenhouse with its riot of escaped plants. She had
picked roses there years ago. She and Sandy . . .

A small core of sanity in the maelstrom of fear that
threatened her whispered that the floor was level, that her
balance was at fault. The gazebo wasn't about to fall.
She clutched at that whisper of calm, breathing as hard
as if she'd been running, focusing on the rioting plants
in what had once been an herb garden. Doreen was Darlene. Henry had known that . . . had paid her. She looked
for rose blossoms. Roses were important. . . . But there
were no roses, only white, trumpet-shaped blooms that
blared triumphantly from their stalks. Trumpets, she
thought. Blowing jazz. The devil's trumpets.

Devil's trumpet. Suddenly she understood.

Someone grabbed her.

She shrieked, feeling claws. The shadows had reached
her. She scrabbled at the sill in an ecstasy of terror, pulling herself over, struggling desperately to escape the
monsters behind her. Below her . . . green. Soft as a pillow, soft green, safe. . . . She felt the air holding her like
a giant hand. Cushioning her. In a moment she'd be free,
would drop gently into that sheltering hand . . .

"Rachel!" The anguished cry rent the mists of mad-
ness in her brain. Briefly.

"Jeff." She shaped the word silently with dry lips,
fighting her traitorous muscles, willing her body not to
fall. He loomed over her, and part of her cringed in terror
at the shapeless menace. Jeff. Monster. The dual visions
superimposed themselves on her retina, and for an instant
Rachel teetered on the sill.

"My God, don't," he whispered brokenly. "Please."

With an inarticulate cry, she wrenched herself back
from the drop, shuddering violently as he seized her and
pulled her back from the edge.

"Poison," she managed to gasp out. "The trumpet. Devil's trumpet..." Then a darkness full of demon faces swallowed her whole, sucking her down into terrible shrieking and the faces of evil.

CHAPTER

16

Rachel faded in and out between dark dreams and a place of bright white light. Body parts hurt and she struggled once, briefly, with hands that hold her, forced her down, Then some of the dark things went away. Her mother's face appeared in the brightness. Jeff's face, too. They talked to her, or maybe she was talking to them, or only thinking. Voices droned on and on in her head, the faces came and went, and sometimes they didn't belong to either her mother or Jeff.

Then finally the bright lights came together, and she found herself staring at the foot of a bed, across white sheets. Time to get up, she thought, but the covers were white, and her quilt was green and gold. For an instant she hovered in that drowsy interval between consciousness and sleep, waiting for memory to kick in and remind her of where she was.

"Rachel?" Jeff's voice. He leaned over her and the carved lines of sleeplessness and worry in his unshaven face jolted her awake.

"Jeff? Where . . . what happened?" She lifted her head and realized she was in a white bed, surrounded by white walls. Jeff hunched on a chair beside her. "I'm in the hospital.'' She swallowed and winced at the rawness of her throat. "The gazebo," she said, struggling to sit up. "The datura. I saw it."

"Easy. Don't rush things." Jeff's arm was around her, and Rachel was shocked by just how much she needed his support in order to sit up. "You had us pretty scared for a while."

"It was datura—jimsonweed. Sometimes called devil's trumpet. That's what killed Henry." She spoke breathlessly, trembling with her need to force the words past the raw swelling in her throat before the dark specks hovering at the edges of her vision rushed in to drown her again. "It was in the lemonade. Doreen made it. She was Henry's wife. That's why he acted so strange before he died. She didn't give him enough to kill him. But it can make you hallucinate. He fell . . ." She sank back, the dark specks swarming across her vision now, hearing Jeff's voice calling for a nurse, oddly distant.

He was still there when she opened her eyes again. Asleep this time, chin on his chest, he looked utterly exhausted. She watched him, very tired, filled with warmth as she took in the two days' worth of stubble on his face, his rumpled clothes. As if he had slept here, just like this.

The door opened, and her mother peeked in. She looked more rested than Jeff, although just as anxious. But her tense expression dissolved into a smile as she noticed Rachel's wakefulness.

"Thank God." She tiptoed over to the bed and took her daughter's hands. "Jeff said you were awake earlier," she whispered. "Oh, thank God, you're all right." Her own hands were trembling. Rachel squeezed them, realizing that she had a little more strength this time.

"I'm okay, Mom. Really." She glanced at Jeff, who still slept. "Poor guy. He looks exhausted."

"He's been here ever since the ambulance brought you in. He made me go home and sleep." Her mother gave him a fond look. "I always liked him. I don't know what made your aunt Catherine take against him so."

"What?" Rachel blinked, trying to put her mother's words into perspective. "Aunt Cat didn't like him?"

"She didn't want to see you get serious about him, that's all. I think she has changed her mind, by the way."

Rachel wondered suddenly about the mail Jeff said he had sent—the mail she'd never received. Aunt Catherine brought in the mail every afternoon.

A puzzle for later. Jeff woke with a start and stared down at Rachel, rubbing his red-rimmed eyes. "Promise you won't pass out this time, okay? I don't think my heart can take it twice in one day."

She smiled up at him. "I'll do my best. Promise." Her smile faltered. "What about Doreen? Did you check the lemonade?"

"Oh, she's locked up safe and sound," Jeff said grimly. "The lab was able to identify datura in your stomach contents and in the pitcher of lemonade in her house. She'd dumped it out but hadn't washed it yet. We were lucky there. And, yes, it's the source of the alkaloid found in Henry. She claims that she only wanted to make him act a little crazy, to punish him for abandoning her. But it turns out she's been regularly depositing money into her bank account. And guess what? The sum equals the one Henry withdrew every month. So it's a little hard to see why she'd be threatening her nice little pension—unless she had a bigger one in mind."

"What about Clyde Montaine?" Rachel started to push herself up on the pillow, which earned her instant assistance from Jeff. She discovered that she still needed it, and his arm felt good around her. "Was he in on it, too? For the inheritance?"

"We don't know yet." Jeff nodded. "Lyle got a warrant, and we searched his motel room and car last night. He wasn't there. He hasn't been back since." He frowned. "I think someone tipped him off we were on the way. I wonder who." He shrugged. "Anyway, we got some mud scrapings from the underside of his car. We sent it to the lab along with soil samples from the hotel grounds and that clump of bushes along the road where your man saw a white car. The lab says that some of the mud on the car definitely came from this area—apparently it's a distinctive soil type. It wasn't fresh, either. We've put out an APB for him—for questioning at the moment.''

Dr. Meier stuck his head in the door. "Is this a party?"

"Come on in," Rachel invited gaily. "I'm feeling better by the minute."

"Good." Dr. Meier smiled a fine bedside smile, but a shadow of worry lurked in his eyes. That shadow made Rachel wonder just how lucky she was to be sitting up and chatting. She shivered, and he saw it. "Yes, it was close," he said soberly. "You're a strong young lady fortunately." He put his arm around Rachel's mother as she caught her breath. "But you'll be fine. They should let you out anytime now."

Jeff had taken her hand, and she returned the pressure of his fingers, suddenly appreciating the summer sun shining through the window in a way she never really had before.

"I think we should go and let her rest." Dr. Meier looked over Deborah's head to give Jeff a quiet smile. "We'll be back later."

"I'll be back this evening with some dinner for you. We ate in the cafeteria." Her mother made a face. "When we do come back, young lady, I have a few things to say about the kind of risks you've been taking lately. Quite a few things," she called back over her shoulder as Joshua Meier ushered her firmly from the room. "Just you wait . . ." The words floated in from the hall, punctuated by a yelp and a giggle.

"I think he's discovered how ticklish she is." Rachel looked after her mother and Joshua with a smile. "They're good for each other." Her smile softened as Jeff closed his other hand around hers, clasping it tightly. "Thank you," she said, meeting his pale eyes. "For saving my life."

"I thought for a minute I was going to be responsible for your death," Jeff said gruffly. "You looked like you'd seen the bogeyman for sure when I showed up in the gazebo. You almost jumped right out the window.''

''I almost did. I think that's what Doreen hoped for—that I'd fall, just like Henry did.'' She looked away, reliving briefly the blind, consuming terror of that moment. ''I . . . it was your voice. Calling my name. It gave me something to hang on to.'' She turned back to him as he squeezed her hand. His eyes met hers, intense, full of shifting light.

His cell phone rang.

''Shit,'' he said softly under his breath. He glanced indecisively down as he freed it from its holster, thumb poised to turn it off.

''Better answer.'' Rachel smiled and tapped his arm lightly. ''We've got plenty of time.''

''All the time in the world.'' He grinned at her, flipped the phone open. ''Price here.'' He frowned, glanced at Rachel. ''Out of the question. She's still in the hospital. I don't care if . . .''

''What is it?'' Rachel asked.

Jeff frowned, hesitated. ''Lyle. Montaine's lawyer just called him. Montaine wants to come in and give himself up, but he wants to see you first. I told Lyle no way.''

''Why not?'' Rachel tilted her head. ''I'd like to hear what he has to say. Besides,'' she added as she gave him a sly smile, ''I'll be safe enough. You're here.''

''Flattery gets you nowhere,'' Jeff muttered under his breath. But he turned back to the phone. ''Okay. Fine. He gets fifteen minutes. She nearly *died,* damn it. Uh-huh. Don't worry. See you in fifteen minutes.'' He closed the phone, his brow furrowed. ''I don't like this much. What's Montaine up to?''

''I guess we'll find out.''

Jeff didn't look mollified.

''Jeff . . . what made you come out to the hotel?'' Rachel reached for his hand again. ''Only Doreen knew I was out there. I'm sure she didn't tell you.''

''No, she didn't.'' He shook his head and gave her a lopsided smile. ''You neglected a resident of the Orchard

View Retirement Village. One Anne-Marie Celestine DeRochers-Smith to be exact. She had a piece of valuable information for you concerning the identity of one Henry Bassinger's wife, and you neglected to avail yourself of it.''

Rachel smothered a laugh. He had Anne-Marie's rather severe voice and accent down perfectly. ''So she called you?''

''Yes, she did. Right after you visited. So I called the Taxi Sisters, got a ride down to your place for my truck, and I went out there. Apparently Lyle had shrugged her off, and she was not pleased. Her ditzy old lady friend—who has a remarkably clear memory and a damned good memory for faces, by the way—identified Doreen from a snapshot I'd brought.''

''You suspected Doreen?'' Rachel's eyes widened. ''I kept telling myself for the longest time that it couldn't be her. She's so nice. But then there was Cass. And her car.''

''Yes. Her car.'' Jeff nodded, his expression grim. ''Actually, I've been wondering about her for a while now. She cleans for some very interesting people. Like Herbert Southern, Henry, the head administrator of the Youth Farm . . .''

''Cass!'' Rachel exclaimed. ''She could have met him there.''

''I wondered why someone would rig Doreen's car to crash—why would anyone expect the kid to steal it? They were either after Doreen or they knew he'd take it.''

''She offered it to him!'' Rachel covered her mouth with her hands. ''That was it, right? She offered him a way out of town and maybe money. Maybe he decided it was safer than turning her in and taking his chances?''

''She's not admitting anything, of course,'' Jeff said grimly. ''But I think you've got the picture. It's certain that the Acura was rigged so that whoever drove the car would go out of control at a high speed. She called the theft in as soon as he left. She probably knew where he'd head—or maybe suggested some sort of haven that could best be reached by the interstate."

"That's how she works, isn't it?" Rachel said softly. "She never kills anyone directly, but she sets up an accident, then lets it happen. Maybe she can tell herself she didn't kill Henry or Cass. They had accidents. Things could have turned out differently."

"I don't know what she's thinking, but I think we've got enough evidence to put in front of a jury that she tried to kill you." Jeff squeezed her hand. "By the way, if we're going to continue this relationship, we need to have a serious understanding—that you do not take the role of murder victim for me again. Okay?"

This relationship? "Okay," Rachel said meekly, "I swear."

He peered at her, and she raised both hands, laughing. "Really. I promise. But you still didn't tell me how you ended up at the hotel just in the nick of time."

"Oh." He shuffled his feet, looking slightly uncomfortable. "Well . . . Madame Anne-Marie has this friend Guy in a wheelchair?"

"I've met him."

"Well—turns out he's a retired detective from Seattle. Moved down here to be near his daughter a few years ago—before his accident. Anyway, he suggested that Doreen probably had a key to the hotel, since she cleaned, and that the safest place to keep any damning evidence would be there, rather than in her house, since the hotel had already been searched. Which I was also thinking," he said quickly. "So I got a search warrant from Judge Cramer—who was not happy at being interrupted on his way out to lunch with his wife, I might say." He looked mildly pained. "But it all worked out. I saw your truck, and when you didn't answer my call inside, I came out back. Just about in time to scare you right over the edge of the gazebo."

"If you hadn't found me, I would have died—even if I hadn't fallen." She laced her fingers tightly in his. "I recognized the datura near the greenhouse. I remember reading something about the extensive herb garden at the hotel back in its heyday. And we've all heard the rumors about old Mrs. Bassinger being a witch. I bet she was an herbalist. Datura isn't a native plant.''

''Why would someone plant something that poisonous?''

''Henry's father had asthma.'' She shrugged. ''Datura was used as a treatment for asthma, but it was so dangerous that people stopped using it.'' She looked up at him shyly. ''Jeff . . .''

''Don't.'' He leaned forward and kissed her, without speaking. The kiss went on and on, and for a while nothing else mattered. Then someone cleared her throat—and they jumped apart like guilty teens.

''Don't people ever knock?'' Combing his hair with his fingers, Jeff turned around to face the amused nurse. ''What happened to privacy?''

''This is a hospital,'' she said with mock severity. ''We don't knock. And there are two men asking to talk with you, Miss O'Connor. Good thing I checked first.''

''Montaine and his lawyer.'' Jeff stood, straightening the neck of his shirt.

''Thanks.'' Rachel smiled at the nurse, who winked, muttered something about being young once, and vanished into the hallway.

''I still don't like this, but we'll see what we've got. Lyle's on his way over. He'll handle the booking.'' He gave his shirt another tug, then followed the nurse out into the hallway. Rachel lay back and listened to his receding footsteps.

He was back in a few minutes, his expression grimly wary, escorting Clyde Montaine in slacks and a casual shirt, followed closely by a round-faced man in an expensive suit. He looked about as grim as Jeff did.

''Miss O'Connor.'' Clyde stopped just inside the doorway and gave Rachel a short bow. ''I figured I might not get the chance to do the apology thing once the shit hit the fan, so hey.'' He shrugged. ''I got a little leverage yet. I'll start with the apology and take it from there.''

"Mr. Montaine, there is no need . . ." the lawyer began.

"Yeah, there is." Clyde cut off his tense words with a chopping hand gesture. "I told you what was going down. I even signed that letter saying you warned me not to do this, and if I did it anyway, you weren't responsible. So you're not responsible. Now shut up."

The round-faced man flushed and gave the musician a brief hard look, but he closed his mouth and didn't say anything more.

"Okay, cop." Montaine turned to Jeff. "Go ahead and do the Miranda bit, so we don't screw this up."

Jeff shrugged and recited his rights. Satisfied, the musician turned back to Rachel. "I'm sorry you got hurt. I don't know if you believe me, but I didn't know what my mother was doing. I haven't seen her since she moved up here." A brief frown crossed his face. "I told her back then that if she wanted to hang out with my dad, then I was through with her. No way I was gonna come see her. So I didn't talk to her for a few years." He lifted one shoulder in a lopsided shrug, his expression apologetic. "I was on the road a lot anyway—doing second-rate clubs with this road band I was with back then. I dunno." He shrugged again. "I guess I got tired of bein' mad after a while. I mean . . . hell, she'd had a rougher time than me—I did okay with Aunt Evangeline. Anyway—I started calling her again. And I got to thinkin' about my dad, and I was doin' pretty well, with the CD just out, and startin' to get really nice gigs. I dunno." He gave her a thoughtful frown. "Maybe I just got tired of hating him. But I woke up one morning, down in Oakland where I've got this apartment, and I just decided—hey, why not drop in and see the old guy while I was up here? He used to play decent horn from what I hear. Just wanted to talk to him once. No accusations, no *schmalz*. So I left early and got into town a day ahead of my gig." He gave Jeff a narrow look. "You gettin' all this down, cop?"

"Yep." Jeff looked up from his notebook and gave him a thin smile. The lawyer scowled.

"Anyway, I drove out to this one-horse town and I asked some kid at a gas station about this old closed-down hotel, and he gave me directions."

Rachel watched Jeff's eyes narrow. All they had to do was find that kid, she thought. Shouldn't be too hard.

"I show up at this dump, and I kind of wonder by now if I'm not making some kind of stupid mistake, so I park in the bushes. Just in case the old boy's a real ass and things get . . . Well, I've sort of got a temper." He spread his hands, his expression sheepish. "I've gotten into trouble once or twice before. So anyway, I didn't see no one around. The place gives me the willies." He hunched his shoulders. "This big old hotel out in the middle of no-where. It's like something out of a Stephen King movie. I knock, but nothin' happens. The door's unlocked, but I look in and it's all shadows, and I think no *way* I'm going there. And I really pound on the door, and figure I'll leave, but then, just for the hell of it, I walk around back. Just to look the dump over, you know." He paused to wipe a sheen of sweat from his face with a handker-chief. "It was weird." His voice dropped. "This tubby old guy's out on this stone patio behind the hotel, and it kind of stopped me—he looked like me. Or maybe like I'd look if I let myself go. It was like a punch in the gut, man. Like I'd never really believed that he was flesh and blood. You know, I used to make up stuff in my head when I was kid. How my dad was really Thelonious Monk or something, and one day some old letters would get found, and the real birth certificate, and everybody would find out." He looked around the room. "Can I get a glass of water?"

"Help yourself." Rachel gestured at the blue plastic pitcher and plastic-wrapped cup beside her bed.

"Thanks." He unwrapped the cup, poured himself some water, and gulped it, visibly regaining his compo-sure as he did so. "Where was I? Oh, yeah—thinking how it hit me that this fat, balding guy was really my

father. He was drunk, too. Early afternoon, and he's staggering like a midnight lush. And then . . . he turns around
and sees me.'' Clyde paused again, shaking his head.
''The guy goes nuts. His eyes get wide, and his face is
all crazy, and he makes this kind of god-awful choking
scream, like an animal or something, and he starts back-
ing up. I ask him if he's all right, figuring he can't know
who I am, or maybe he does, maybe Mama told him, and
he figures I'm here to kill him. So I grab hold of him,
and he starts fighting me—I mean, really swinging and
kicking, you know? So I let go, and I yell that it's okay,
that I just wanna talk.

''And he runs.'' Clyde's eyes widened. ''Like he's
seen the Devil hisself, he turns and starts running. He's
running along this weird sort of boardwalk stuck up
along the side of the damn cliff, and there's this fancy
little picnic shelter at the end . . .'' He stopped, ran a
finger inside his collar. ''Halfway there, he sort of
spreads his arms and . . . he jumps.'' Horror glazed his
eyes. ''He just . . . jumps. Like he thinks he can fly.
'Cause . . . he saw me.'' He swallowed, his eyes on a
vision they couldn't share. ''I'm never gonna forget
that,'' he whispered. ''Not if I live to be a hundred. And
you know . . . I'm sorry. I wanted just once to meet him.
Tell him I didn't hate him anymore.'' He shrugged, then
gave his lawyer and Jeff a defiant stare. ''So I'm done
here. I didn't kill Henry Bassinger. Not on purpose, anyway. I didn't know my mama had anything going on with
him—didn't even know she cleaned for him. But, yeah,
I was there. That's all I'm guilty of, you got that?''

Jeff nodded at somebody out in the hallway. Lyle, in
uniform. The lawyer put a hand on Montaine's shoulder,
who shook it off brusquely and turned back briefly to
Rachel. ''I hope you're okay.'' He smiled at her. ''You
take care of yourself.'' Straightening his shoulders, he
walked out into the hall, his posture full of confidence.

Rachel and Jeff watched him go, walking between
Lyle and his lawyer. ''So.'' She let her breath out in a
sigh. ''He's got a lot of presence.''

Jeff grunted.

"Do you think it's like he says? That he really didn't know what his mother was up to?"

"We'll sure try to find the crack in that story. He knew enough to get himself a quick alibi when we came asking about his father."

"That could be because he knew Henry was dead," she said thoughtfully. "He was there, after all."

"Maybe." Jeff nodded shortly. "By the way, we talked to Darlene's sister down in Los Angeles. Guess what their father did for a living in Louisiana?"

"I'll bite." She smiled, although the beginning of a headache was nibbling at the back of her brain.

"He had a dinky little crossroads garage. He was the mechanic, and his two girls pumped gas. Evangeline—this sister—told us that Darlene used to work on the cars with Daddy—that she was a real good mechanic. We found the cutters she used to cut the Acura's sensor cable. They were in a drawer at the hotel. She missed one fingerprint on the handle when she wiped them clean."

Poor Cass. Rachel looked away, tears stinging her eyes. He might have started to turn his life around. Willis had thought so. She felt Jeff's arm go around her.

"What about Herbert?" she asked. "Poor Sandy—he was involved, wasn't he?"

"He came to us as soon as he heard about you." Jeff stroked her hair. "He was devastated—told us everything. Yeah, Doreen was spending the occasional night with him. She got Henry to consider an offer on the hotel. Herbert promised her a percentage if the deal went through. He planned to develop it—already had money lined up. Then Alex came through with a promise of financing, and Henry was all hot to work with him. Maybe she overheard him promise Alex he'd leave him the hotel in his will. I guess all these years she'd counted on Clyde inheriting it. I guess she decided to hurry things along—and hit her son for a share of the profit for connecting him with Herbert. That way she'd pick up money from both of them. And from the insurance money he left her." He shook his head. "I don't know how she acted around Henry, but she hated him. She sure didn't try to hide it."

"Because he didn't stand up to his father," Rachel said softly. "Because she had to quit school."

"Maybe. I don't think she'll tell us. You need to rest." His breath tickled her neck. "I'll come by later."

Rachel nodded, already slipping down into the sheets, too tired to argue with him. "So who will get the hotel?" she mumbled as she closed her eyes.

"That's a good question." Jeff's lips brushed her forehead. "I don't think anyone will know the answer for a while." He kissed her fingertips and laid her hand down on the spread.

Rachel smiled and let herself slip into slumber.

CHAPTER

17

September

Four days of unseasonably early fall rain had made the finishing touches to the Meier property a nightmare of wet bark dust, tender new lawn, and careful raking. And mud. At least the dual wells hadn't run dry. At this time of year, many local wells did, and they'd been pulling a lot of water for the new plantings. Rachel wished she could feign deafness as the overwrought Elaine hovered, and worried, and asked the same questions over and over again.

"It'll look fine," Rachel assured her through a haze of exhaustion. Both she and Julio were working from dawn to full dark—attending to final details on the beds, watering, spreading the bark dust, raking the graveled paths smooth.

Rachel wasn't sure if she should pray for rain to continue so that the reception would take place indoors, or hope for sun so that they could finish without the mud. The sun finally decided to shine, but they didn't get the last load of bark dust spread until the morning of the wedding.

"Let's get out of here," she told Julio and began to gather up her tools with great relief. Joylinn's crew was already setting up tables along the deck and carrying in crates of dishes, silverware, and glasses. It promised to be a lovely day—not too hot, but clear skies.

Joylinn set down an armful of tablecloths and waved. "Aren't you coming to the wedding?"

"It's not until eleven." Rachel glanced at her watch. "I have two whole hours to get dressed."

"I still can't believe it—that it was Doreen who killed Henry. And tried to kill you." Joylinn shivered. "I'm so glad you're okay."

"Not half as glad as I am."

"How awful." She shuddered again, arms wrapping around herself as if the day had turned suddenly cold. "How did she know to use that stuff . . . What did they call it in the paper? Jimsonweed?" She shook her head. "I never even heard of it."

"Doreen studied medicinal herbs." Rachel closed her eyes briefly, remembering the dark terror that had seized her, and the shadows of monsters at the edges of her vision. She dreamed about them some nights. "It causes hallucinations," she said slowly. "I think Doreen had been giving Henry small doses of it in her lemonades for some time. That would explain his erratic behavior at times. Maybe she was building a case for suicide?" Rachel picked up a plastic crate full of wineglasses. There were plenty of places to fall to your death along the rear of the hotel. And Doreen must have known how much time Henry spent out at the gazebo or wandering along the edge of the cliffs. Rachel shook her head, angry at this woman who had simply and quietly made the decision that a lonely and inoffensive recluse should die.

"He paid her money every month from the day he left her," she said as she carried the glasses over to the growing stack of crates on the deck. "I guess Clyde never knew. She told him that his father abandoned them. I guess it's one of the reasons Clyde has been cooperating. He really regrets that he never met his father."

"You know, Doreen came into The Bread Box all the time." Joylinn sat down on the deck steps and pushed her hair back from her face. "She'd stop for a roll and coffee on her way to early jobs, or come in for a sandwich for lunch. I used to talk to her. She just seemed quiet . . . and nice. It's scary to think of her mixing poisonous plants into her lemonade—plotting to kill an old man. And you!"

"I don't think she ever forgave him." Rachel let her eyes follow the shining ribbon of the Columbia River until it disappeared into a haze toward the Dalles. "Henry had to choose between his family and her, and he chose his family. I don't think Henry was ever able to stand up to his father. But he never divorced her." She looked at Joylinn. "I wonder why they kept it secret—that she was his wife. Maybe she was planning to kill him from the beginning." They'd never know. "Jeff talked to her sister—the one who raised Clyde. She told him that Doreen—Darlene—could hold a grudge forever. That she always got even."

"Well, I guess she did." Joylinn got up. "She spent her life doing it. Wonder if she feels it's worth it." She glanced around at the trestle tables and the piles of linen and glassware. "I'd better get cracking. I've got a couple of vanloads of food to bring over yet."

"I can't wait to try everything." Rachel grinned and patted her stomach as she got to her feet. "The way I've been working the past couple of weeks, I figure I can eat anything I want today."

"My dear, you look positively skeletal." Joylinn eyed her with mock severity, then laughed. "I hope you like what I fixed. For that matter, I hope the Dragon Lady does." She rolled her eyes. "I must say, I won't be sorry to get the check and say good-bye to this job." Joylinn waved and hurried off in the direction of two of her crew who were setting up tables and folding chairs on the rear deck. "Not there," she called. "We're setting up the bar against that wall. . . ."

"The tools are in the truck, *señorita*." Julio appeared at her side. "All is ready."

"Thanks, Julio. We did good." She grinned at him. "Are you coming to the wedding?" Joshua had personally handed Julio an invitation one afternoon while they were putting in the water feature.

Julio had stared at the gold-embossed card and stammered his thanks in Spanish, which Joshua Meier turned out to speak fluently, much to both Julio's and Rachel's surprise. "I was in the Peace Corps," he explained. "In Guatemala." He had spent a few weeks in the town where Julio's family had lived.

"I . . . will come." Julio smiled shyly. "My sister did not believe. Then I show her the card. She says *el señor* is a very nice man."

"He is." Rachel nodded and smiled. Julio was almost his old self now that Henry's murder had been solved. But he still watched Jeff warily when he showed up. "We'd better get going, then." She picked up the rake she had been using and tucked her gloves into her belt.

Climbing into her truck, she drove Julio home, then went on to her apartment to get ready. Fresh from the shower, she ignored Peter's demands for attention as she donned the new linen dress she'd bought for the wedding. A soft jade color, it brought out the auburn highlights in her dark hair and went well with her tawny complexion. "If you put a run in these stockings, no tuna for you for a month. You hear me, cat?" She shook an admonishing finger at Peter.

He yawned at her, hopped up on the sofa, and curled up in a sulky ball, flattening his ears as someone knocked on the door.

"You ready?" Jeff's voice sounded from the far side of the panels. "Your escort has arrived."

"Actually, I *am* ready." Rachel opened the door. "Unless Peter goes for a flying attack on my way out the door." She grinned up at him. "You look great."

"You look stunning." He bent and kissed her, then recoiled in mock fear. "I'm afraid I'll muss something."

"Oh, come on, muss!"

"Here." Laughing, he reached for something outside the door. "It even matches. Aren't you impressed with my ESP?"

The white cardboard box held an orchid corsage. The ivory blossoms tied with pale green ribbon did indeed match her dress.

"Sandy couldn't be a part of your ESP, could she?" Rachel admired the waxy, delicate blooms, then handed the corsage to Jeff so that he could pin it on her dress.

"Do you trust me?" he asked with a straight face.

She laughed, remembering the junior prom, just before Jeff had left for Los Angeles. He had brought her a corsage, had given it to her at the gym where the prom was being held. He had stuck her with the pin as he fastened it to her dress.

"I can get bloodstains out." She smiled as he deftly fastened it to her shoulder, eyes half closing at the sure pressure of his fingers against her flesh.

Taking his arm, she closed the door on the pouting Peter and went hand in hand with him down the narrow steps.

The wedding took place in the Blossom Grange Hall. Rachel sat with her mother, Dr. Meier, and Jeff—and Julio, whom she had spotted standing awkwardly at the edge of the well-dressed crowd entering the church. For all Joshua's friction with his daughter, there was no mistaking the pride on his face as his son-in-law walked his granddaughter down the aisle. She wore a long gown with a lacy train and carried a bouquet of pink roses. She had an immature face and an expression of petulant triumph that Rachel found less than engaging. The groom looked about as young as she—seventeen, maybe, she thought. He was actually nineteen, she recalled. Jeff gave her a brief questioning look as she sighed, but she merely shook her head without answering. *You are too young,* she thought as the couple ascended the low dais between banks of flowers. *Way too young.*

The ceremony was brief and very ecumenical. A Unitarian minister performed a sectarian service—although the flower-covered marriage canopy and the glass that the groom stomped on and smashed added a touch of Jewish tradition. Rachel noticed more than one disapproving face among the well-dressed guests. The minister didn't say a word about the soft swell of a pregnant belly beneath the gathered front of the bride's ivory brocade gown.

Afterward Rachel ended up in the reception line on the steps outside, alongside her mother. Shaking hands with the smiling men and women who greeted her and appraised her and sometimes kissed her cheek, she felt very much an outsider. Her mother seemed to be enjoying herself—returning greetings and kisses with an easy, relaxed manner. She was willing to bet that her mother's marriage to Joshua was more the news of the moment than the wedding itself. To judge by Elaine's expression, she had come to the same conclusion and was not at all pleased with it.

She and Jeff finally escaped to the reception. As they walked up the driveway from his truck, she paused, eyes sweeping the finished landscape. Couples chatted, glasses in hand, around the long tables set with food, glasses, and plates. Soft harp music filled the air. Banks of roses perfumed the afternoon, and water trickled over rocks in the tiny pool, adding its delicate note to the harp music. A tiny green frog sat on one of the wet black stones, its ivory throat pulsing, then dived off as Rachel and Jeff walked nearer. For a moment Rachel let her vision blur, seeing the young saplings as they'd be in ten years' time, seeing the gaps filled in with huckleberry and salal, lost in a vision of the mature space.

"It looks great," Jeff murmured in her ear. "They ought to put this in one of those fancy home and garden magazines."

"I'm pleased." She smiled up at him. So was Dr. Meier. He had given her a nice bonus. She sighed contentedly as Jeff ushered her along the new paths. Next year the lawn would be starred with blossoms.

"Don't tell me you lust after this kind of affair." Jeff regarded her with mock alarm.

"Not at all." She squeezed his arm. "I think eloping is a perfectly fine idea myself."

"Runs in the family, I guess." He sounded relieved. "Maybe we should try it someday." He spoke lightly, but there was a serious glint in his eyes.

He was letting her laugh it off as a joke if she wanted to. Giving her space. She looked up, met his eyes, and said nothing for a few moments. Then she squeezed his hand, unable to come up with the words she needed. A figure waved from the fringes of the crowd, then hurried over, a champagne flute in one hand.

"I thought I might run into you here." Alex Creswell saluted them with the wineglass, then leaned down to kiss Rachel on the cheek.

"I just want to tell you how grateful I am—that you stuck with this case and finally found the real murderer," he told Jeff. "And I'm so glad you weren't injured." He turned back to Rachel, taking both her hands in his. "I would have felt responsible—like I enticed you into this mess by passing out on your floor."

"You didn't." Rachel shook her head. "What about the hotel? What's going to happen to it?"

"I don't know yet." Alex frowned into his glass. "Uncle Henry definitely left the property to his son," he said stiffly. "If the property had been under development, it wouldn't have mattered. The contract would have had to cover that possibility. But we hadn't drawn up a contract yet. And Montaine's status is . . . equivocal at best." He made a rocking motion with one hand. "I spent the afternoon with him yesterday. Actually it was a three-some—he, his lawyer, and myself." He gave them a wry grin and took a sip of his champagne. "His trial is scheduled for early October. His lawyer seems to believe that he'll at least be acquitted, if not found not guilty outright." He shrugged. "If that happens, we're in the clear.

It turns out that he's very interested in my plans to develop it, you see.''

"That's great." Rachel smiled at him. "Henry's ghost will be happy."

"Probably not." Alex cleared his throat. "Clyde is much more flexible than Uncle was—and much more modern in outlook. He's very interested in my ideas about turning the property into an upscale retreat targeting the jaded execs who want the personal touch and guaranteed privacy. I've got the contacts to get us off the ground, I believe.''

"Not a genuine restoration?" Jeff drawled. "Henry will haunt you."

"Just don't say that around prospective guests." Alex laughed uneasily. "Uncle lived in the past. He wanted to re-create his father's hotel—but that was an artifact of the thirties. This is the nineties. We're going to do the same thing—in a modern way. Uncle couldn't quite understand that.''

"I'd like to see the old place fixed up," Jeff said slowly. "We let too much of our past slip away."

Rachel gave him a brief glance, but he was smiling, his thoughts hidden.

"I hope it works out." Alex sighed. "Sometimes I just want to walk away. And forget.''

"I'm sorry," Jeff murmured.

"Me, too." Alex looked at the glass in his hand as if he'd forgotten why it was there. "It's so odd—meeting Clyde. I felt . . . betrayed, you know. In a way.''

"Betrayed?" Rachel paused as one of Joylinn's waiters offered a tray of champagne glasses. Jeff took two, and she accepted one with a smile, clinked its rim with his.

"To Henry." Alex chimed his glass against theirs as she echoed him.

"So what about this betrayal?" Rachel sipped her champagne, savoring the tart, sparkling tang of the wine.

"Well . . . I never really came out while Mother was alive, you know?" He placed his empty glass on the edge of the deck and snagged a fresh one from a passing waiter. "She would have done all the dramatics—thrown a fit—generally made life hell. I mean, I just didn't feel like being the straight man for yet another round of her theatrics. God knows Grandfather had served her well enough." He made a face, then grinned. "But it was too easy—coming out to my friends and the people at the firm. I had to come out for my family before it would matter. And there was Uncle Henry. We'd always been close." He sipped meditatively at his champagne. "I . . . had a feeling he'd understand. In fact, I wondered . . ."

Rachel managed to keep the surprise off her face.

"Anyway . . . he was supportive." Alex looked up and gave a lopsided shrug. "He never admitted anything, you know. But he started telling me about the musicians he knew—who went home with whom. That kind of thing. I always figured that was his way of admitting to me that he was gay, too. I thought he was trusting me with something he'd never shared with anyone. I felt . . . special, For the first time in my life, I think. But I was wrong." He shrugged and tossed back the rest of his champagne. "It hurt a lot more than I would have expected."

Rachel took a sip of champagne. That explained his stubborn refusal to believe in Darlene's existence.

"But Clyde is a savvy guy," Alex was saying. "We speak the same language—money. Means power, you know?" He chuckled. "You Paul Bunyan Northwesterners haven't quite figured that out yet, have you?"

"Who you callin' a Bunyan, city boy?" Jeff said with mock anger. "Just 'cause we use beaver pelts for money around here . . ."

"Hey, wish me luck." Alex laughed. "You may have Bill Gates stopping into The Bread Box for a Danish and coffee."

"As long as he behaves himself."

"We need to talk about that . . ."

"No bending rules for rich kids."

"I didn't mean that. I'm thinking more in terms of security . . ."

Rachel watched the two of them head toward the bar on the deck, deep in conversation. Jeff looked back and mouthed, "Can I bring you something?" but she shook her head. She had a feeling that they'd do better without her. She looked around the now crowded garden. Yes, it looked good. Guests stood about the trickling pool with their drinks and their food, obviously enjoying the gold-fish.

Her stomach rumbled sharply, reminding her that she'd made do with only a bagel and instant coffee this morning, in her rush to get over here and finish the last details with Julio. The laden tables caught her eye, and she began to make her way over to the nearest one. Platters of Brie, Stilton, sharp cheddar, and Havarti, vegetable cru-dités, dip, smoked salmon, savory pastries, crackers . . . She picked up a plate, trying not to drool. Calories be damned. She had just forked slices of pink lox onto rounds of Joylinn's dark tangy rye bread and was adding wedges of baby Gouda to her plate when someone cleared his throat behind her.

"Hi."

She turned and found Willis Bard facing her. He looked thinner, his face all angles and bone, as if he'd dropped pounds in the past few weeks. "Hello," she said.

"I never realized you knew Josh, until I finally made the connection between his new wife's name and yours." He grimaced and offered her his hand, balancing a glass of beer and plate of cheese and crackers in the other. "Sorry, I'm being gauche. I'm a nephew of his—on his first wife's side. Which you probably didn't know. And I'm really glad he married again, by the way. He's a cool guy, and I think your mother is just right for him. Is she really your mother?" He grinned. "You two seem more like sisters."

"She'll be delighted to hear that. Or should I be insulted?" Rachel raised one eyebrow, trying not to laugh as Willis blushed crimson.

"Oh, God, wait a minute while I get my size ten out

of my mouth. No, no, she just seems so young. . . ." He
narrowed his eyes. "You're teasing me. Okay, I deserved
it." He grabbed for his beer glass as it threatened to
topple. "I heard you were poisoned." His expression sobered. "Are you all right?"

"I'm fine now." She was also the proud owner of a
comprehensive encyclopedia of poisonous plants—the
missing book she had spotted on the evening of the accident. Sandy had returned it to her. She had found it
under a bush in her backyard—had thought Rachel might
have left it on the night of the party. Doreen must have
tossed it over the fence, to retrieve later.

"That whole affair with the van . . . it was a mess."
Willis stared at his plate. "The Baldwin woman cleaned
for Ross, the administrator, out at the Farm. Did you
know that?" He gave her a searching glance and
frowned. "He's middle-aged and divorced. He . . . he resigned last week. For personal reasons."

Another middle-aged bachelor client? So Doreen had
had the opportunity to meet Cass.

"Anne, our history teacher, is a little too lax," Willis
went on. "I guess she had been checking the van out for
a few chosen students she considered responsible. One
of them was Cass. We need an overhaul of the staff."
He nodded. "I've applied for the job of administrator. I
don't know that I'll get it—I'm pretty young for that kind
of post. But I want it. The Farm works." His eyes
glowed. "It really works—and we can't afford to let
scandals tarnish it. We were just throwing those kids
away—we teach them how to be better criminals in the
detention centers and then we punish them for learning
the lessons. Sorry." He ducked his head, busied himself
with the cheese on his plate. "I'll get off my soapbox."

"You don't need to." Rachel nodded. "From what
I've heard, I think you're right. I sure hope you get the
job."

"Me, too. Thank you." His grin returned, then he set
his plate down on the deck. "Just stay there a minute—I
want you to meet a friend of mine." He disappeared into

the throng around the food and returned a moment later, towing a short, barrel-chested man with a thick auburn ponytail and red suspenders holding up his suit pants. He looked familiar, but for the moment Rachel couldn't place him.

"Phil, this is Rachel. She did the landscaping here. Nice, huh? Mostly native plants."

"Hi." He offered her a hand. "I'm Phil Ventura—and no quips about the Jim Carrey movie." He lowered thick dark eyebrows in a theatrical scowl. "I'm the face on all those neon-colored flyers you've probably thrown away without reading. You know. The *other* candidate."

"I actually read them." Rachel laughed, recognizing him now. "I gather you really worry our noble mayor and feed store owner."

"I'm trying hard. The latest poll—self-conducted, so it doesn't really count—says I have a chance." Ventura grinned. "Ferrel is still living in the fifties. This town can't go on making it on fruit-growing only. The population is changing. People are moving out here—telecommuting to Portland. We either ride the crest of the wave or get sucked along in the ebb—getting sand in our britches." He made a face at Willis, who was humming "The Times They Are a' Changing" under his breath. "I'm waiting for Ferrel to show up at my door and challenge me to a shoot-out at high noon."

"Maybe if we were farther east." Rachel laughed. "Actually there was a genuine gunfight on Main Street way back when. Nobody died. We're not very good shots. And I agree with you that we need to think about the changes that are going on. Looks like more houses will start going in east of town."

"Time-share condos. And the influx has just begun. I heard a rumor that Blossom is going to get written up in the Portland paper as an undiscovered gem. After that, the rush will really start. You wait. Well, I'm impressed with what you've accomplished here." He looked around, his gaze lingering on the rock-filled pool. "I

know that this was old orchard land—in fact, I used to
hunt rabbits here when I was twelve."

"I didn't know you grew up around here," Rachel
said, surprised.

"Nah. But we used to come out to spend the weekend
with some friends of my dad. Bob figured every red-
blooded American kid should know how to hunt. Since
my dad hated guns, he taught me. My hunting stories
have convinced more than one good ol' boy that I'm not
just a city upstart." He grinned at her. "Although the
rabbits never had much to fear. Tell you what—vote for
me for mayor. If I get elected, I'll give you the contract
to make the city center look pretty with plants and maintain it. We need a nice Main Street."

"Are you offering to buy my vote, sir?" Rachel
drawled.

"Hey, I offer a good price." Ventura's eyes twinkled.

"Well, you got it anyway. But I wouldn't turn down
a city contract." Rachel didn't even permit herself the
luxury of considering it. That kind of steady income
would go a long way toward making Rain Country Landscaping solidly solvent. "So go work on getting
elected," she said, winking at Willis. "If I get a city
contract, I could hire one of your kids."

"All right—you've got to win now." Willis slapped
Ventura on the shoulder. "You heard the lady."

"I'll do my best." Ventura winked at her and strolled
off to fall easily into conversation with a couple of orchard owners at the bar.

"Actually I can probably afford to hire one of your
kids next spring," Rachel told Willis. "At least for part-
time work." Julio needed more hours for his growing
maintenance clientele, and he didn't want to ask her for
the time.

"That's great. I'll call you in February and remind
you," Willis said soberly. "I think Phil is going to win.
Even the old-timers can see that the world is changing.
Everyone except Andy Ferrel."

"Here's to Phil." Rachel lifted her champagne glass

to him, then headed over to her mother and Joshua, who
were surrounded by Portland guests. Her mother looked
a little tired but still seemed to be enjoying herself. She
was chatting easily with a tall, red-haired woman wearing
a diamond and emerald necklace and a white silk shift
that made her tanned skin glow.

"Ah, Rachel, there you are." Her mother excused herself and made her way over to her daughter. "Whew!
Thank you for the rescue." She laughed and plucked a
cluster of black grapes from a fruit platter.

"Are you having fun?"

"Actually, yes." Her mother's eyes danced. "It's like
being the new girlfriend at a family reunion—everybody
wants to know who your parents are, what they did, who
you're related to. And, of course, why Joshua married
me—but you don't ask that outright." She made a face
and laughed. "The price of community, but hey . . ." She
spread her hands. "That's the way it is. And one
woman—Carrie Shay, a reporter for the *Oregonian*—is
distantly related to your father's family. Oy." She rolled
her eyes. "The world is such a small place."

Rachel laughed. "You're proud of yourself, lady. Admit it."

"I'm proud of Joshua, and yes, I'm proud of myself."
Her smile softened. "Because we knew in our hearts that
this was right for both of us, and we didn't let our
brains—or relatives—interfere." She touched her daughter's hair lightly. "Don't play it too safe, sweetheart.
Your father and I would never have gotten married if
either of us had acted sensibly. Sometimes you have to
leap on faith alone."

"I won't forget, Mom." Rachel patted her mother's
hand. "You're a good role model."

"I don't know about that." Her mother looked
vaguely alarmed. "But just keep it in mind." She
glanced past Rachel and smiled. "Joshua's giving me
that 'you need to meet this person' look, which means
it's probably more family." She sighed. "We're taking
off for a week at the beach as soon as this is over. I'm

ready. And you've done wonders with this place, you know. Your dad would be terribly proud of you." She kissed her daughter on the cheek, her own face glowing. "Jeff's alone again," she murmured. "He looks bereft. You'd better go save him."

Rachel smiled as her mother walked lightly over to where Joshua stood with an elderly couple, smiling to herself. She could certainly understand Willis's comment. Her mother would seem young even when her hair was snow-white. And Jeff was indeed looking her way— although she wouldn't describe his expression as bereft, she decided. Lustful was more like it.

"What are you grinning at?" He tucked his arm in hers and offered her another glass of champagne, which she declined.

"I'm grinning at you. And my mom."

"She looks stunning." Jeff looked over at her and shook his head. "She could be Dr. Meier's daughter."

"Yeah, I think that bothered Elaine some. Where's the wedding party?" She looked where he pointed and found Elaine and her small, pursed-mouthed husband shaking hands and chatting with a circle of people on the deck near the bar. The bride had changed into a clingy black dress that showed off her belly and her multiple piercings to very visible effect. The new husband lounged sulkily on a wooden deck chair with a bottle of beer.

"Lovely couple." Rachel shook her head and smiled up at Jeff. "And in-laws now. Any chance I could pry you away from this party?"

"Show me the door," Jeff said fervently.

Hand in hand they slipped around the back of the house, avoiding Alex, who was gesturing lavishly as he talked to Phil. "He's not a bad guy," Jeff commented as they threaded their way through chatting clusters of guests.

"I hope the hotel deal works out." She climbed into his truck.

"Me, too. Where shall we go, lady?" Jeff slid behind

the wheel and started the engine. "Your wish and all that . . ."

"Your place," Rachel said. "Let's sit on your back porch and watch the sun set." She gave him a slow smile. "I left Peter extra food."

Jeff's smile matched hers. "Sounds good to me," he said softly. "I'll apologize to Peter next time I'm there." He leaned across the seat, brushed her lips with his, then put the truck into gear. As they pulled away, her mother waved from the deck. Rachel lifted her hand in return.

Sometimes you have to take the leap on faith.

LANDSCAPING TIP

If you're planning a lawn, consider an herbaceous seed mix rather than a traditional sod or seed lawn. This is a blend of low-growing grasses, clovers, wild-flowers, and herbs. It needs less mowing, fertilizing, and watering than a conventional lawn, has less thatch buildup, and provides a lovely springy turf studded with flowers—ideal for cloud-watching on your back on a warm summer day. Ecological Grass Mixes specific for your climate can be purchased from Nichols Garden Nursery, 1190 N. Pacific Highway NE, Albany, Oregon, 97321.